Forgotten Souls

Gordon,
Thanks for all the patience,
and help along the way.
Best,

Forgotten Souls

T. G. Arsenault

Five Star • Waterville, Maine

First Edition
First Printing: November 2005

Published in 2005 in conjunction with Tekno Books and
Ed Gorman.

Set in 11 pt. Plantin by Minnie B. Raven.

Printed in the United States on permanent paper.

Library of Congress Cataloging-in-Publication Data

Arsenault, T. G.
    Forgotten souls / by T.G. Arsenault.—1st ed.
      p. cm.
    ISBN 1-59414-383-8 (hc : alk. paper)
    1. Women librarians—Fiction.   2. Spiritualists—
Fiction.   3. Cemeteries—Fiction.   I. Title.
PS3601.R754F67 2005
813'.6—dc22   2005024288

This novel is dedicated to those I have recently lost: Bella L. Vye, Randall B. Vye, and George E. Arsenault. You will never be forgotten . . .

EVERLASTING

As the day dawns without me there,
Just smile and know to say a prayer,
'Cause soon you'll know as I do,
"There is a God" who keeps his promise true.
In Heaven above, He's there with "everlasting" love.
And like a snow-white dove, touched by an angel,
We fly to our home with heartfelt joy,
To our place in the sky, in that Heavenly dome,
"And we'll never, ever, ever be alone."
Yes, in God's Heavens up in the sky,
You'll see me again 'cause we don't really die.
We go on forever in love so sublime,
In God's tender care till the end of time.

Randy Vye
(1944–2001)

Author's Note

My Uncle Randy was an aspiring poet who was taken from us before being able to reach his lifelong dream of becoming published. In placing his poem here, a poem I believe fits well with the theme of my novel, I hope to fulfill a dream of his while fulfilling one of my own.

Acknowledgements

I would like to thank the following people for their contributions in one form or another (sometimes the occasional kick in the rear) in making my first novel become a reality: My wife and son for their complete understanding of the many hours locked away in my room. Mom and Dad and my brother, Jeff, for the continued support and motivation over the years. Carol Bourgoin for creating an idea in my mind that simply refused to go away. And Pauline Berube for letting me use her kitchen table to pen the very first chapter. I'd also like to thank some writers and friends I've met along the way who were always there to help and answer some very off-the-wall questions at times during the writing of this novel: Brian Knight, T. M. Gray, James Newman, and Teri Jacobs. Special thanks go out to John Helfers, my editor, Gordon Aalborg, and everyone at Five Star Publishing for their faith in my work and the fifty feet of rope to scale those vertical walls of my learning curve and making a dream come true.

Chapter 1

Whispers of the dead passed through his little fingers.

Hushed exclamations suddenly erupted from all sides, echoing a fury of tangled words into a common center of boiling excitement.

It's him! It's him!

She could almost see their translucent fingers being pointed at the boy standing before her, their misty shapes surrounding him with arms that wanted, but were unable, to embrace him within the halo of their presence. They existed at the periphery of her vision, like the faint illumination of distant stars, quick to disappear if she should look directly at them.

He's the one! The bellow of a man's voice—commanding, powerful.

Oh, sweet goodness, it's almost time! Quivering syllables of an elderly woman on the brink of ecstatic laughter.

The Chosen One is here . . . A subtle whisper soon swallowed by the surrounding fever of discovery.

More whispers. Rising in pitch, quickly becoming shouts and screams of joy. They traveled the lengths of her fingertips, found their way through the tingling surfaces of her arms, neck, and head.

And entered Andrea Varney's mind, sending pleasant ripples of recognition fluttering through her body with searing pinpricks of heat, enough to all but eliminate the cold winter air the boy had brought with him inside the library only a moment ago.

Andrea felt her heart rise a few inches within her chest,

and her eyes widen as if she were about to be hit by a truck. Severed breaths hitched within her throat as the boy began to remove his nervous fingers from her hand. His mouth opened in a silent gasp and cheeks flushed a slight shade of red.

He felt it too.

In the flash of time before their fingers lost contact, the moment so intense she felt her teeth painfully squeeze her lower lip between them, Andrea began to recollect her past.

Memories resurfaced and burned scarlet visions into her mind of the little girl she once was, making weekly rounds of visitation to the few cemeteries residing on the hillside. Cemeteries infested with massive overgrowths of grass, weeds, and whatever else that needed only sunlight to grow unhindered. Where headstones leaned at different angles and inscriptions were faintly visible, if at all.

Many of the plots she walked upon bowed upward, the caskets below rising a few inches, sometimes a few feet, in protest to the yearly erosion and frost heaving. But she didn't like to think about that. Instead, Andrea imagined the pocked and weed-filled curve in the ground as the roof of a new house, which the dead now occupied. Unsightly to some, but the glorious, frescoed arch of a Romanesque chapel to a certain eight-year-old little girl.

Soon enough, the visits became daily.

Andrea thought herself to be a *different* girl, not *strange,* as she so often heard from others. She knew she didn't do everything any normal girl would do at her age—too boring. At least, she didn't think it was strange. She only felt an obligation to pay these visits to the deceased, as no one else ever did. A big word for such a small girl, but one she understood.

At first, she just thought they were lonely.

10

She wasn't too young to notice during her frequent strolls through the hillside that very few people ever paid their respects to the dead. Aside from token flags being placed at headstones on Memorial Day, or the occasional burial she spied upon from the edge of the forest, a single visitor was extremely rare. A single rose, lucky enough to be placed next to a headstone, would soon wither and crumble, and at last scatter into invisible fragments with the slightest breeze, along with the memory of the individual below.

During the summer, daily visits grew into all-day adventures as she recited names she was able to decipher, had one-sided conversations with each, and placed gentle hands upon the chipped and weathered surfaces.

Every time she sat by the headstones, fingers tracing faded inscriptions, a cool chill swept completely through her body, as if these people actually knew she was there to visit. It wasn't a chill that scared her—not at all. In fact, it comforted her, as she thought the dead were speaking to her in their own special way, in a language only she could understand.

Sometimes, she even remembered to bring a damp cloth from home to wipe away any grime that had gathered since her last visit. And should moss creep along the base of a stone, a plastic knife kept in her back pocket could be used to cut away its congested fibers.

From each headstone she visited, and certainly only from those that allowed her the liberty without causing any more damage, she pried away a tiny, brittle piece of stone. Then blew loose particles of dirt from its edges and cleaned the entire piece with her shirt before placing it into her pocket. The stone eventually rested inside its own protective compartment of an old shoebox that hid underneath her bed. But, more importantly, it found a place inside a little girl's heart. And memory.

This produced a happiness inside of her that couldn't be achieved through her dolls or playhouses, a feeling which became the reason for her to return at every chance. To Andrea, these people were friends that wouldn't laugh at her and surely never tease her. They understood her. And would always be there to talk to. Always.

Soon, she began to hear their whispers.

And learned of a partner she must wait for, of a journey that needed to begin. Of the number of souls that needed to be remembered, and what happened to the unfortunate souls whose memories had been allowed to dwindle into the slightest flicker of a passing thought in the minds of their friends and loved ones.

The ultimate price civilization would have to pay on account of its negligence.

It frightened her.

The ring of the service bell released Andrea from the tightening clutch of her memories.

"Excuse me, miss?" Phil Jacobs said for the third time, muffling the bell with a large palm.

"Oh, I'm . . . I'm sorry. I guess I had . . . my mind on other things," Andrea stammered, words not coming out exactly as she had hoped. She picked up a small pile of papers and placed it back down, found the strength to smile before looking into the face of the man before her.

Her hands were shaking and she quickly brought them out of sight to toy with the brass handle of a desk drawer. It was something familiar, something she was used to, like home. It calmed her, and her nerves began to settle. She looked past the boy and his father, and let her eyes linger

upon the shape of the card catalogue; computerized direc-
tories had yet to establish a need in such a small town. It
was like admiring the antique table in her home that her
grandmother had passed down. Familiar. And cherished,
Andrea's fingers never tiring of the endless flipping through
bent and ink-smeared cards. Fingers that were . . . now
steady, no longer trembling.

Not completely relaxed, but close.

Andrea noticed the boy standing on his tiptoes, peering
over the edge of the large mahogany desktop with a happy,
but concerned look on his face. He rubbed his fingers together, inspected them with a gaze that quickly went from
her to his fingers, then back again. Tufts of dirty-blonde
hair wiggled on the back of his head in response.

"No problem. I was only getting concerned," Phil said,
changing the stern look on his face to a friendly grin. "We
just moved into town and I'd like to get my son, Darren, a
library card," he continued as he placed a hand on his son's
shoulder and gave a gentle squeeze.

Darren smiled.

"Absolutely," Andrea replied, trying her best to smile in
return, fingers fumbling for the proper form. "If you'll just
fill in the required information, I can get him one right
away." The words sounded slurred and sluggish, like lead
weights rolling off the end of her tongue and falling dead at
her feet.

Phil nodded and chose a corner reading desk to use.

Darren watched his father with eager eyes, the episode
between him and Andrea forgotten for the time being.
Eyeing the thousands of books that occupied the small library's bookshelves, most beyond his reach, he waited on
the balls of his feet for the nod of approval to explore this
new territory.

13

Attempting to look busy behind the desk, Andrea kept a furtive gaze fixed on Darren. She couldn't help it, nor could she believe it. He caught her on one occasion and tucked his body into the side of his father, pulling his eyes away from hers, suddenly inspecting the toes of his sneakers.

Andrea wanted to know everything possible about the boy she had just met. Sure, he would be back again to take out more books of his liking, but she wanted to know everything *now*. The whispers of the deceased had never told her how long she would actually have to *wait*.

Andrea thought she had a right to know, since Darren Jacobs, still yet to see his teenage years, still yet to see a single hair magically sprout from his chest or reddened blotch of acne invade his forehead, would be that partner for the rest of her life.

Though only in her twenties, Andrea had grown up fast, and at times felt as if she had lost a lifetime to waiting.

The same year she graduated from high school, icy roads on the interstate killed her parents, leaving her alone with a house, a mortgage, and bills to pay. Except for the occasional night class, she had postponed college and found herself lucky to live in a town where a college education wasn't yet required to be a librarian.

Children. How she longed for them. But she knew the kids who frequented the library were the closest she would ever come to having any children. She treated every one of them as if they were her own, but a burning void would always exist and probably never be filled.

She only watched, amused, as mothers brought their bachelor sons to parade in front of her, thinking they were helping her, but in fact, were only making her that much more depressed. Of the few relationships she did manage to have, each had lasted only a few weeks, months at the most.

She was terrified to settle down, to have a family, fearing the day she would have to pack up and begin a journey. Now, she just preferred to be alone.

And there was still a wait ahead of her.

Anger built up inside Andrea, but she managed to control it with minimal effort. The fact was simple: Darren was the *Chosen One.*

The *only* one.

With the completed form in hand, a glimpse of Darren's face remained as an afterimage as Andrea turned around to type up the library card.

She produced two loud clacks from an outdated Zenith typewriter when graying fingers suddenly clawed at the boundaries of her vision with hooked, blackened tips. She grasped the edges of the typing desk as an oncoming blackness surrounded her. Then swallowed her. Knuckles losing color, she fought to keep her breaths steady, counting the seconds in between.

The blackness pressed into her from all sides and pushed her through a shrinking, suffocating tunnel, like hundreds of giant fingers moving her along—poking, prodding. The deepest regions of the tunnel gave birth to a slight flicker of light, but complete darkness embraced her like the arms of a rotting corpse as the light extinguished.

A sickening groan formed within her throat and almost escaped. Her fingernails dug into the sides of the desk—the snap of one was the only piece of the real world she heard before that faded as well.

Andrea fought for control, now unable to count any time between breaths.

If pitch black could get any darker, it did.

Without warning, the face of Darren Jacobs swelled from the darkness, appearing as a milky image, undefined at the edges and strangely out of shape, eye sockets filled with a deeper shade of black than that from which they grew. Almost as suddenly, sparkling charges of energy rotated within the empty spheres, like swarms of bright, visible molecules, before developing into the clear blue eyes Andrea had seen only minutes ago.

The rest of his body grew from the base of his neck and expanded into the little boy she had recently met: young and unknowing, waiting to be filled with the knowledge of the world.

She watched as Darren aged.

It was as if he were an elastic form, expanding and distorting as he got bigger, like a comic strip image a child would pull and stretch on some legendary Silly Putty with a smile of satisfaction on his face.

Darren slowly expanded into an adolescent, wearing what looked like an athletic uniform: probably a hockey or football uniform, the image was too deformed to make out. A second later, he was wearing a graduation cap and gown.

Andrea had to smile, because she thought he was pretty handsome, distorted or not.

With another gradual change in his appearance—features swelling, melting, then reforming again—she witnessed Darren as an adult: suit and tie, the whole bit.

The image lingered only momentarily, as did her smile.

A frown trembled on Darren's face and a glimmer sparkled in his eyes. He seemed to be looking down at something, restraining his emotions with considerable effort. She wanted to reach out with a warm touch to his cheek, tell him everything was going to be all right, prevent that first tear from falling.

Her own emotions rising and falling, twisting and turning along the webbed grid of her nerves, she combined all of them into one: horror.

Hair disheveled, face burning with anguish, Darren appeared to be reaching with an outstretched arm for help, a frozen scream covering his face, pulsating veins straining at his temples.

Growing shapes and shadows were moving behind him, lumbering toward him. Reaching . . .

Andrea started to panic.

Hours seemed to have passed since she had lost contact with the outside world. The physical world was right under her feet and all around, but seemed to be on the other side of a magician's black curtain, waiting. She feared the surprise that would be unveiled when the curtain finally dropped. And the laughter that would surely follow.

Her self-control began to chip away, piece by jittering piece.

Remembering where her physical self *really* was, Andrea bit off an oncoming scream and only hoped whatever was happening would end soon.

It didn't.

Completely enveloped by this alternate reality, she squinted to see another flicker of light beginning to appear at the end of the tunnel. She released a sigh of relief, but sucked it back in just as fast, and held onto it. The light was not the fluorescent light of the library. The light she saw was red.

Fire red.

An unbearable heat penetrated her body, locating every pore, every orifice that led to her inner self, seeming to cook all of her inside organs, melding them into one. Something forced her closer to the light, the heat. The closer she got, the clearer her destination became.

Flames licked at the opposite opening of the tunnel like

the slithering tips of serpents' tongues, the first step into the acidic bowels that craved her.

Closer, closer.

She was in Hell. She knew this with the same certainty that she'd sink to the darkest regions of the ocean if her legs were encased within a barrel of cement.

Hell. No other place could be this horrid.

Or as foul. The stench immediately brought tears to her eyes and an unpleasant clamminess to the back of her tongue, threatening to release her gorge.

Wiping stinging droplets of sweat from her eyes, Andrea stared into a blood-tainted sky, its horizon nothing that would place it under the laminated covering of a postcard. The land below looked like one vast, violent country, appearing to grow even as she watched, breeding within its very own shadows.

Smoldering stakes, each much taller than Andrea, lined the landscape, continued until they were mere inches above the horizon, and continued some more. Between some of these stakes, human flesh was stretched: taut, tanning.

An ominous presence remained unseen, but she could feel it pressing into her skin, tasting her, wanting to crawl under the thin layers of her flesh and consume her.

Andrea gazed with eyes that refused to blink and welled with sorrow.

To the right of where she stood, people, *real* people, were being burned on the stakes, surrounded by separate circles of figures clad in hooded robes. A muffled chant rose and fell in time with the crackling from each pyre and the screams emanating in piercing warbles.

From within one of these circles, a young girl searched for help. Her mouth was pulled from all directions, her teeth bared into an ugly attempt at a scream. The half-beautiful, half-charred face of a woman in front of her yearned for freedom from the stake to which she was bound, from the flames that swept across her face. The resemblance of the two was uncanny. The little girl could only kneel at the woman's feet and look on, open hands catching the crimson fluid that dripped from her mother's toes.

Andrea's body remained in place, yet somehow she got even closer.

The woman's skin blistered and popped, turning into a molten mess that began to sag. Andrea saw the burning, smelled it, the sharp odor burning holes into the tender flesh of her nose. She gagged then fell to her knees, vomiting until it felt like her insides were being ripped out with each convulsion, one organ at a time.

She stood back up.

Unable to endure the sight of the dying woman or the helpless child without another battle with her insides, Andrea turned a shamed face and ran.

Running, running.

Something followed her with thunderous footsteps she could feel as well as hear; powerful explosions that found their way into the inner caverns of her brain and squashed exposed nerves.

Running, running.

Refusing to look back, Andrea continued into the darkness ahead of her, the way she had come. Hundreds of questions probed her mind like invisible tentacles prodding for a source, searching for answers.

She remembered the whispers of her dead friends and searched for strength: *Do not fear the presence, it only fears you.*

Then why was she running?

The darkness fell in sheets around her.

Her shoulder-length brown hair hung in disarray, the underside of her bangs now sticking to her forehead. Blood pumped with heavy beats inside her ears, seeming to mask a fit of laughter.

Bewildered, Andrea stared at the completed library card.

The card slipped through her fingers as she tried to hand it to Darren's father. She had to push it across the desk.

Phil Jacobs mumbled his thanks, then disappeared into the Children's section with strides quicker than Darren could keep up with.

Pulled in tow by the hand of his father, Darren turned.

And his eyes locked onto Andrea's.

He smiled.

Chapter 2

Chin in palm, elbow resting against the arm of her office chair, Andrea watched the December sky darken early—and quickly, as though a cloak were thrown over the sun as an afterthought. A cold wind caused the window to buffet and chatter within its frame.

Hiding herself in the back office, Andrea had asked her assistant to work the desk for the rest of the day, claiming weeks of papers needed filing. She didn't want to encounter Darren or his father as they checked out . . . she'd be apt to buckle at the knees.

But, as she heard the deathly silent hush that comes when the last of the patrons have left for the day, she did wipe away frost from the window. And took one more look—as he climbed into the car by the sidewalk—at the boy who would change her life.

Andrea glimpsed an unsteady pile of books resting on Darren's lap before his father shut the passenger's door. His hands were casually placed on top of the pile. Not toying with the edges, not flipping back and forth between illustrations. Not running a finger slowly beneath each word as he read.

He wasn't even looking at the books.

His eyes seemed locked in position, locked straight ahead, only able to look elsewhere. As though being forced, his head turned slowly and faced the library's office window, cheeks much too red to be suffering from just the touch of winter.

Andrea turned away.

Tension filled her body and numbed her fingertips. She repeatedly grabbed the air at her sides and allowed her brain to develop a stunning mirage of a gin and tonic producing drops of moisture upon her desk blotter. The mere thought of the drink made her smack her tongue against the roof of her mouth in heavenly anticipation.

The tension began to ebb.

Andrea helped close the library with her assistant, ignoring the strange looks that were sent in her direction. She wasn't about to explain.

She grabbed her winter coat, scarf, and purse, making sure everything met her approval before leaving. Locking the door behind her, Andrea braved the cold December bite, heels clicking on the sidewalk as she ran to her car.

Just that brief time in the cold plagued Andrea's fingers with a very uncomfortable sting. She had a rough time trying to get her key to fit in the tiny hole of her car door. The key worked against her, as if refusing to succumb to its inevitable demise, thrashing within the grip of her shaking fingers. She finally managed, adding to the plethora of small jagged scratches that surrounded the keyhole, then hurried to open the door and escape the punishment of the cold.

Throwing herself into the car, the driver's seat producing a long, wheezing noise as the frozen vinyl settled around her position, Andrea slammed the door. Jammed the key into the ignition, refusing to let it fight against her, and willed the engine to start when she turned the key.

Like clockwork, her knees knocked together while she gunned the accelerator to bring the car to a weary winter idle. She cranked the heater full blast, waiting for it to build up steam, extremely grateful the aging Plymouth Duster still liked to keep her warm on the many cold nights she drove home alone. In a few minutes, Hell would be pouring from the blower. Until the car actually sickened beyond any fruitful attempts to fix it, she wouldn't even think about purchasing another. It was her first, and would be hard to part with.

She rubbed her hands together and thought about all that had happened. An unexpected surprise that almost left her breathless, the events of the day had really wiped her out. As much as she hated to admit it, she wasn't ready for this to occur *today.*

Andrea had gone about her business, leading a somewhat normal life, sometimes wondering if everything the deceased kept telling her was true, or if she even heard them at all. Maybe she really *was* crazy. She wanted to believe them, but after a while, she had almost lost hope, thinking she had only imagined everything, her growing mind refusing to filter out the imagination of her young self.

A wave of guilt now swept through Andrea, creating a frothing tide of shame for distrusting the only *real* friends she ever had. But it was quickly dispelled as the faces of those she had remembered began to appear, called up from distant memories, always forgiving. And she started feeling better, knowing that it was all indeed true.

The journey would someday begin.

It would make everything she had done, or not done, all worth it.

She spent much of her time at cemeteries, especially the older ones, knew the name on each stone and the person buried beneath it. She researched the past of each one— part of the reason she took the job as a librarian, knowing no better way to gain information than knowing exactly where each document existed that the town had produced.

Not that it was strictly necessary . . . her deceased friends enjoyed telling her of their lives directly.

Her fingers tingled as blood began flowing within them, the numbness slipping away.

Knowing the car wouldn't stall, she placed it into drive and, looking over her left shoulder, pulled onto Gerard Street, heading home. At the only set of lights in town, she turned left onto a brittle section of Route 202 and forced a breath through tightened lips in an effort to relax for the somewhat long and bumpy drive home.

She listened to the monotone babbling of an unenthused deejay at WORC, a station just outside of town, known for its orchestra, while replaying the scenes of the afternoon over and over in her head—Darren's happy face, his distorted features, her visitation into Hell. What kept forcing its way to the forefront of her mind was the suffocating feeling of an unseen presence. She loosened her collar at the very thought of it, immediately angry with herself for even acknowledging the power it might have over her.

Despite the heat now pouring into the car, a shiver reached its icy fingers to the base of her spine.

She had started humming to a piece by Vivaldi when the radio station disappeared and only static crackled from the speakers. She looked down, confused—eyebrows coming together—and turned the dial all the way to the left, then to the right. Nothing. She was stunned. The idea of WORC going off the air diminished. Every station remained silent except for the venomous hiss that oozed from each frequency. Something was wrong.

"What in the . . . ?" Three words, the rest silenced when her head struck the steering wheel. The squeal of tires echoed somewhere in the distance as they locked up and slid upon a mixture of sand, snow, and rock salt.

She swayed back and forth, fearful of passing out. The world around her began to shimmer at the edges, but came back into focus at a pace equivalent to a caterpillar becoming a butterfly. And she *did* feel like a butterfly—one splattered on her windshield in all possible directions.

Andrea pinched the bridge of her nose in an effort to relieve the pain. It didn't work.

She still held onto the steering wheel with one claw-like hand that refused to open. Wincing, she felt a lump beginning to take shape in the middle of her forehead.

The car was silent. No lights. No power.

No heater.

Her breath soon appeared in front of her, forming a haze just thick enough to dim the glow from a single streetlight that stood alone for miles. Shadows seemed to grow from all sides, leaving the forest on spreading bellies, crawling over, through, and around the snow banks, closing in.

"Damn car," Andrea muttered, hitting the steering wheel with a balled fist. She looked outside for any oncoming vehicles, but saw none. Snow banks and pines on either side of the road outlined the black, patchy pavement. She instantly hated winter's insistence at being dark by five o'clock.

She tried to start the Plymouth again, but it politely denied her the favor.

Frustrated, she looked outside the rear window in desperate need of help. Turned the ignition a second time, a third, but again the car disapproved. Before her fourth attempt, she placed the car in neutral, jiggling the key as she turned—a trick that sometimes worked. Only a slow whine moaned from the engine and soon returned to an eerie silence.

Getting scared.

Andrea leaned back against the headrest and closed her eyes.

She brought her cussing to a halt as a high, painful screeching sound came from in front of her.

Peering between squinting lids, she looked at the windshield and brought her head up with a painful snap of her neck. She rubbed her eyes with a vigor that didn't help much, bringing pain to her already aching head, and disbelieved what her eyes wanted to show her.

From outside of the car, her windshield was shattering under the pressure of steadily dropping temperature. Or so she thought. At first. When she noticed the peculiar way lines were forming within the glass, curving where needed and intersecting where appropriate, she also realized it wasn't shattering at all, but was being carved into.

The sound was almost deafening amid the blackened silence of the winter night. Andrea covered her ears with quivering hands and watched, eyes performing a wild dance within their sockets, as a message appeared. Very abstract, but it was there.

Among a series of scratches was the word: *Dare.*

"Oh shit! Oh shit!" Her pulse increased. She could hear it in her ears, feel it in her chest as short breaths grew in succession.

With a final squeal that threatened to shatter the windshield, the word was underlined.

She screamed.

Chapter 3

From the distance, the soft buzzing of a vehicle turned into the dull roar of Frank Carlson's Camaro.

He was on his way to the library to look through the *Help Wanted* ads once again. In a way, relief came with seeing Andrea's car on the side of the road—it could only mean the library was closed. A slight grin perched on his lips, knowing that his parents couldn't bitch about him putting job hunting off one more day.

Two years and counting since he had quit high school as a senior, he didn't think his parents would mind him still living with them for a *little* while longer. He had looked through so many classified ads from various newspapers around the state that he thought he would vomit black ink onto the snow-covered ground and create the world's most unusual novel.

Thoughts of what to do the rest of the night quickly entered his mind: pick up a girl, get a quick high with his not-so-intelligent friends, see a movie. Or his ultimate fantasy: slipping under the sheets with Andrea Varney, the kooky librarian with the gorgeous body.

With this last thought doing a joyful jig in his mind and an expanding grin covering his face, he pulled over in a skidding halt to help in any way possible. Maybe some sort of reward would follow.

How could he be so lucky? *Fate—gotta love it.*

Stretched lips connected each ear and revealed stained, uneven blocks of teeth. He groped for the comb inside the rear pocket of his jeans, slicked back his hair. This was the ultimate chance to prove to Andrea he wasn't just a kid anymore. He had what she needed—right between his legs. And someday, *someday,* he'd give her the works. Make her scream in pleasurable pain as he thrust, bucked, slapped . . .

Lighting a cigarette unworthy of a brand name (it was all he could afford), and leaving it between his lips as he puffed, he put up the collar of his leather jacket, consulted the rearview mirror one last time with the aid of the dome light, opened the door, and stepped out. All in one fluid motion—smooth as a cat's ass.

Frank's imitation python-skin boots made small, crushing sounds as he stepped onto the pavement. The mixture of sand and salt hid the road's icy condition well. If not, Frank Carlson would have fallen on his ass as soon as his heels hit the ground.

Left thumb hooked into a belt loop, he took one long drag of his cigarette and tossed it to the ground, crushing it beneath the worn-out sole of his right boot. A growing tendril of smoke followed him as he crossed the road and knocked on Andrea's window.

She didn't move until the third knock.

Behind a foggy window, Andrea mouthed words he could not hear, and appeared startled at seeing him standing there. She opened her window, flinched at the intruding cold air (or his stunning presence?), and gaped, looking deep into his eyes, as if they contained the answers to all of her questions.

"Something wrong, babe?" They were the first words that Andrea's mind seemed to actually register—somewhat, anyway.

"Huh . . . what?"

"I SAID is there something wrong, BABE!" Spittle flew

from his lips and decorated his chin. He was quick to wipe at it with the back of his hand.

Andrea jumped back a few inches, apparently stung by his words. She looked from Frank to the cracks in her windshield and back to Frank, as if wondering why he didn't notice. She pointed to the window, but withdrew her gesture just as quickly, seemingly afraid she might touch it.

"What? What the hell are you looking at?" A brief look was all he needed. "Looks like a rock took out your windshield!" His words came like impatient bullets waiting to be released from the barrel of a gun.

Why couldn't he see it? Andrea's mind screamed. *It's right there!*

With splayed fingers and a quick look to each end of the deserted road, Frank ran a hand through his hair. His chest heaved and released a long cloud of visible breath. Andrea shied away, stealing a gulp of air as Frank's hand then came forward.

Mumbling soothing words she barely heard, Frank touched her cheek with the back of his hand. Andrea cringed, taken by surprise, but was too shocked to back completely away from his reach.

She did her best to endure his touch—as if his fingers were the legs of a hairy spider—trying to move as little as possible, hoping he would ignore her and scurry away.

She wasn't so lucky.

Andrea wrinkled her nose at the sharp odor of nicotine coming from his fingers in bitter wafts, envisioned a pallid shade of yellow being drawn against her cheek if he rubbed any harder.

Frank moved his hand to the back of her head and caressed her earlobe with his thumb.

Andrea shuddered, tensed.

Tracing a line from her ear, he paused at her jaw and rubbed with small circles that were a little too rough to feel comforting. A jagged hangnail scratched the side of her neck as his fingers continued downward and lingered at the base of her throat.

She stared at his arm, the cracks in the windshield seeming to laugh at her from the corner of her eye. Then followed the crinkled and peeling leather of the jacket sleeve to his face again, shivering at the gleam his eyes now contained—a gleam that contained more than just the hint of a Good Samaritan pleased to be helping her.

His hand still lingered, and was that a slight increase in pressure? She imagined his grip slowly crushing her throat, cutting off her air supply until her eyes bugged from her head and skin turned a pale blue. Consciousness would fade and . . .

With a sudden surge of energy, she grabbed the handle for the window and rolled it up with quick, jerking rotations. Frank's arm flopped around like a speared fish, finally free of Andrea's throat, before he managed to pry it from the rising window.

"What the fuck!" he screamed, rubbing the crook of his elbow, eyes livid within their orbits. "I just thought I'd see if you needed any help—fucking whore! Since you don't, I'll just leave your prissy little ass here!"

"Wait," Andrea tried to call, immediately realizing she would still be alone, but the word only developed into a grunt within her throat. She swallowed hard.

Frank turned his head and uttered a final word, determined to get the last word. "Bitch!" he shouted as he stalked away into the night.

The word stung as it echoed, but thoughts of being

stranded in the dark, alone, and frozen to death by morning, held the power of an ice-pick being driven straight through her heart, each thought a heavy blow to the butt end.

Andrea pictured her corpse still sitting in the driver's seat, eyes permanently frozen open, pupils cracked down their centers, and snot forming twin stalactites from each of her nostrils.

When her mind summoned the image of her black, frostbitten fingertips clinging to the steering wheel, it also—magically—conjured up the low rumbling of the car's engine and the soft music of the radio returned. A sonata. The glow coming from the dashboard did little to hide the ashen look on Andrea's face when she looked in the rearview mirror.

Andrea forced her heart back into her chest.

She stared beyond the cracks in her windshield, beyond the end of the road, beyond the vague distant tree line. And wondered what awful thing could be doing this to her.

The roar of Frank's engine and tires spinning before gaining enough traction to move forward were the last things Andrea heard before she grabbed the column shifter and pulled with an arm that felt heavy, lifeless. The only thing on her mind now was gin (forget the tonic), and more gin, to relieve the numbness that now flowed through her body with undulating vibrations.

Andrea turned the radio off and gripped the steering wheel in both hands, trying to look past the cracks, through the cracks, anything to avoid looking at them. At the edges of her vision, they mocked her with a malevolent grin, at times appearing to stretch and get bigger. She refused the temptation and kept her eyes locked onto a space a few inches above the road.

She arrived in her driveway with a sharp turn and a loud squeal as the tires cried against the sudden change in direction. The hood dipped toward the ground and rose again as she placed the car in park and lifted her foot off the brake pedal. Releasing a long breath mixed with anger and frustration, she craned her neck from side to side, heard it pop from tension, and closed her eyes.

When she opened them, the cracks were gone.

She felt the glass with just the tips of her fingers at first, then the entire palm of her hand. Smooth as a well-polished stone.

She had fought them back, refused to let them out until she was in the safety of her own home. But now, as hard as she tried to do otherwise, the tears began to fall.

Chapter 4

Durbin, Maine: Population 2562, and decreasing with each passing year.

Where the cold chips away at your bones during the harsh winter season and humidity suffocates you in the summer as its own entity, stealing your breath with hot, tangible waves.

Where nothing spectacular ever happens. Unless you include the time old "Mr. Happy" pranced around the town square naked, a sagging and very large belly thankfully hiding his most precious parts. Or the time Mrs. Ducharme finally crossed the border into Alzheimer's disease and insisted her cat was lost, knocking on every door of the neighborhood in search of Cuddles, then asking for directions across the street to her home. Her feline companion had passed away ten years prior.

Where the years of a childhood are spent outside, rain or shine.

Or snow.

During the winter, each child inevitably challenges the other to stick their moist tongues against frozen pipes, light poles, or anything their tender flesh will adhere to. Without fail, both always oblige, then take off screaming in separate directions (a sizeable layer of their tongues bleeding, while another layer is missing altogether), only to do it again once healed.

During the summer, with the Auburn Mall too much of a pain in the ass to get to without a ride, children seem to overtake the town, cluttering front lawns with toys, gadgets, and the occasional invention, which usually turns out to be a combination of both.

While some children choose to stay within the safety of the neighborhood, others decide to explore the wooded surroundings in search of new things, meandering through majestic pines that act as legendary sentries at the edges of town.

Six months after his first encounter with Andrea Varney, Darren Jacobs did just that, still discovering how to get around town. Taking an alternate way from the usual always seemed to add to the flavor of his adventures.

With visions of tiptoeing through the jungle while his foreign enemies tried to capture him, Darren veered off Whipple Street and onto a very peculiar-looking path.

Surrounded by overhanging trees that looked like they were about to pay a visit to tree heaven, rotten branches gently scraping the ground below, the path was pretty well hidden. But not for Darren; the point man had to notice everything!

Darren started to evade with an invisible M-16 tightly gripped between sweaty palms, thinking the enemy might be very near. Scratch that—an M-60 now hung from his arms as his muscles (very large and glistening with a sweaty sheen) allowed him to hold the huge weapon at his waist. Exploding mines and flying shrapnel surrounded Darren, but always missed him, being the immortal soldier that he was.

As he continued to make his way with silent steps through the trees, he remembered the times of playing Army with his friends in Auburn. Darren missed their journeys into the woods behind the local park, missed the friendships he had gotten used to, never thinking he would actually *move*. Those friends were gone now, seemingly hundreds of miles away according to his small feet. He had made friends quicker than he had expected in Durbin, but they would never replace the first friends he had ever come to know.

Sadness pulled at the corners of his lips, but vanished when he noticed an area cluttered with beer cans, sunlight almost unable to reflect a shine off their long-since-rusted surfaces. And cigarette butts—hundreds of them. This was a very familiar sight . . . he and his friends had found many of these spots in Auburn. It was a place the local teenagers came to drink their blues away and smoke their brains out secretly. Darren still couldn't find reasons behind any of it.

As he looked around, trying to see if he could find anything of value, he noticed a dilapidated wood sign leaning against a tree. A star-shaped hole in its center suggested the sign had once been nailed to the tree. But now, probably after a teen had fallen in a drunken fit, the sign rested against the trunk, left to rot. The words were almost invisible, as the changing of the seasons had definitely given the sign a beating.

Darren glanced at the faded letters, trying to make some sense of them. After connecting the letters to their missing counterparts, he discovered the sign read: *Cloud Nine.* He stared at it and wondered who would think of such a name—the place was a dump.

On a nearby tree smothered with carved initials and dates, a pair of once-pink panties was hanging from a protruding stub of a branch. On the ground beside the same tree lay a bra and a pair of men's underwear on top of a stained and mildewed mattress with springs poking through the cigarette-burned fabric. Darren's eyes enlarged as he tried to picture the scene and he could barely stifle a giggle.

Seeing absolutely nothing to take home as a souvenir,

and surely nothing his parents would like to see, Darren continued on, visions of being an immortal soldier now gone.

The knee-high grass brushed at Darren's pant legs in gentle swipes as he made his way deeper into the path. It swallowed him whole. On occasion, he stopped to have a look-see at articles left behind by those who had traveled this same path, but nothing held his interest for more than a second or two. After a few hundred more feet of glancing side to side, a faint glimmer of light caught his attention. He tilted his head to better his view, and it changed. The glare appeared larger, now emanating a brilliance that couldn't come from a rusted can. Or anything left behind by anyone, for that matter.

It began to take on an abstract shape, as if a mist were pushing its way through the grass, rising from the earth and flooding the ground just above the surface. It grew, and sparkled with energy around a milky center, demanding to be seen.

It pulled at Darren's curiosity.

With his gaze fixed on the mist, he climbed over trees that had met their dying day and pushed away overgrown branches that hung from the green ceiling above, unmindful of scratches beginning to cover his arms.

He couldn't keep up with it.

The mist withered like a shadow beneath the sun at noon. He tried to touch it, but it pulled back quicker than his reach, teasing him.

He laughed, immediately seeing the makings of some sort of game.

Darren followed the mist akin to a hound following the scent of a rabbit, eager to find its origin. Two quick steps and he touched the very edge of it. And pulled his fingers away in surprise. His fingers were out of the mist even before he heard the sharp snap of electricity. A gasp shot from his mouth.

Then something pulled at his leg and wrapped tightly around his ankle.

Darren's arms flailed at his sides, searching for balance. No use.

The air left his chest in a violent *thump* as he hit the ground. Thoughts of suffocating to death in a place nobody would ever find him entered his mind as he fought to inhale that small amount of precious oxygen that would keep him alive. Dinner would be waiting on the table and cold before his parents thought he might be doing something other than not paying attention to the time. And then it would be too late. He would be gone, buried within the weeds that now surrounded him.

Eternity seemed to pass before a trickle of air found its way into his lungs and allowed them to expand. Once, twice, breathing at last.

Through hair dangling in front of his eyes, through long blades of grass that had since turned brown, a marble headstone stared sadly at him. Another inch and his forehead would have caught its edge.

Blowing a small gust of air in front of his face to move his hair, Darren looked to see what had taken hold of his ankle.

A tangled mass of a thick root had emerged from the ground, revealing a surface that had split with no room to grow any further. The root formed a semicircle, rising from one point in the ground and reentering a few inches away, enough to let his foot pass through and snag his ankle.

Darren pried his foot loose, removing his sneaker in the process. After pulling his sock out from between his toes, he put his sneaker back on and stood up, brushing dirt and grass from the front of his clothes. He noticed a grass stain on one knee and knew he had to look forward to a verbal lashing from his mother when he got home. But, until then, he would investigate his new discovery!

The headstone's surface was covered with cracks similar to the dotted lines his father had shown him on maps of old logging trails of Maine. Brittle pieces, outlined by jagged edges, waited for a small tremor to tumble from the stone.

Darren bent to touch it, but pulled back as he remembered what had brought him here. He tried to decipher the name faintly engraved in the stone, but it was concealed beneath layers of dirt and weeds that had grown around it and clung with fierce determination. He wasn't about to touch it.

Other stones lay forgotten and scattered about, some well hidden, others not. In some areas of the cemetery, the grass would be able to tickle his nose.

Looking down at the headstone, he didn't know what to think. He couldn't explain the sorrow he felt as he looked at this old, weathered rock. And joy . . . but not just the joy of discovery. It was more like an empty hole in his life had just been filled.

A small gust of wind ruffled his hair, its sudden appearance changing everything around him.

Darren felt a sudden weight of responsibility pulling him down, as though he had aged many years. He could almost feel time carving wrinkles of wisdom into his flesh and implanting memories that didn't really seem to belong to him. He rubbed at the sudden bumps that appeared on his arms, as if pins and needles had fallen from the sky and covered his body in a gentle descent. Darren felt a change, a feeling in the pit of his stomach that told him to expect something. Something big.

For a single moment, he knew everything about the people that rested below his feet.

Actually, he didn't think they were resting at all.

Then, the moment was gone, leaving him with a queasy stomach and a touch of confusion.

But Darren knew there was something to be done involving those who once walked the Earth as he. Something *magnificent*. What to do was beyond him, but the curiosity was set in him like the fine lines at the corners of eyes age will bring, getting deeper as time passes.

After a quick jab at the stone proved he wouldn't be struck down by a sudden bolt from the heavens, he picked a small, brittle piece from the headstone—making sure he didn't actually break it himself—and placed it into his pocket.

The wind grew a bit stronger, and as suddenly as it came, it went.

Beneath twitching eyelids, a tomato plant (of all things), attacked Darren as he slept. But this was no ordinary tomato plant. Far from it—this one had thorns. As though it were a hybrid of some demented gardener, a new species developed under the secret windows of a backyard greenhouse.

Its stem pulsed from the ground, growing in sudden bursts. The green surface expanded, then retracted. Expanded and retracted again in a continuous cycle—breathing. Covered with jagged spikes that leaked smoking fluid from their tips, the stem wrapped around Darren's ankle and pulled him down, the ground giving way beneath his weight, sucking him in.

He felt thorns pierce his shins and burn as venom spread from each wound. Then his legs, and his chest as the stem coiled upward. It found his throat, creating hot flashes of pain as thorns punctured and sank into his flesh. When thorns wrapped around his head, he wondered if he was supposed to be nailed to two adjoining pieces of wood in the shape of a "T."

The green cord began to squeeze the life out of him.

Through bulging eyes, Darren saw the quivering end of the stem swell as if pregnant, the green skin turning a shade darker as it began to split and give birth to a tomato with a violent popping noise.

A dancing sphere of crimson bounced on a shaky tether of green stalk that couldn't support its weight. The smooth surface of the tomato's infantile skin beaded with clear fluid that gathered quickly and rained down all sides. Darren could have taken a bite of the dripping tomato if thorns hadn't been driven completely through his lips.

The surface of the tomato blistered, then split open, skin curling and turning black at the edges.

Venous innards glistened beneath its skin, producing a substance that fell onto Darren's nose in stinging drops. He tried to struggle, tried to keep the thorns from cutting into his eyes, but the stem grew tighter still. Shadows grew from the edges of his eyes and . . .

The buzzing of his digital alarm clock rescued him, the pounding in his chest slowly beginning to match its steady rhythm.

Sweat fell onto his nose, pulled down by the tightened crease between his eyebrows.

And for a moment, it stung.

Chapter 5

During the years following his first visit to the Durbin Public Library, Darren frequented the small building at least twice a week. He weaved through narrow hallways only getting thinner as books began to encroach on walking space; ran fingers along crowded shelves; and sometimes, if the scent was strong enough, precariously balanced a few feet from the ceiling in search of a book.

The smell got to him first, assailing his senses with intoxicating fumes upon the opening of each book. On occasion, he'd sneak around a corner and actually place his nose into the exact center of a book and breathe deeply, eyes closed, savoring the aroma. Darren tried this at a bookstore one evening, but found it wasn't the same, almost artificial. He liked the old books, the ones that crackled as he stretched the tough binding.

He'd leave the library with the maximum number of books he could check out (usually five, but sometimes up to seven, since Ms. Varney knew he was a trusted customer) and returned them well before they were due, read at least once, sometimes twice, while in his possession.

As he approached his teenage years, his love for books turned into a crush on Andrea Varney.

Darren didn't will it to happen, wasn't expecting it in the least. He hated to admit it and had never disclosed this vital piece of information to anyone, save himself, when even his own thoughts were hard to believe.

It had happened as he was leafing through an ancient medical textbook, amazed at things that could happen to

41

people, enthralled by the black and white images of bulbous tumors, swollen appendages, and rotting flesh. Alerted by the squeaks of the book cart's wheels, he looked up to notice movement in the aisle across from him.

A space between *Gray's Anatomy* and another book provided him the view of a lifetime.

Ms. Varney was leaning over, her shirt hanging from her body at the center of her chest. A medallion of sorts hung from her neck and twirled and twirled. But he wouldn't fall for it. His eyes wouldn't be lured away—they had found their target: the white cotton mesh of her bra. Maybe it was a tad too small, but Darren could almost swear that half of a nipple was peeking over its edge.

He couldn't believe it!

Then, the unthinkable happened.

The tingling sensation he felt in what he and his friends called a *nutsack* made him shift in position as his skin tightened and balls began to ache. Before he could even fathom what was happening, his penis started to grow at feverish speed. Thinking his skin would peel open at the sudden hardness, he let out a muffled groan as he pressed on it. The shock of how good it felt squeezed another centimeter from his tightly stretched skin.

Rock hard. Painful. Yet rather enjoyable.

Darren wanted to leave immediately, avoiding anything that resembled eye contact with anyone, but soon realized he would have to walk home. Then the entire town would see that Darren Jacobs just had his first "legitimate" woody—sporting the morning wood (due to a full bladder) didn't count.

He waited until she finished putting books on the shelf and departed to the front of the library before choosing a book big enough to cover the entire front of his jeans.

He had a hard time meeting Andrea's eyes at the checkout section of the desk, knew that his cheeks were glowing, was dead-set certain that she *knew*, that she had to know. And when he did steal a look into her eyes, he noticed a change in them and knew he was busted. Why else would she look at him like that? With that smile that wasn't a smile, but a grin that said she knew what he had seen? Almost in confirmation, Ms. Varney plucked at the button that secured the opening of her shirt.

While she scanned his library card (a recent addition to the library—computers), he pushed the lower half of himself against the desk in order to hide his new friend. And loved the feeling. A trickle of sweat fell down the center of his back, pausing at his waist before falling into the edge of his briefs. If he had leaned in a little farther, he might have punched a hole right through the sturdy mahogany.

When Andrea bent over again, he had to look away.

Darren wobbled home, book held in front of his jeans in the most casual way he could find, but still he thought he looked like a dork.

When the journey home finally ended, he locked himself inside his room with imaginary images of Ms. Varney and an open shirt—minus the bra. Closing his eyes, she instantly peered at him through hair that hung over her face as she leaned over. Behind loose strands, her eyes sparkled in their brilliance, a shade of green as calming and serene as a tropical lagoon. When she pulled at the opening of her shirt, fingers gently peeling the fabric away from her skin to give him a better view, he soon discovered the sticky stuff that can come from the tip of your *Jimmy* (or whatever you decided to name it) in quivering spasms if you touched it a certain way.

It took him a few days to go back to the library. When he

finally summoned the courage, he wished he had waited a few more.

As he strolled through the entrance, Ms. Varney's gaze seemed to penetrate him, causing his skin to flush in color. She wanted to say something—he could see it in her eyes— but chose to remain silent, letting him stir in his guilt.

And his jeans.

Chapter 6

A football traveled in nimble arcs between pairs of hands, somehow defying physics and missing a lamp, several picture frames, and a glass trophy of a quarterback frozen in mid-pass. Listening to heavy-metal music blaring from vibrating speakers, Darren and three other boys enjoyed their first year as legitimate teenagers.

It was June 10th, the first of many days before school started again.

Darren's parents were still at work, and the house, for now, was Darren's very own. Mischievous tones seemed to emanate from the very walls that surrounded them, entering their brains with a likeness to mass hysteria.

Mark Simpson leaned outside an open window, taking a drag from a cigarette he'd swiped from an open pack left by Mr. Jacobs. It was his first. Much to the delight of those watching, the coughing spell that followed was impressive.

Almost as impressive as the sudden shade of green Mark's face turned. Cheeks ballooning to contain their contents, he hung over the windowsill just in time to deliver the ground his innermost thoughts. He flicked the burning butt into the small puddle of bile directly below Darren's bedroom window and turned to meet laughs thankfully hidden beneath the raucous music.

Sitting comfortably on the floor, Craig Aldridge kept the football to himself. His head bobbed up and down to the heavy rhythm of a song by Metallica, with long, curly hair almost concealing his entire face. He looked like a mop with a human body attached and dancing happily—his body was almost that skinny.

With an attitude clearly defined by his appearance, Simon "Spike" Wilson paced slowly back and forth. Darren's room was littered with posters of rock bands and Spike carefully examined each one, apparently looking for clothing items he thought he'd look good in. Spiked belts and bracelets were but a few of the items he liked to wear. His jet-black hair, always standing on edge, could be spotted easily in a group of a hundred or more.

Darren kept up with the beat of the drums by tapping his hands on a stereo speaker, looking for another CD to play among many. He found one by AC/DC.

The changing of CDs created a thick silence that smothered any sort of conversation allowed by the ability to finally hear each other. Leave it to Spike's sarcastic and raspy voice that sounded more like muffled grunts than intelligible words to break the silence before anyone else. "Man, let's get the fuck out of here."

"Yeah man, let's fucking bail," Craig agreed, grinning at the still-fresh taste of a cuss word.

Mark slowly nodded in approval, perhaps afraid to disagree with Spike. His hands were wrapped around his upset stomach, but his face was finally hinting at its original color. He always tried to fit in, but most of the time didn't seem to get it quite right.

"Hey Darren, got any more of those cool books I could borrow before we go?" Mark asked, referring to Darren's collection of horror paperbacks with gut-wrenching covers Darren had gotten him addicted to.

"Sorry, man, you've already read them all. I'll let you have the one I'm reading as soon as I'm done," Darren said as he clapped Mark on the shoulder. He knew Mark used the books to escape a world that dressed him in checkered shirts that buttoned high enough to give his neck a rash. A world that had him up at dawn to eat breakfast (even on Sundays). Where homework assignments existed even during the summer.

Though three out of the four clearly wanted to leave, no one moved.

Spike cleared his throat. Looked everywhere but at Darren, foot tapping against the wall, waiting.

Spike may have been convinced he led this small group, but all of them, including Spike, followed and admired Darren. At thirteen, Darren had the build of a freshman in high school and his close friends had silently elected him leader. At first, merely because he could kick any one of their asses. It didn't take them long to realize Darren was also the cool voice that prevailed when any of them got into squabbles, intervening before any punches were thrown or feelings hurt.

Darren hit the power button on his stereo and the LED display faded.

Spike snapped his fingers and clapped his hands, most likely delighted to have seen the signal to leave at last.

They meandered along the back roads of Durbin, a town that once tried to flourish and failed, for what seemed like hours. Boredom can do that: take time and pull it from both ends, stretch it between two points into such a length that people have trouble filling it in with activity, especially newly-christened teenagers in a small town.

Sporadic conversations varied from the latest rock groups to the hottest new girls in town (not many in the way of new arrivals or good-looking ones). When they came to the beaten structure of an old warehouse, they paused, almost perplexed that something had gotten in the way of

47

their travels, wondering what to do next. Four pairs of eyes craned toward the sky, squinting as they reached an edge of the roof partially hiding the sun.

The warehouse towered above them all and appeared to weigh heavily on supporting pillars that leaned just far enough to notice. The floor of the warehouse rested on these pillars, creating a shadowed world beneath that resembled a gaping maw and stank like mildewed breath.

Darren wasn't the least bit surprised to see the Cheshire grin Spike cast over his shoulder before walking into the unknown. It was just Spike's nature to be the first at everything. The look alone meant Darren had to keep a watchful eye and, unfortunately, this meant having no choice but to follow him into the darkness.

There was enough room for all but Darren to stand fully erect under the warehouse. He resorted to a slight hunch to avoid impaling himself on nails that jutted from wooden support beams and bypass cobwebs that hung limp between each.

With one more look over his shoulder, Spike ran ahead, a fading giggle trailing behind him like a stream of toilet paper stuck to the crack of his ass. He stopped ahead of the rest of them and appeared to work feverishly at completing a task before any of them could see what he was doing. His silhouette bounced back and forth between the shadows, bending down every so often only to hurry back to a common area. It could only mean trouble. Darren tried to hurry without falling. Mark and Craig were at his side like wingmen, behind and to the right. One of them had kicked a can, and the sudden noise caused Spike's silhouette to freeze briefly before continuing its strange dance on the edges of the shadows, punctuated occasionally by a mischievous giggle.

Spike's hazy shape slowly grew into greater detail as Darren approached, and revealed a crazed teen frantically searching his pockets for something. Darren was still too far away to intervene, but a few more tactical weaves around scattered debris would have him at Spike's side momentarily.

But not before a Zippo lighter trembled within Spike's fingers as if it were the Holy Grail.

Seeing Darren getting closer, Spike quickly opened the lid with the snap of his thumb and middle finger, brought his thumb down over the wheel, and stared into a flame in a matter of seconds.

Then placed it on the small pile of leaves he had gathered.

The flames spread in all directions, blue and yellow fingers rippling among the leaves to create a small fire. Spike's bugging eyes reflected the dancing flicker with malevolent wonder as he absently rubbed at his crotch—a disgusting habit he had every time he got excited. Something everyone knew but never talked about.

Spike never looked five minutes into the future with anything he'd done, and subsequently failed to realize the structure above them would become a towering inferno in less time than it took them to get out from under it.

Darren brought his foot from the shadowed surroundings and down upon the fire with a heavy stomp.

"What are you, nuts?" Darren asked in a tone that dared Spike to take it any further, still tapping at lingering ashes that refused to die.

"Damn you guys! Can't you just let me have a little fun once in a while?" Spike shouted, but his defiance was short-lived beneath a glare stronger than his. Simon Wilson soon lowered his head and turned away.

Mark broke the deadened air. "Hey, look over there, it looks like smoke or something, coming out of those leaves."

They turned to where Mark was pointing.

"Wasn't me," Spike immediately chimed in, eyes wide.

"What the hell?" Craig marveled, still tasting a new vocabulary.

"Come on, let's check it out."

They gathered around a perfect circle and stared into a multicolored center of autumn leaves. A small haze of smoke rose from under, outlining each leaf with silent, wispy fingers of gray. All breathing ceased, all words swallowed for the moment. A drop of water found the stagnant puddle beneath it and echoed somewhere beneath the warehouse.

Darren watched the tendrils of smoke lengthen, intertwine, and sway before him like the watch of a hypnotist. His eyes began to burn and water. Part of him wanted to squeeze them shut and wipe at the fluid building at their corners, but he could only stand transfixed as an image began to appear within the smoke.

From the outside edges of wrinkled skin, a face developed around thin, deflated lips and a nose that appeared to be bigger on one side than the other. Pale eyes grew from swirling pockets of smoke and searched for answers, searched for understanding. They were the saddest eyes Darren had ever seen. As if any type of life force that once existed had been sucked from behind them, removing their energy and their sparkle.

ALBERT.

Darren knew the man's name without knowing how, as if it were just whispered into his ear. He thought he saw one side of the man's mouth curl up into a grin before the image shimmered, like the surface of a pond stirred by a breeze, and then vanished.

A hand slowly moving up and down in front of Darren's eyes broke his concentration, made him blink.

"You okay dude?" Craig asked. "What's wrong?"

"Hmmmm?" Darren's words were distant even to his ears. "Oh . . . nothing. Just wondering where the smoke's coming from." He pushed Craig's arm away, looked toward the center of the leaves. Whatever he had seen, if anything, was gone.

"Aren't we all," Spike said as he picked up a large rock. Two of the others waited curiously. Darren was somewhere else entirely.

"Watchya gonna do with that rock?" Mark asked, his voice timid.

"See if there's anything under there, dumbass!"

Spike threw the rock directly toward the center of the circle before anyone could stop him. As the stone drifted through the air, they all watched with held breath and slackened jaws as it tumbled in flight, one slow rotation after another.

And waited.

The impact proved not to meet any of their expectations.

There wasn't any.

The stone broke the surface of the leaves and fell and fell and fell. A sudden gust of heat made each of them step back, alarmed, eyes burning, as if a seal had just been broken.

They stood with their heads turned, ears toward the hole in front of them, waiting for the rock to hit bottom.

Silence.

Until a faint but audible warbling pricked at their ears and turned into the rise and fall of a chant that thrummed within their souls.

Far below the surface of the earth, hooded figures surrounded an elderly gentleman bound to a stake.

On the surface, four teenagers ran like little boys.

Chapter 7

Summer vacation.

Raining.

The small aisles of the library were silent except for the click and shuffle of an elderly woman perusing the Romance section. When she paused to examine a book—a seemingly endless amount of time—Andrea could hear the occasional rumble of thunder, the hum of the fluorescent light bulbs overhead, the ticking of a clock.

An old newspaper had been pulled for someone's research and now rested on the front desk, its yellowish tinge making it appear as though sunlight were entering a window and covering it in a wash of dull rays. The paper waited for Andrea to gather enough energy and place it in the filing cabinet just a few feet away.

Andrea picked it up, but instead of placing the paper into the cabinet, she turned to the second page, a page she knew well.

She wondered how long ago the second page of the *Durbin Sentinel* was dedicated to the obituaries. As though the people that died, most having spent their entire lives here, some even dedicating themselves to its development, were not worthy of front-page news. The road to being forgotten, it seemed, started the day after one took a last gulp of air.

On March 23, 1935, Albert Fontaine had started down this same well-traveled road.

His eyes . . . That was the small detail that caught Andrea's attention, pulled at her from the yellowed picture.

There appeared to be something hidden behind his eyes. The rest of his expression revealed a happy life: laugh lines around the mouth, eyebrows raised as if someone had just told him a joke and he struggled not to laugh. However, his eyes revealed a profound sadness. Like he knew he would someday be lost from the thoughts of those he loved most.

A forgotten soul. One among many.

Darren, it's almost time.

Rain pelted the window of Darren's room, creating small streams of water against the pane of glass that distorted the world outside. Claps of thunder made the house shake. The darkened sky, with condensed shafts of rain stark against a gray background, acted as a cage that prevented him from spending the day outside.

Darren sat at his desk and let his fingers pulse their way toward a paper clip, pick it up, and bend it beyond all recognition. Bored again.

Another crackle from the skies stirred him from his lethargy. He opened his desk drawer in search of . . . in search of anything to occupy his time. He shuffled past countless numbers of pens, pencils, highlighters, and note cards, many of them yet to be removed from the cellophane.

He reached beneath all of this and dug deep inside the compartment his mother had termed his *junk drawer*. Seems there were plenty of these throughout the house, as she constantly fought to rearrange them, taking one pile of junk and moving it to another, more organized pile. She left Darren's alone, and for that he was grateful.

Deeper still into the darkened area of the drawer, while he picked things up, felt familiar shapes and sizes, and let them fall back in place. Until he came upon an object he rolled three times within his grip and still couldn't figure out what it might be. He squeezed it, rubbed it, and squeezed again. Cool to the touch, partly smooth on one side, coarse and rough on another.

His mind drew a blank.

Seeing no better time to amuse himself with a foolish surprise, he closed the object within his hand and removed it from its darkened home for the last . . . he didn't know how long. He brought his hand under a lamp and closed his eyes.

Let his fingers uncurl before chancing a look into his hand.

And managed a slight peek before his eyes flew open. A severed finger he had saved for whatever reason would have produced the same effect.

He gazed upon an almost-forgotten piece of headstone, watched it shake in response to his shaking hand, then tumble to the desk as memories flooded into him. People suddenly appeared inside his head—for only an instant, but clear as recent memories.

Memories that didn't belong to *him*.

The storm, the music he had turned on just to fill in some space, and the world around him fell into the distance. His heart knocked hard against his ribcage. Scraping the legs of the chair against the floor, he hurried to stand up. Then pressed his fingers hard against the sides of his open mouth, trying to understand what had just happened. He pinched his lower lip without feeling it, ran a hand through his hair. The more he thought about it, the more ludicrous everything became.

There was only one way to prove what had happened—a way he didn't really like.

He opened his door and looked toward the living room. He heard the soft murmur of the television and the crinkling of a bag of chips. A page turned in a book and the hard plastic of the remote banged upon an end table. His parents were occupied with a lazy day off.

Sitting himself back down at his desk, he eyed the stone. Minutes ticked by. His CD player played a final song before becoming silent, as if in anticipation.

He encircled his hands around the stone without touching it, the sides of his palms against the desk, fingertips together, hands rising above it. Using his thumbs, he pushed the stone toward his pinkies. Still able to breathe, heart still beating, he grasped the stone between a thumb and forefinger. Rubbed the smooth edge of the stone, feeling a gradual change take hold of his body in a gentle caress that wasn't frightening at all.

People began to appear again, slower now, less startling, as if they were making introductions instead of jumping right in front of him and saying, *Boo!* An older man first, then a woman just as old tucked in close against him, and two young girls that looked exactly alike sitting on each of their knees. They were smiling, as if readying themselves for a portrait.

Darren felt a chill run through his body and emotions not entirely his own tug at his heart as Albert Fontaine presented himself and the cherished moments of his life. Disbelief kept him rubbing the stone until his body grew numb and slouched, eyes falling heavy.

The images kept changing.

The girls now swung beside each other with Albert pushing from behind, their faces flushed with delight and happiness, their hair lifting to reveal saucer-like eyes as they gained speed. Darren flinched when a vision of Albert lying in bed intruded on their happiness, silencing laughs and chuckles of excitement, bringing with it a deep sense of sadness as he died in a sleep of peaceful dreams.

The nightmare began when weekly visits to his burial plot turned monthly. Then yearly. Until they were ultimately forgotten.

Darren felt Albert being released from his current state of being, as a happiness far outweighing any misery he may have been subject to chewed away at his pain and ate the shadows that surrounded him.

Beneath the surface of a small town, Albert Fontaine slowly disappeared from the stake to which he was bound.

Chapter 8

If cemeteries could speak, many questions would possibly be asked in silent lamentation, perhaps causing their rusted gates to shutter in protest, their entrances to creak open a fraction of an inch. Iron flakes, peeling away with the mournful groan of a hinge or the rare touch of a human hand, fall in fragments as distant memories. Elegant spires, spaced evenly apart, once protected the perimeters of these cemeteries in rigid splendor, but now often slump and stagger along jagged ground, as if in defeat from a battle that has been waged for far too long. Once lush green, neatly trimmed lots are overgrown with yellowed grass, and clumps of weeds sparsely add to an increasingly pallid flavor.

Burial processions are sad. Sadder still, when most people make their last visits to a cemetery the day they bury loved ones, friends, acquaintances; unmindful of the fact that they too will eventually be buried beneath these same grounds, some right next to the person they had just tossed a handful of dirt onto and said a final goodbye to.

Did they think that was it? Buried in a pine box only to wither and decay into nothing?

Abandoned cemeteries around the world try their best to keep souls within crumbling gates, to protect them from the sinister force that consistently pulls from beneath. Of course, they are only material objects, built by the same people they hold below their shriveling lots. The *living* need to keep these souls wrapped within these gates until they are allowed to move on to a better, higher existence. People

. hold this responsibility. People need to remember.

And they have no idea.

Why don't they come and pay their respects as they once had, ideals of tradition and honor falling at the wayside?

Why can't they remember the people they have buried?

A few do, but unfortunately they are trying to do the work required of thousands.

Time is running out.

Again.

Chapter 9

Graduation was the scariest day of his life.

From behind maroon gowns and tassels ahead of him, Darren listened as the other members of his student class (a whopping seventy-three) had their names announced, received their diplomas, and were led off the stage with a small blurb stating the college or trade school or branch of the armed forces they would be attending in the near future. A round of applause followed, with an occasional cheer from family, friends, or just some wiseass.

The school authorities moved them like cattle, pausing ungodly amounts of time between students. Otherwise, the entire ceremony would have lasted no more than fifteen minutes. That was fine with Darren—he had no desire to cross the stage, feel the warmth of the spotlight on his back. When he received his diploma, the applause would be short, polite, the infamous golf clap from people wanting to move on to someone with a future. Not someone who'd be spending his life making piecework at Knapp Shoe.

Two more shuffling steps and a cowbell chimed in his head. He imagined bits of grass jutting from the corners of his mouth as he chewed. The spotlight now basked on a shorter guy in front of him who just happened to be going to Harvard and had a strut that emphasized the point. How could he compete with that?

The light touched the tips of loafers he'd probably never wear again. Darren stepped back and heard an involuntary cluck in the back of his throat. Pretty soon it would be shining upon him and him alone.

Another diploma, the Harvard blurb, another round of applause—splendid.

The spotlight swiveled on an unseen bracket, searching for him, a tether of light ready to pull him toward the stage. His breaths got shorter and his heart beat faster. Trembling fingers picked at the edge of a thumb's cuticle to the point of actually oozing a drop of blood, something he couldn't seem to prevent when he was nervous.

He took the first step and . . .

Somehow, he survived, even heard his father throw in a hoot for him. The round of applause was louder than he would have ever expected.

For the ten days leading up to that dreaded day, he had paced. And paced, wherever he happened to be, wondering what to do. With no SATs completed, no applications to college, and absolutely no idea what avenue to venture down, Darren didn't know which way to turn.

To approach his parents would be to admit defeat, unable to make any decisions on his own—still a baby suckling his mother's breast. He shuddered at the thought.

His future was a popular topic at the dinner table, but he found ways to skirt around it, spouting with false confidence about wanting to experience some of the world before delving into a future of doing the same thing day after day. But his eyes never seemed able to leave the mashed potatoes on the plate in front of him. Sure, he had plans, but suddenly it was time to talk about the weather. He was amazed at how fluently his mouth would spew this information, refusing to mention the one word that terrified him: help. To ask for it meant he was incapable of being independent. He wanted his parents to be proud, not ashamed.

Graduation completed, diploma stuffed in the bottom of a drawer, he paced yet again (the living room this time). He found the remote and turned on the television, deciding to fall into the couch, hoping it would take him into another world—one where you didn't have to work for a living.

Surrounded by swollen cushions and pillows, he clicked and clicked the remote. Thoughts barely registered the newscasters, weather photos, and cartoons that appeared for a moment before being dispelled into the realm of the television's subconscious with yet another click. With each heaving sigh, he sank deeper into the couch.

When an advertisement displayed for a nearby vocational institute, he turned off the television with a heavy press of a red button. Static crackled from the surface of the screen and the house seemed to yawn at the sudden silence.

Mustering all the strength he could find, he pulled himself out of the upholstery, resisting the urge to fall back in and go to sleep until the next century. With a sigh that echoed off the walls and through the hallways, he left, heading for the library to look for answers that always seemed to exist just out of reach.

Andrea wasn't surprised to see Darren come through the doors of the library with his head down, feet dragging. This entire week he'd been in and out, searching every possible career guide available, and always left without saying a word. She really wanted to help him, but was torn between wanting to tell him about the journey as soon as possible and letting him discover his own desires. If she only knew how long the journey would actually take. *Probably close to a lifetime,* she thought miserably. And there was surely no financial outcome from this trek into darkness—another miserable thought.

She watched Darren walk toward the back aisle of the library, his favorite spot, eyes pointed at the floor in front of him while his hand swiped blindly at the edges of books, and wondered when she would finally summon the courage to tell him. She had waited all this time and now the moment was here, waiting. It had to be soon.

NOW, she said to herself. *Now is the time.*

Her stomach tightened the way it used to when she was about to speak in front of a crowd of people, almost to the point of cramping, muscles twisting. She bent at the waist, holding her breath until the feeling passed, then wiped her palms on her slacks.

Thoughts and images went through her mind as she tried to arrange how she would approach him and put it all into words. How would she even begin?

Forcing herself to get a folder under the desk, she pushed herself ahead before she could change her mind.

Darren stared into a pile of open books that lay in disarray on the table in front of him. As usual, no matter how many times he turned the pages or scanned through the index, he found nothing that held his interest even for a few minutes, let alone the rest of his life. At this point in time, he was convinced a future existed as a bagperson, spending his days pushing around a shopping cart and standing in line at the soup kitchen. He cringed.

Frustrated, he pushed the books away and laid his head on the table. He found comfort from the blackness as he closed his eyes, letting the world slip away as he listened to his slow, steady breaths and relaxed. No sooner had his breaths begun to lull him, than sleep turned blackness into hazy images.

A hand on his shoulder startled him and pulled him away from a dream that left a familiar aftertaste, existing just outside the edges of a memory.

". . . trouble, Darren?"

"Hmmm . . . ?"

"Having some trouble?" Andrea asked, her voice soft, as if she were part of the dream that kept nagging at the back of his mind, but would never present itself.

"Oh . . . sorry. I must have dozed off for a while," Darren said. The folds of his sleeves were imprinted on the side of his face. He rubbed at the tenderness.

"Having a rough time trying to decide on a career, eh partner?" Hearing that last word sent shivers of surprise through his body. "I wish I could help you, but you've got to decide that on your own," she said. And in afterthought, "Sorry if you've heard that enough already."

"Yeah, I know. I just don't know what to do," Darren said, hands rising above him at his sides, as though waiting to catch the answer from the heavens. "I never gave it much thought. I thought the future was a lifetime away and—"

"Don't worry too much. Everybody goes through the same thing. In fact, it took me a few years just to decide I wanted to be a simple librarian. And there's something about the smell . . ." Andrea said, seeming to drift off into her own daydream.

"At least you have something you'd like to do the rest of your life. I have nothing."

A deep frustration dulled his eyes, pulled the focus from them.

"That's what I wanted to talk to you about, Darren," she said. She placed a folder on the table and left it unopened.

A glimmer of hope flashed in Darren's eyes as he listened for what she was about to say next.

"You see Darren," Andrea said, "I've been waiting to tell you this for a very, very, long time . . ."

He listened. Right now, anything was better than nothing.

The words fell from her lips, as if she had memorized an entire speech. She described how she became friends with people who once inhabited this world and how they needed to be remembered and saved from the anguish of being forgotten. How *they* had told her of a partner so many years ago, and the feeling she got the first time he stepped foot into the library and shook her hand. After this last mention, Darren rubbed his palm, flexed his fingers. *And remembered.* She continued, words flowing from her mouth almost as if she'd rehearsed them.

Darren listened curiously, intently. He found this, true or not, very interesting, but still didn't understand his role in all of it. Why had she waited for *him,* a soon-to-be factory laborer?

As he stared at what Andrea took out of a manila folder, his surfacing skepticism quickly vanished.

The man in the obituary seemed to look right through him. Darren's spine quivered, icy fingers crawling up each vertebra, one at a time.

"I've saved this for a long time, so I could show you what I mean," she said, using her thumb on the paper as though caressing the face of the man in the picture. "When I first looked at this obituary a few years ago, I could see that there was unhappiness in his eyes, like he knew he would be forgotten. But a few days later, I looked again and saw happiness within those same eyes. I thought that my feelings might be wrong, so I saved this to show you, thinking you might get the same feelings . . . Darren?"

Darren continued to stare at the picture, mesmerized, mouth falling open. Albert Fontaine stared in exchange. They had met again. He could almost hear Albert giving his thanks for being remembered, released from his pain.

A flash of heat started at his toes and gently pervaded Darren's body, seeming to fill every nerve with a burning coil. Darren looked up, finally able to pull away from Albert's gaze. Andrea was smiling, and doing something he couldn't quite put a finger on. The intensity of her eyes made him turn away.

"Can you feel it, Darren?" Andrea asked. "Can you feel the power between *us*, too?"

A nervous twitch of a grin perched on Darren's lips.

Silently, he accepted a journey that would take him to regions of the world he could never have imagined.

And beyond.

Chapter 10

Darren sat at the kitchen table, eyes fixed on the *goodbye* letter he had just finished, and felt like a child as tears gathered and threatened to spill. The security that surrounded him in the form of a roof to live under, warm meals provided no matter what time his mother came home from work, and a bed he had long since gotten very used to, were about to be removed from his life. His reverie brought him to a time when his father had first removed the training wheels from his bicycle and urged him down the small stretch of road in the front of their home. Only now, memories of the dead urged him onward, the stretch of road suddenly looming larger. And he couldn't see past the curve.

Writing this letter was tough, tougher still that he didn't have the guts to face his parents for a proper farewell: a warm hug from his mother or a firm handshake from his father. Nor did he think that's what he would have received.

More than a few pieces of crumpled paper had found their way into the wastebasket. He made sure to shove them all the way to the bottom, past last night's spaghetti and meatballs, in the event his parents would unravel them and try to understand what he *really* meant to say amidst the erasures and scratch-outs. Truth be told, he had absolutely no idea what he wanted to say, only that it was something he needed to do and he loved them both. So that's exactly what he decided to write: two quick sentences after many long starts. He avoided saying he was sorry, though he came pretty close. He felt it would undermine any strong determination he wanted them to know he had.

A single tear, unable to be restrained by pure will alone, fell onto the paper and spread the ink that contained the first two letters of his signature. He didn't attempt to dry it, didn't crumple it up and start over, but left it alone.

He had even tried to bring it up at the dinner table the last couple of nights, but what came forth was a senseless babble about a personal journey to find himself.

It really didn't matter what he decided to tell them. Darren noticed the grins and glances his parents shared as he attempted to tell them what he planned to do. Their thoughts were boldly printed across their foreheads: *Okay, Darren honey, when you leave I'll make sure to keep dinner warm, just in case you decide to return early. Uh . . . son, you sure you don't want to go fishing this weekend, so maybe we can discuss this man to man? Where are you going to get money; you think everything in this world is free?*

Yes, Darren could tell from their glances at one another that that's what they were thinking. In a rapidly developing ritual, he would excuse himself from the table, deciding against discussing the matter any further. They wouldn't understand. He didn't dare tell them he had taken the entire 1500 dollars from his savings account, but did vow to pay it back once he returned, whenever that would be.

Darren also opted against telling them that he'd have a companion by the name of Andrea Varney. They would surely be more interested then—a little too interested.

Humidity followed her into the car and she unrolled both windows, trying to let the stale air pass through the car instead of surround her with its thickness. It didn't do much, as beads of sweat immediately began to form on her upper lip and brow. Air conditioning hadn't existed when she first bought the car and was considered an extreme luxury in this part of the country at the time.

As she peeled her blouse away from her skin, she wondered if it was only the humidity and not the excitement she felt in the pit of her stomach that caused her insides to boil. Today was a day that had always kept on the heels of a setting sun. No matter how much closer she thought she was getting, the distance seemed to stretch equal amounts in between.

At long last, the time had finally arrived and a barely harnessed energy now filled her insides. Alongside this excitement, anxiety ran parallel, knowing they would soon be walking a shady path, in fear of what might lurk in the shadows.

Like the long drives that used to accompany family vacations to Bar Harbor when she was younger, Andrea immediately assumed the roles of her parents when she left her driveway. Her thoughts drifted back to all she had brought with her, checking off the imaginary checklist in her head. She fought the temptation to turn back around and make sure the stove was off, the doors locked. God bless her parents and the idiosyncrasies they passed on to her; she just had to laugh. She would never forget them.

She didn't know how, but her Plymouth still kicked beneath her, albeit with slightly less punch on acceleration. She only waited for the kicks to pump spasmodically in a dying gyration before she had to finally replace the engine, an engine well over its first 100,000 miles. She patted the steering wheel, rubbed the dashboard, and said, "Just a little longer, Betsy." Looking through the windshield, she remembered a cold winter night, but said nothing.

The car protested with squeaky shocks after passing over even the smallest of potholes, but went unnoticed, as the noise had become part of the car's personality. As much so as the road she traveled to and from work each day, knowing when each dip in the road would occur and how much she had to slow down and when, without even thinking about it; all part of the glories of living in the boondocks. As much as she hated the same long drive that would bring her to Darren's home, she welcomed the time it allowed her to think.

Darren wanted her to arrive while his parents were still at work to avoid any questions. She knew it was hard for him, couldn't imagine making the jump into adulthood again, especially in the way he was, with so many unanswered questions. She hoped to at least answer a few.

The last couple of days were spent making sure everything was taken care of during her absence, however long it might be. She was fortunate enough to have planned this gradually over the years. There was enough money to pay her bills for a long while if need be, with still enough for her and Darren to use on the road. Where that road would take them still intrigued her. Money was not the first of her priorities during this ordeal, but she'd need it to get anywhere.

Her first concern was to make this journey as safe as possible for her and Darren. She had no idea how dangerous this might prove to be. Darren's life was just beginning, and if it was taken from him, she couldn't even imagine the guilt she would feel for the rest of her life. *Unless, of course, they left the world together.* Andrea shook her head to disperse this unwelcome thought, not believing she was even thinking about such a thing.

She had gone to work yesterday as usual, but spent most of her free time wrapping up her research. At the end of the day, she had compiled a list of cemeteries for the entire state of Maine that still amazed her. So many cemeteries, so many people to be remembered. So many forgotten souls.

70

She wondered if they would even get out of the state of Maine at all. Could they do it alone? She knew it would be a mission almost impossible for anyone to ever finish, but at the very least, she and Darren could perhaps spread the word to people who would listen and follow their lead.

One step at a time, she thought. *One step at a time.*

She had found it difficult explaining to her assistant librarian that she didn't know when she'd be back. Luckily, Shelly Colban understood, somewhat, and said she'd love the extra hours. Said she just hoped that Andrea wasn't in any kind of trouble. Andrea had told her with a wink of an eye that it would be a vacation with no known end date. That was as far as she'd go in explaining the situation. She didn't want anyone to know what she planned to do, close friends or otherwise. She could clearly envision the fellas at the State Loony Bin chasing after her with a syringe full of happy juice. Andrea promised to call every so often and see how things were going. That seemed to relax Shelly and stop her from giving Andrea that funny look that said she knew something was wrong.

At home, she had finally finished packing and forced her last suitcase closed shortly before midnight, leaving only one thing left to do.

The box was on the top shelf of her walk-in closet, buried beneath a growing pile of sweaters. She couldn't remember the last time she had actually opened the beaten old shoebox and looked at its contents. Looking up at it, part of her was hesitant to take it down from its resting place. She had been so young when she put the box together, how could she have known?

With unsteady hands, she grasped the bottom of the box and slid it gently from beneath the sweaters. She placed it on her bed, stared intently, as if trying to see through it in-

stead of taking the lid off. By doing so, she would be re-
living so many memories, slicing them into a layer of her
consciousness that would sting like a freshly opened wound.

She gripped the lid of the box within the palm of her
hand. The hollow gong of the grandfather clock in the
living room made her jump.

Midnight.

Sipping a nervous breath, she opened the box. Let it out
slowly as she surveyed the small pieces of headstones that
hadn't changed since she had placed them there. She
picked one up, let the small charge of energy pleasantly
numb her fingers, and then closed it tightly within her
hand. She closed her eyes and let the images and memories
flood her mind once again.

She did this with each of them, letting her friends no
longer of this world know the time had come to begin the
journey.

Among them: Ellen Sampson, who died of a heart attack
during a Thanksgiving Day dinner; Justin Berube, mur-
dered one night following the robbery of a convenience
store he was tending; Robert Maheux, frozen to death after
falling asleep in an ice-fishing shack on Lake Thompson;
Henry Demers, who suffered severe head injuries in an accident involving his car and a moose. Kimberley Larkin, who,
at eight years of age, had her life taken after her drunken father had beaten her, then sent her flying down a set of
stairs.

With eyes ready to spill, Andrea remembered the deceased telling their individual tales as she sat quietly in
front of each headstone and listened.

She wiped the now-flowing tears with her sleeve and
gently placed the cover back onto the box. She thought she
had everything she needed when she remembered a crucifix

her mother had given her, passed down for generations.

She took it out of the jewelry box, catching a glimpse of herself in the mirror. Her face appeared long and drawn-out, almost scary. She asked her reflection if she was actually ready for this, but turned away before it could answer.

Andrea hung the chain from her fingers and watched the crucifix twist and turn, glimmering in the soft bedroom light provided from a lampshade that captured the harshness of the bulb. Three generations and it still looked relatively new. She placed it around her neck and a cold shiver sent the hair on her neck on end.

And did so now, as she unmindfully caressed the crucifix within thumb and forefinger, staring at the road ahead.

Anxiety transformed itself into a ball of unease as she passed the small houses of Durbin on either side of the car. It was a town she loved, never once giving a thought to moving. Though some of the residents considered her a bit eccentric for not getting married and having children, most were very kind to her and appreciated all the work she had done at the library.

It was the sight of children playing that gave her the sudden, unsettling feeling that things soon would not be the same. As she watched them on their front lawns, some bouncing on trampolines, others huddled in groups of three or four, she felt a strong tie to them, a tie that might tighten and eventually snap, separating them altogether. She recognized most of the kids, but had a wary precognition that all of their futures were dependent upon what she and Darren were about to accomplish.

The sky darkened as a cloud drifted over the sun, casting shadows among the children, eliminating their features.

Andrea hoped they were enjoying the day, and the days ahead, to the fullest extent possible.

* * * * *

Darren heard the door close on Andrea's car, but made no effort to get up and greet her. He knew it was time to go, but his feet remained glued to the floor.

Eyes distant, he looked around the house from his regular seat at the table. Tomorrow morning he wouldn't be eating cereal and watching cartoons from here—a habit he had yet to outgrow. For the last three years, he couldn't wait for the day he would move out and finally be on his own, that it would be no problem, a cakewalk. Now, he wasn't so sure.

Her knocks came softly at first, but he couldn't open the door to another part of his life just yet. Almost. Receiving encouragement from a lump in his pocket, he reached for it between the folds of his jeans, once again feeling the stone that was about to change his life.

Her knocks came heavier, her shadow dancing vaguely behind the door's beige curtain. He reached for his bags and opened the door, then closed and locked it quickly behind him, before Andrea could see the note on the table.

"Are you ready for this?" she asked in a voice just larger than a whisper.

He kept his head down, still needing time to himself, and hoped she didn't see the mixed emotions that were surely emblazoned on his face. Wanting to appear strong, Darren took a deep breath and fought to bring his gaze to meet Andrea's. She held an expression that he had grown to love: part smirk, part pout, with her lower lip extended just so, in an effort to say she understood what he was feeling.

"As ready as I'll ever be. Let's get out of here," he said, trying to smile and failing miserably.

Chapter 11

A light breeze stirred from an afternoon sun, relieving the air of its thickness while clouds formed and spread their masses, together bringing the temperature down a few degrees in preparation for a cool summer night.

They were spending the night at a Best Western, an hour outside of town, to put their plan together. Far enough away from Durbin to sever the ties that kept them there, ensuring they didn't turn around. New surroundings for a new life they were about to live.

Together.

Darren agreed to share a room with Andrea, though it was a bit uncomfortable, knowing it was the cheapest way for them to travel. Although it didn't take much coaxing on his part, he couldn't help but feel a bit embarrassed about sleeping in the same room with an older woman. What would his parents have to say about *that?* Then again, what would his friends say? He tried to mask a very large smile, and was thankful his shirt hung below his zipper.

As they walked into the room, the first thing Darren noticed was the smell—nothing unusual, just different. A clean but stale smell came from the room being empty, without a reason to run the air conditioner. He turned it on and opened the window to cycle in some new air.

Darren had only spent the night at a motel once, after a high school football game in Augusta, with roads too hazardous to risk the two-hour drive home. This was different. He was on his own now—except for Andrea, of course. But he was sure she'd let him make his own decisions and try

75

not to assume the mother role. At least he hoped so.

There was a kind of excitement building in Darren as he placed his overnight bag on the bed he unconsciously selected as his, the one nearest the window. A mixed feeling of adventure and a hint of fear at being unsure of what might happen in the next few days or weeks. He looked around the room wondering what to do, how to take it all in. His parents weren't here to tell him what to do. A new world waited. Could he do it? The phone caught his attention from the corner of his eye. He turned away from it, but felt a tug of guilt just the same.

Andrea was outside, trying to free her overnight bag from heavier bags she had mistakenly placed on top. Darren looked on for a short time, amused.

"Need some help?" Darren asked, trying to hold back laughter. He almost lost it when she blew at the hair that had fallen across her face.

"That would be swell, if you could do so without laughing."

He managed to get her bag out, amazed at how much stuff a woman could fit into an *overnight* bag. He handed it to Andrea and followed her inside after wrestling a trunk from the back seat. *Must be more woman stuff,* he thought.

He placed the trunk on the bed Andrea would be sleeping in and went to shut the window. He turned the air conditioner on low, surprised at the speed at which it brought a chill to the room.

"No better time than the present," Andrea said.

Darren turned from the window and joined her on her bed.

The trunk wasn't filled with the woman's essentials he originally thought were in there. It must have taken Andrea years to compile what they were looking at. From what he

76

could see, the trunk was stuffed to the top with maps, books, newspapers, and charts of some sort. And that was just the visible top layer.

"I've been getting ready for this for quite some time," Andrea said, hands digging below the surface. "Things are easier to get when you work at a library and know where everything is."

Darren looked on, amazed at the amount of material.

"I've gathered everything I could find on every cemetery located in Maine. Of course, I'm sure there are some that haven't made the books. Those will be the toughest ones to find. If I don't have something by now, there isn't anything to get."

"Wow," was the only thing Darren could think to say. He looked at Andrea for approval and then began leafing through the contents. Andrea left him alone while she unfolded a map, did her best to flatten the creased squares, and began to highlight certain areas.

"Looks like we'll just head north and start around Fort Kent and work our way east and then south down I-95. That seems to be the easiest way I can figure," Andrea said, perusing the map.

"Sounds great," Darren said, briefly looking up from a picture of a cemetery. "Some of these cemeteries are pretty creepy-looking. I don't know if I'll enjoy spending a lot of time in one."

"Those are the best to visit," Andrea said with a sly grin. "On a serious note, though, those are the cemeteries that really need us to visit. They aren't being kept up or visited the way they should be. After all, the dead can't hurt you."

Or can they? A thought left unvoiced.

"Yeah, I guess I see what you mean. But you didn't say I had to actually enjoy going into these places."

"No, I guess not."

Darren looked again at the picture he held in his hand. There was something else that kept nagging at him besides it being just creepy-looking. Something about this particular cemetery, located about five miles east of Fort Kent. *Evergreen Cemetery.* He had heard the name before, or seen it. It must have something to do with his family; otherwise, he didn't think he would have remembered the name.

It was time to call home.

Darren went outside to a pay phone for want of fresh air, but mostly so Andrea couldn't hear. He already knew how his parents would react, but needed to get rid of the ugly feeling picking at him for leaving just a note.

His mother picked up after the first ring, her voice high-pitched and filled with worry. He let her vent before trying to fit in any words of his own.

After what seemed hours of explaining to his parents (each of them taking a turn at the phone) how he was *finding* himself, his parents were still left angry and confused. He attempted to explain the purpose of the journey, but his parents weren't really listening to the details. In a way, he thought that was a good thing.

Finally, he got them calmed down enough to where he could talk about Evergreen Cemetery. It took his father a few seconds to place the name.

"Your grandfather's buried there—why?" It was his father's turn on the telephone.

A family photo album, Darren pictured it clearly now. He remembered seeing the obituary of his grandfather displayed behind a plastic page curled with age. That was where he had seen the name. He had never been there himself, though.

"I'm looking at a picture of the cemetery right now, and

I thought the name rang a bell. I guess I was right. I'll be paying my first visit to him, soon," Darren said.

"Darren, what the hell are you doing? Your mother's worried sick."

"I'll explain everything when I get home, I promise."

"You'd better start explaining things right now, young man," Phil Jacobs said. "And where are you anyway?"

"Look dad, I . . . we don't have any time to lose. We—" That did it. He knew what was going to follow.

"And who's *we?*" Darren's father cut in rather loudly.

Darren took a deep breath and let it hiss between clenched teeth, a hand running through his hair, eyes closed. He could see his dad pacing in the kitchen while his mother twisted a dishtowel in her hands.

"Andrea Varney, remember her? The town librarian? We're doing this together."

"What!" Darren pulled the phone away from his ear.

"Dad, I'll call again soon, love and miss you both," Darren said as fast as he could spit out the words, and hung up, his eyes starting to water. He couldn't take any more.

On the way back to the room, Darren blinked back the beginnings of tears that caused a burning at the back of his throat and made his nose run. He entered the room to see Andrea still going over some detailed maps.

Andrea took a peek at him, but said nothing.

Evening approached quickly as they buried themselves in the mass of information. One map they had was covered with red stars, hastily drawn, marking each cemetery in Fort Kent and the surrounding area.

"If all these cemeteries are just in this area alone, it'll take us years to go through the entire state of Maine," Darren stated with the hint of a sour note in his voice. "I don't know if we'll ever finish this thing at all."

"I know it doesn't seem possible, but at least we can do what we can. That's all we can ask of ourselves, isn't it?" Andrea asked. "And we don't have to do it all at once. We can always go back home to stay for a while before planning another trip. Let's just see what happens."

The thought of returning home released a visible tension on Darren's brow. "I know, I'm sorry. I guess it's just the pessimist in me."

He tried hard to keep his mind on the matter at hand, but kept going back to the episode with his parents. If only he understood things better himself, maybe then it would be easier to tell his parents exactly what was going on. *Well,* he thought, *at least I tried.* He even felt better at contacting his parents. They knew he was okay—that was the important thing. Someday they would understand.

It was then that Darren decided to keep a journal.

He preferred taking his showers in the morning and used the time while Andrea was in the shower to change into some sweatpants and a tee shirt.

Awkward. There was no other way to describe the way he felt. Once under the covers, he turned the television up loud enough to drown out the noise of Andrea in the shower, afraid of where his mind might take him. When he heard the shower faucet turn off with a whining squeal, he turned the TV down, placed the remote on her side of the table in between the two beds, and turned toward the window, feigning sleep with the covers pulled up to his ears.

Sleep found him before the bathroom door opened and Andrea stepped out in her pajamas.

At the final closing of her eyes, Andrea drifted into a fitful sleep.

A nightmare once buried beneath the passing of time

was allowed to enter, but not without her mind trying to fend off its blows. Her eyes cinched against this sudden intrusion, trying in vain to seal its source of entry as tears were squeezed from their corners and trickled to the pillow.

Hazy figures soon gained clarity as they circled a victim fastened to a makeshift stake.

Again, she could smell the putrid odor of burning flesh and see flames devouring the fine hair of a woman. The popping and hissing of exploding blisters screamed with a voice of their own, but she couldn't find her hands to cover her ears. Pushed by something other than curiosity, she moved closer. Her pace quickened, as did her heartbeat, when she got within a few feet of the burning stake. Her eyes were pried open against her will and she was forced to look upon the sacrifice.

At a blackened face that belonged to her!

Her own screams as the flames licked at her feet and crawled up her torso awoke Andrea with a start. She clutched her face as if protecting it from unseen flames. She lay in a pool of sweat, sheets sticking to her flesh, outlining her figure. Her nose was saturated with the unpleasant odor of charred remains.

She breathed through her mouth, unsure if it was to avoid the odor or slow her breathing with large gasps of untainted air. When her chest finally expanded and deflated in normal intervals, she coughed into the pillow, still trying to get rid of a nasty taste.

With only the glow of the moonlight shining through a crack between the curtains, she peeled away the sheets and grabbed a tissue.

She looked over at Darren, heard the steady rhythm of his breathing.

In the bathroom she blew her nose, almost gagging at the

acrid flavor her phlegm produced.

As is the habit of any person, she peeled away the two sides of the tissue.

And stared at a sooty substance standing out in black streaks against the white paper.

Chapter 12

They checked out, ate breakfast, left.

Headed north on Interstate 95.

They scurried through a two-mile stretch of road in Bangor, Andrea defensively driving around people going to work and college students a few days behind in leaving the University of Maine at Orono campus for the summer. In a matter of five minutes, civilization all but eliminated itself from their view.

All traffic northbound diminished, leaving Andrea's car the only vehicle visible on the interstate more often than not, as though they had been plucked by God's fingers and placed into another part of the state, or the world, for that matter. If not for the occasional large green signs telling them the distance to the next town, they wouldn't have known which direction they were traveling. Mile after mile of majestic pines, birches, and maples outlined either side of the interstate, towering over them, eliminating the visible compass of the sun.

It was hypnotizing. Beautiful. When the fall season approached and the spectacular changing colors of leaves took place, it would be that much more spectacular. The trees would be consumed by shades of red, yellow, and orange to be awed by everyone. Tourists would flock across the entire state of Maine just to witness the event.

The air changed as well, allowing them to unroll the windows an inch or two without suffocating. Fresh and clean, plumes of factories seemingly nonexistent in this part of the state.

Andrea had never been this far north. She was amazed at the feeling of freedom it produced, not to be closed in by any structures, any people. Durbin barely registered as a town itself, but once you took away everything that made it a town, it was enough to give you a whole new view on life. Out here, where nothing seemed to exist, existed all the possibilities. There simply wasn't anything to stop you. You could start over, get rid of all of your mistakes, leave behind everything you disliked, shed your old skin and find a new one. You could become a pilgrim of a different era.

The only station the Duster's AM radio picked up faded into unpleasant static. Andrea turned it off, preferring to listen to the wind. An overcast day let the sun shine through the trees occasionally.

"I guess I should have invested some money into a real radio, huh?" Andrea asked.

"Nah, that's okay. The quiet is actually kind of nice. How much longer to Fort Kent, anyway?"

Andrea sighed. "Oh, I don't know, maybe another three hours or so if my foot's feeling heavy. And I believe it is." She hadn't seen a trooper for miles. She arched her back, envious of cars with lumbar support, and let out a small gasp as the seatbelt tightened across her chest. The edge of it plucked at her left nipple and created a tingling sensation that twirled within her stomach. It had been so long since she had experienced this same feeling that she hadn't realized both of her nipples were pleasantly hard. *What have I been thinking about?* She pulled her blouse away from her chest, felt a blush coloring her cheeks. "We'll probably want to stop for lunch in Houlton and take a break. I'll have to fill up, too. Sound all right?" She did her best to keep the flutter out of her voice.

"Yeah, sure. But I have a feeling I'll have to visit a

restroom long before that. Sorry."

"Let's see how far the next rest area is. A few more signs should be coming up soon. I hope."

Darren nodded and reached toward the back seat, and pulled a notebook and pen out of his bag.

Andrea watched his hands produce meaningless designs and cartoons. Then his forearms, as they flexed to grip the pen, veins jutting from the insides. She noticed the way his tee shirt clung more tightly to the top of his chest than the bottom, the bulge in his biceps. The way his . . .

She looked out her window, suddenly interested in the increasing speed at which the white lines passed on her side.

Chapter 13

Doodles, happy faces, faces with their tongues sticking out, and sad faces were scribbled onto the first page below the date. It was all he managed to write in a journal that held all empty pages as they drove. And they drove. The only thing he could think about was an increasingly painful bladder, ready to tear at whatever held it together and run in a hot river down his legs. He couldn't hold it much longer. He stared at the page of his childlike artwork, refusing to look outside at the absence of any exits, any off-ramps, anyplace to take a leak!

An hour ticked by and he undid the button at the top of his jeans—a little less pressure, but still there.

"Finally," Andrea said, squinting at a sign that appeared in the distance.

He couldn't help himself, had to see what she was looking at. As the sign got closer, he began to fidget. The weight of his bladder was almost too much to handle. He was about to explode. Sudden cramps made him twist in his seat and mumble under his breath. Hot flashes swept across his face.

REST AREA CLOSED—NEXT REST AREA 56 MILES, a sign displayed almost covertly below the actual REST AREA sign.

"Well . . ." Andrea started.

"Pull over somewhere, this can't wait," Darren said between clenched teeth.

She pulled over to the shoulder of the interstate, crossing a solid white line riddled with reflective bumps. *The emer-*

gency lane, Darren thought, and would have broken into a fit of laughter if his bladder wasn't threatening to burst with any change in pressure. Before the car was even at a complete stop, he was gone, running into a large patch of woods.

Somewhere below the surface of the earth, maybe another world altogether, a woman writhed and screamed as she burned.

And burned.

A crowd had gathered to watch her be engulfed by flames for her sins, each piece of blackened flesh that fell away payment for the terrible things that had happened in the town. They were gawking, staring, yelling, and chanting at her as she was violently dragged to a wooden pole surrounded by large amounts of timber and anything that would catch fire. She remembered seeing a child's doll, all the fun played out of it, spaces visible where there should have been hair, placed at the outer reaches of the kindling.

They were angry with her, but why?

Shortly before, she had been nestled into bed, looking forward to a good night's rest after a long day of work on the farm, a farm that wasn't going to produce its desired yield for the first year in many. Her hands were cracked, her feet bleeding, and she needed the time to recuperate for yet another hard day that would start before the sun even broached the horizon.

And then they came in, forcing the door open and knocking over anything in their path as they went for her.

Men. There were four of them, yelling and screaming. What did they want? The reverend—why was he here? The mayor—what did he want? Her father? Her loving husband?

Before she had time to wipe at the crust that had built in

her eyes, she was thrown out of bed and pulled by the hair to the crowd that waited anxiously outside. What would the children think?

But her children were there as well, leading the festivities, pointing their tiny, accusing fingers, throwing things at her. Her mind had no time to deal with the sudden horror of her own children against her as the pain came suddenly, her flesh leaving her body as the flames grew beneath her, eating her alive.

Surprisingly, almost at the onset of immeasurable agony, the pain faded into a numbness she could handle. Her body remained, but her mind found itself another world to occupy, a world where no pain existed, a limbo she found confusing. Why was she here?

She didn't know how long she had stayed in this world that existed in its own separate reality. She seemed to just float around and wait and wait and wait. For what, she didn't know.

At times, she could see things.

She recalled looking up at the sky and being surrounded by trees. She saw animals walk right over her, oblivious to her presence, saw snow fall in wispy flakes. At times, she saw the sun beaming down on her. Other times, she could almost feel the rain as it tried to reach her.

And sometimes, she saw her children.

She watched them approach slowly, cautiously, as if they weren't supposed to be there, peering through tear-stricken faces. They made their way directly above her with small steps and knelt down.

Sometimes, they brought flowers.

They talked to her, but she couldn't hear them. She tried yelling back at them, but no sound ever left her lips. She cried, but no tears ever came. She reached out to touch her children, wipe at the trails of tears like she used to, but had no hands to use.

Her children came for a while, still cautious and almost secretly. But eventually, the visits dwindled and came to a halt altogether, leaving her to her own world, staring up at the trees, the skies. The heavens.

That was when something took her from this secret limbo.

And she burned again.

Darren felt as if Andrea were watching, spying around every shape of a tree or shrub, wanting to steal a look at him. He couldn't go. He stood there with his thing in his hand and waited for nature to work its magic. It didn't. He felt ridiculous and embarrassed that he wasn't able to take a simple leak in the woods. He knew she couldn't see him and he'd gone far enough into the woods not to be seen. He heard an occasional car swoosh by and when he looked back, he couldn't even see the highway.

He started whistling in an effort to relax, imagined himself under the comforting inundation of a waterfall. A few seconds went by and a slow trickle developed into a steady stream. He pushed hard to ensure it didn't stop. The gates were down and he was flowing!

As his supply depleted itself, Darren took the time to breathe in the fresh air the forest seemed to produce. For miles around, he noticed, the forest was using the tops of heavy pines to protect its inner organs. The shade was refreshing. He could smell the moisture.

There was a pause in the flow as his reserve supply was about to kick in. Looking around, willing his bladder to release what remained, he noticed a space in the green ceiling above. That part of the forest seemed to be almost on fire as the sun found this entrance and scorched the ground below. From where he was standing, it produced a solid beam of light about ten feet wide. Darren decided to take a closer look after shaking and zipping, walking over to the light while avoiding fallen trees, stumps, and holes that magically appeared and could do a number on an ankle.

The rise in temperature first caught Darren's attention as he walked directly into a solid ray of sunshine and looked up into a clear sky. His feet crunched on the surface of the forest floor, but he couldn't take his gaze away from the sky to notice. The tops of gigantic pines created a perfect circle. Amazing. Two birds darted from one side of the circle to the other in a blur of flapping wings and warbles. He looked to the ground and found that the bases of the trees also produced a perfect circle and were evenly spaced. He had never seen anything so peculiar.

Until he looked at what he was standing in.

Beneath his feet, the ground appeared to be charred. Black chips of burnt wood were strewn about, forming an inch-thick carpet. Grass didn't grow. Young trees didn't grow. Nor was there any sign of plant life.

He found it hard to believe that sunlight itself could produce this. There had to be some kind of evidence among the chips. Maybe some kids just used this area to have campfires or something.

He didn't really want to get down on his hands and knees to look, so he casually kicked at the chips as he walked around the circle, not expecting to find anything.

Darren worked his way around quickly, ending up in the middle of the circle with still nothing unearthed. He shrugged and decided to leave, knowing Andrea was still waiting.

With only one more step, his foot struck something solid.

He bent down on one knee and brushed away blackened chips of wood that were concealing an object finally able to emerge for the first time in many years.

Darren let out a small sigh of regret as he discovered a polished stone at his feet, just a little larger than his hand. Smooth striations decorated its exposed surface, as if it had just been pulled from a nonexistent stream. It didn't look like it belonged here in the middle of the woods, but still was nothing more than a rock.

He picked it up and pulled his arm back.

As Darren was about to throw the stone half-heartedly, his fingers grazed a different surface of the stone—coarse and jagged, unlike the smooth surface he had first set his eyes upon. He returned the stone to his side for another look.

But was allowed only a glimpse at its underside.

Something pummeled Darren from behind like a blind-sided tackle he knew well from football. A grunt escaped his throat as he fell forward. The stone was at once of no concern and tumbled from his grasp. He tried to look behind and see what had hit him.

Before his head struck the stone, he saw only the trees sway and darkness probe the edges of the forest beyond the circle.

With no sign of Darren coming out of the woods, Andrea shut the engine off and decided to get out and stretch. She wondered what was taking so long, but also didn't want to walk in on something she might regret. Maybe he had decided to go the leaves route and finish some other business. She knew it was easier for men to do that sort of thing. She would wait a little longer.

Twenty minutes passed before Andrea decided to see

what was taking Darren so long. Maybe he had fallen and needed some help. *No,* she thought, *I would have heard him calling.* Maybe he was hurt. She tried to shrug this thought off. After all, he was only going to pee.

"Darren?" Andrea meant to yell, but what came out was only a strangled shout.

Minutes passed.

"Darren!" Her voice was now clear and sharp. And scared.

No answer.

Andrea had gone farther into the woods than she would have liked when she was overcome with fear, a sense she could almost taste on the back of her tongue, like the sour taste of bile. She swallowed hard against a dry throat.

Where is he?

A patch of light cut a hole into the forest, standing out among its surroundings like a beam from the heavens.

Feet unfamiliar to the forest's floor of stumps, bushes, and rocks, she stumbled more than once before she knew she had to slow down. Forever, it seemed, to get to this light.

It seemed to get a shade darker when she saw Darren lying face down, unconscious.

She ran.

Andrea fought hard to push back tears and the worst of thoughts away as she arrived at his unmoving body, thoughts that were entering her mind as fast as a train would speed over the rails below it. She wondered how she would face Darren's parents and tell them that she was responsible for taking Darren on this journey. Maybe Darren wasn't really the one. Maybe she had just killed someone that shouldn't have been here in the first place.

She knelt down beside him and brushed back the hair off

his face. There was a small amount of blood on a stone beneath his head. She moved his head gently, reluctantly, not wanting to injure him further.

A small amount of warm air blew against her hand and she let out her own breath, relieved.

There was only a minor cut on Darren's forehead, almost a scratch. His eyes flickered as he began to regain consciousness.

"Darren, you okay?"

"What happ . . . OW!" Darren shouted, placing both hands to his head. "What happened?" He started to sit up, but thought better of it and lay back down.

"I don't know. I found you like this. You must have tripped and landed on this," Andrea said, pointing to the rock.

He looked up at the circle of trees.

"Let me see it," Darren said.

"Why? It's just . . ."

"Let me see it!" Andrea flinched. "Sorry. Can I see it . . . please?"

She handed him the rock.

As Darren saw the red stain, he immediately went to his head, groping. Then rolled dried blood away between his fingers. He turned the rock over.

Andrea couldn't understand exactly what he was looking for, but watched quietly.

Then stared in surprise.

A word—*WITCH*—had been crudely chiseled into the small stone with uneven, jagged letters.

Something was happening. Things were changing all around her.

She no longer felt the burning in her right leg, then the

93

left. The darkness beyond the licking flames was now illuminated with bright lights of all shapes and colors. It was like the Northern Lights she once remembered.

The pain now left both of her arms, and her body felt like it had been placed in a cool mountain stream. In her mind, she bathed in its soothing waters.

Though she couldn't see any part of her body, she felt bindings suddenly starting to loosen from her ankles.

Then her arms. She imagined herself flying away into the lights that surrounded her, letting the beautiful rays of hope caress her body in loving strokes of energy. She tried to smile but couldn't tell if she was or not. Either way, it felt wonderful!

The bright colors slowly began to diminish and revealed something she wasn't expecting.

A perfect circle of trees exposed a sun shining upon her from a cloudless sky.

Out of nowhere, a young man appeared. He was going around in circles, doing something she couldn't quite figure out.

He stood directly on top of her now, hands deep inside his pockets. She couldn't really see his face. At the moment he wasn't looking down at her. She knew he didn't see her, didn't even know she was there. She knew better than to waste the effort of trying to call to him.

As she watched him, something began to go terribly wrong.

The circle of trees unexpectedly came to life with a strong wind and the boy was pushed violently from behind. She almost thought he had tripped, but knew he hadn't even been moving.

And then the trees were still again, but something lingered in the darkness beyond.

Almost as suddenly, something tugged at her body, her soul, whatever she was. Her legs and arms were immobile again as they were secured with something strong and heavy.

She was pulled into the darkness. She could smell the heat.

Soon, she knew, she would feel it.

She accepted the fact that she would burn forever, for what she didn't know. To struggle would simply be another wasted effort. She succumbed, letting an unseen force take her into the abyss. Her destiny. She felt herself limp in a body that she could not see.

She felt the flames feeling for her feet, imagined closing her eyes in defeat.

Then, without warning, everything seemed to stop. She was no longer traveling to the waiting fires below. She didn't feel the heat penetrating the air around her. Memories seemed to be pulled from her mind by a stronger force and carried her upward. And then she saw them, holding the marker of her fate within their hands, sharing her pain.

She was lifted higher, weightless. A brighter light, brighter than anything she had ever seen before, shone into her eyes. She forced them open against the brightness, feeling real tears forming and spilling down her cheeks.

People began to appear out of nowhere, people she knew. She couldn't remember the names, but the faces were all too familiar, even after all this time. They were faces that begged for forgiveness.

They were reaching for her.

With an impromptu lesson given by Andrea, Darren joined her in holding on to the stone and sharing the memories of the woman who was buried in the ground beneath them.

It seemed she had led a beautiful life, but one demanding lots of manual labor. Nonetheless, she was happy. Happy until the day she was forced from her home, her life—her family—and brought to the stake. They were taken aback by the visions of the sacrifice, but a feeling of peace eased its way into their minds and the pressure lifted as the soul of the woman was released.

A hum similar to the buzz of a power line transformer emanated from the air around them, intensifying, and then cresting at a steady drone. The buzzing came from the ground, the air, the forest as if it were breathing in monotone, a constant exhale. When they felt the ground stir beneath their feet, they jumped back in surprise.

And gawked at the blackened chips as they began to quiver on the ground like a pile of burnt popcorn still trying to pop in a pan of hot grease.

Small sprouts of grass in their infantile stages quickly developed into stunning blades of the brightest shades of green, hiding the blackened chips of another time. As they stood awestruck, the carpet of fresh grass continued to grow before them, each blade shining and glistening with moisture as it reached to attain its fullest height. Not only grass grew, but other kinds of plant life as well. A rare flower, the lady's slipper, bloomed throughout the floor of plush green carpet, giving a pinkish glow to the surface.

Andrea's eyes sparkled with a green that could make someone turn away from their brilliance. The beauty paralyzed her. If life could be measured in shades of green, this small clearing would be the healthiest life one could ever ask for.

From the same location Darren had found the stone, a single rose bush thrust from the ground in an explosive burst of energy, sending blackened chips spitting away from it. Multiple roses in immediate full bloom proudly displayed their beauty as petals glistened under a circular section of blue sky.

While they watched life blooming before their eyes, an occasional breeze through the forest brought the fragrance of a million roses from this single bush. The smell tickled their noses and brought smiles to their faces, as if the woman so horribly sacrificed at this very spot was sending them a heartwarming message.

THANK YOU!

They both heard the message as if it were whispered in their ears. Raw, heartfelt emotion exuded from the ground and into their bodies. They had corrected a wrong, or as best they could have, giving them a feeling of such satisfaction that Andrea's eyes started to well up with tears of joy. As much as Darren might have wanted to contain himself, he couldn't completely, as a single tear from each eye left a moist trail down each cheek.

The blackened chips weren't there anymore, and if they were, they were buried beneath this beautiful site, as good conquered evil in a very just manner, if not an unusual way.

Hours could've passed and they wouldn't have known. Looking at the small clearing seemed to make time stand still. A small world in which there would never be any seconds, minutes, hours, days . . . years. In fact, if they were to visit this same site in the winter, summer, or fall at anytime in the future, they would find this place exactly as it appeared to them now: a circular section of the world devoid of the elements. This now sacred place would remain untouched by seasons, man . . . time.

They both looked toward each other in amazement, in fulfillment. This was yet another reason to continue their journey, to be looked back upon when things went wrong, when they felt the need for encouragement, for meaning. Another passage in an epic they were creating each time they remembered another forgotten soul.

Soon, others would follow. Soon, others would *have* to follow.

"Well," Andrea said dully, fatigued, "I don't think there's much more we can do here."

Darren looked back at the picturesque scene, taking a deep breath. "No, I think we've done what we were meant to do."

They each took the time to observe the colorful clearing one last time, wanting to place the picture deep within their minds.

"I think we ought to start taking a camera," Darren said.

Andrea smiled, nodded in agreement, and turned to go.

They exited the forest and could see the top of the car on the interstate. No words were passed between them—they weren't needed.

Darren would have plenty to write about.

Chapter 14

For the third time, Darren said nothing as Andrea pulled the car away from the emergency lane.

This, only after the small, square bumps of the emergency lane passed under the right tires, bumps that reminded him of Braille for a blind driver. As he watched her nibble on her lower lip, he knew where her thoughts were: the same place his were having trouble leaving. Thoughts that kept flashing to horrid images of that poor woman being sacrificed while her family members watched the procession—eyes wide, teeth bared—in eager anticipation of her death.

What were they thinking back then?

He tried to reassure himself, knowing they had freed the woman from her misery, had righted a terrible wrong, but felt like they'd just released an innocent person that had already spent a lifetime in prison. The reward just seemed to fall short. Though happy at what they had done, he couldn't stop wondering how long this soul had been discarded, forgotten, left to burn. Again.

Caught within a reverie of his own, picking at an already-hardening scab on his forehead, Darren thought the experience frightening, yet exciting, and sad. Giving him more than a solid reason to participate in this journey, it also confirmed his suspicions that something did exist beyond the world in which he lived. Mixed emotions left him overwhelmed with a feeling of smallness, of being nothing more than a flea upon the earth, searching for a reason to exist, before it decided to shake him off. Money, fame, the

American dream—nothing really seemed to matter in the grand scheme of things. *From the day we are born,* he thought, *we are all merely finding a way to bide our time until our impending death.* And whatever came afterward.

Someday, he too would die and face his time to be remembered.

God help him.

The car drifted again—past the Braille bumps, past the edge of the pavement, and into the start of a ditch on the side of the interstate.

Clumps of grass spit from the right side of the car as the rear end fought for traction and started to fishtail. Dirt and rocks rattled inside the wheel well, striking the undercarriage below Darren's feet, pulling him from his daydream with the same speed he'd pull his hand away from an open flame.

"Andrea!" Instinctively he reached out to grab the steering wheel. His heart pounded in his throat, then returned to his chest as he felt Andrea begin to regain control with a startled shriek.

"I got it! I got it!" she screamed, then relieved pressure from the gas pedal and steered into the skid. With a sudden jolt, the car rocked on its axles with creaks and groans, straightening as the tires clutched at the pavement with ear-piercing squeals. "Holy shit!"

"Man, what happened?" Darren's voice came in short, tremulous bursts of air he didn't know he'd been holding.

"I don't know. I just . . . I don't know," Andrea replied, still trying to catch her own breath. Both of her hands—now at the ten and two o'clock positions—shook around the steering wheel. She formed a fist with each. "I DO know that I'm done driving for the day. Next exit, we pull over," she said, leaving no room for compromise.

"Hey, sounds good to me."

Andrea stared ahead, blew at the hair covering her eyes, hands never leaving the wheel.

They seemed to crawl toward the next exit as Andrea refused to allow the speedometer to creep higher than ten miles an hour *under* the speed limit. She sighed, sounding relieved, when a sign announced the exit to Sherman Mills. Then hissed with obvious regret as another soon boasted: NO SERVICES.

She turned, anyway.

A rotting piece of wood with hunter-orange letters greeted them as they came to a stop at the end of the off-ramp. The word MOTEL had dripped and dried at the bottom of each fading letter, in some places like long, trailing tears. In the shape of a cross, the makeshift advertisement leaned as if ready to topple, its base once driven into the ground by an optimistic entrepreneur. Now, barely hanging on with the changing of many seasons, it clung to a thick tangle of grass that held it up like intravenous lines, trickling just enough life into it to greet one last visitor.

It leaned toward its required direction.

Andrea followed.

A change in temperature breathed relief into the car. Overhead, trees on both sides of the road seemed to be introducing each other with gnarled and twisted branches, embracing over the road. The shadows were deep, the shade cool.

A dirt road soon cut into the thick woods as if it didn't belong, its entrance marked by the rusting shell of a pickup with the same hunter-orange paint covering the door. Andrea turned and the Plymouth sent plumes of dust into the air that twinkled after catching shafts of sunshine between the surrounding trees.

"Sure ain't the Holiday Inn," chuckled Darren, trying to break the silence and relieve a tension he felt building.

She didn't catch on to his feeble attempt at humor. For a moment, the only reply was the crunching of gravel beneath the tires. "Mmmm. Well, it's only for one night."

Darren opened his mouth, but closed it before something came out that he might regret, instead choosing to admire the empty parking lot and shingled siding of the motel he could only describe as shit brown.

They slowly rolled by one wing of tenant units.

Ripped and hanging screens, sometimes none at all, occupied the outer frame of the windows. Some of the windows contained cracks that ran from top to bottom. Paint on the shingles seemed to exist only in patches. Groups of them had separated altogether and still lay where they had fallen, decorating the dirt and gravel of the parking lot like dried-up cow chips.

Not surprisingly, at the center of two wings attached to it, the main office had the most upkeep, with only one tattered screen on one window and a perfect, undamaged screen on the other.

Darren made the decision to get the room even before the car had stopped. He had seen Andrea trying to drive with shaking hands and, at times, not even looking at the road ahead, but to some other place. She'd barely talked to him during the last hour. He wanted to say something, but was at a loss for words and uncomfortable. He remained quiet until the car rolled to a stop in front of the main office of *Velora's Motel . . . A Comfortable Place to Stay.*

"I think I'll check us in this time," Darren said.

Andrea hung her head and nodded, hair hanging at the sides of her face. She curled her fingers around the steering wheel and her body shuddered.

Darren jumped out of the car and left the door ajar. "Be right back."

Behind the office's one good screen was a small pile of dead flies and a HELP WANTED sign that had spent too many days in the sun. Its once-white background behind large, red letters had turned a dull yellow and looked burned at the edges.

A cowbell produced a barely-audible *thunk* as Darren pushed the door open and entered the cramped foyer.

Humidity immediately wrapped around him like an extra layer of skin. He wiped at the beaded droplets on his forehead and felt like he could barely draw a breath. Overhead, a ceiling fan with only one of three bulbs illuminated slowly churned as if each rotation would be its last. The harsh smell of trapped smoke brought reason to the faded, yellow walls.

The front office was empty. The sound of a television came from behind a curtain of purple beads that hung from a doorway behind the front desk. The faint theme music of a game show trickled into the foyer.

As he listened closer, waiting for someone to appear, an ugly, squeaking noise that sounded like a chair shifting under the weight of its owner made him tense. He had a sudden feeling that he wasn't supposed to be here, like he was sneaking into someone's home. He fought the urge to run, as a violent coughing fit erupted. Congested sounds of phlegm being cleared from a throat echoed through to the office, loud enough to make the curtain of beads sway in the doorway.

Silence. A contestant asked for Shakespearian Tragedies for two hundred dollars.

Darren hit a silver bell on top of the desk.

The sound pierced the quiet air of the office, making

103

him squeeze his eyes shut and bring his shoulders up to his neck in protection. The chair creaked one more time and then crashed as it was probably pushed against a wall in surprise.

A muffled cry of astonishment came from the hidden room.

More phlegm gurgles.

Footsteps.

A fragile man parted the curtain of beads with hands curled from arthritis. Darren looked down at the man, at last able to relax, but turned his attention away while the man picked at the seat of his pants with one crooked finger.

Thrown into a tar pit, he would surely come out weighing close to eighty pounds. A leather belt cinched around the man's waist held up green trousers that would fall to his knees if he held in his breath. A sweat-stained tank top clung to his withered body and protruded out of his open fly.

Darren had to work at not breaking into a smile, but felt sorry for the old man.

"You scared the bejesus out'a me, son," the old-timer said. His voice consisted of words that were linked together by crackles of syllables trying to break free of the phlegm. "If you're here for the job, there ain't one. Just don't get any business these days." His pale blue eyes seemed to exist in another dimension of time. Something about them caught Darren's interest.

"No, I . . . uh . . . just want to get a room for the night," Darren said, bringing the old man back to reality. The man's eyes grew large, then focused.

"A room? Are you lost?" More coughing. His eyes seemed to size up Darren almost as if he were a threat. It was hard to tell—one eye was looking in a direction totally opposite the other.

"An old knife wound . . . if you're wondering."

"No, I . . ." Darren began, embarrassed because he didn't know which eye to look at.

"Happened a long time ago." Both eyes now appeared to be swimming in their sockets, not knowing which way they were being told to go. "I thought I'd throw a knife to the ground and see how close I could get to a sidewalk without hitting it. Damn near poked my eye out the first time it bounced back at me." He produced a small exhalation of breath, free of phlegm this time. "I tried again, and you can guess what happened. Ran to the house trying to hold my frickin' eye in my head as I yelled for my mother. A grown boy crying for his mommy, for Chrissakes! They ended up giving me a glass eye. Want to see it?" The old man started to take it out.

"No, please. That's all right. I get the picture," Darren said, not knowing if he was going to puke or burst out laughing. "All I want is a room for the night and I'll be on my way."

"Oh, yeah, hee-hee, almost forgot. Have any one you like, nobody else here. Hasn't been since a few years back when a young couple got lost trying to find Mattawamkeag Lake. Said they were going to a family reunion or something." The old man seemed destined to keep Darren there a little longer. His dentures began to produce an aggravating, clicking noise.

Darren noticed a calendar on the wall behind the old man: 1952.

"Been here running this thing since I can remember," the old man answered. "Used to be the wife and me, but she passed away . . . lung cancer, they say. I still think she

105

died of depression. Thought we'd make a killin' being right off the interstate an' all. Didn't happen. Nobody ever stopped here. Barely made enough to eat. Yeah . . . she was a bit depressed, all right. Now it's just me. Good thing too . . . one of us would have starved to death, anyway."

"I'm sorry mister. Could I get a key?"

"There I go again. You're the first person I've talked to for quite a while."

I can see that, Darren thought.

"Here, room seven. Cleanest one we . . . I have. Right around front to the right, can't miss it," said the old-timer, finally handing him a key. Darren grimaced as a curled finger rubbed against the palm of his hand. "Guess I'll talk at'cha tomorrow." Another bout of coughing followed by more clicking of his dentures.

"Yeah, sure," said Darren.

Key in hand, he escaped.

The cowbell hanging from the door made its last clunk of the day.

A blast of hot air rushed past them as Darren blindly searched for the light switch.

A single light bulb hanging from the ceiling provided just enough light to see with and enough of a beacon for a single, dancing moth. Before going any farther into the room, he opened the thick and musty old curtains at the window to let the remaining sunlight dispel the gloom.

An inch-thick blanket of dust covered just about everything in the room; he found it hard to imagine what the others looked like. A vintage Zenith television with a rotary dial, the knob missing, occupied a major part of the room, like a mammoth on exhibit. Next to it, a table stood at an angle, with one leg resting on a folded piece of cardboard. A nightstand containing a small lamp separated a set of twin beds. To his surprise, no dust covered either of them.

Andrea was silent as she unpacked the small number of things she had brought inside with her. Darren let her be with her thoughts. He had begun to notice that her lips would tighten if she was thinking too hard, and she was doing that now. In a funny way, he thought it made her look very attractive.

When she bent over and her blouse dropped slightly away from her chest, his thoughts peeled away layers of time and exposed a scene that was still engraved within his mind. Her very motion provided a sudden gust of oxygen to a burning ember that had always existed within him. She might be an older woman, but her small physique still held all the right curves. Her hair, which she sometimes wore in a small ponytail, held a shine he wouldn't mind investigating with splayed fingers, and surely an aroma he'd do anything to breathe in. The small, laughing indentations at the corners of her mouth reminded him of other unique crevices her body contained in places he couldn't see unless . . .

Before the smoldering fire could develop its first flame, he turned around and soon heard the bathroom door close.

Darren listened to the first sounds of water, coming in sudden spurts and then a gurgling flow. He couldn't avoid imagining Andrea in stunning detail as she took off each article of clothing—slowly, of course, just like before. Relishing the tingling in his loins, he realized she was naked, or soon would be, and only a door separated them.

He shook the image away, stepped outside to get some fresh air.

Chapter 15

Twilight came with a steady increase in shadows. Pastel colors spilled across the sky, and crickets began their evening symphony.

His feet led him in a direction of their own while his mind still presented him with seductive images of Andrea in the bathtub. The cool air intruding on the humidity gave him a very welcome and comfortable chill and did well in putting out the fires threatening to blaze inside his lower half.

Darren walked past a dumpster overstuffed with cardboard boxes, past an aluminum tool shed that leaned in one direction, and came to a stop behind the motel. He looked up from his feet at a full moon still low in the sky. It radiated an orange glow as it captured the rays of the sun, and seemed to let them look out from the inside.

In the middle of a field, hidden behind the two wings of the motel, stood a majestic and aging willow tree. A small breeze caused the drooping branches to rattle like skeletal fingers groping for the ground below. On the lowest branch, now out of reach of human hands, was a rope that may have once had a tire tied to its end. The tree had grown over the rope, making it appear like a bulging vein beneath its wrinkled skin.

Darren went back to a time when he and his friends would spin as fast as possible on a tire swing and see who would be the first to vomit on themselves. And Spike, in his infinite wisdom, would run around with a paper sack waiting for one of their green faces to spew hot liquid.

Darren laughed at the memories, laughed more at the fact that they had finally rid his brain of Andrea for the time being.

He walked toward the tree in search of a comfortable place to sit. Crickets filled the evening with more music . . . an allegro, perhaps.

As he ducked under the hanging branches, a glint of light twinkled in front of him, coming from the base of the willow and within a clump of grass. Darren squatted on his haunches and parted the grass, hearing some of the strands rip from the ground. A shovel was buried in the thickness, its shape easily discernible. The metal blade was reflecting the moonlight.

Reaching for the shovel, he wondered if Andrea was out of the tub yet. He could sure use a hot shower, or maybe a cold one to get his mind completely off her. He grasped the shovel handle and tried to pry it from the hold of the intertwining blades of grass.

"Help me." The whisper raised his hackles, sent a shiver down his back, so close he felt the cold breath on his neck and hair stir near his ears.

He turned quickly, bringing his hands up to protect himself.

And stared at the motel, at the weak light coming from his and Andrea's room, at the dumpster, the tool shed. There was nothing else to see—he was still alone.

A sudden gust of wind sent the branches of the willow into a frenzied chatter of conversation around him before becoming silent once again.

"Help me," the voice cried again, louder. Darren turned again, back toward the willow, and heard the start of sobbing. It was a woman.

He let go of the shovel and stood up. Walked slowly in

random directions, straining to hear past the small thuds he heard in his ears, trying to determine the source of the voice. For what seemed eternity, he listened. Only the voice of the wind, the rustling of the grass, and the music of the crickets touched his ears.

Silence.

He was almost sure he had imagined it. But not quite. Knowing a sudden change in the wind's pitch can turn a normally silent evening into one filled with shouts and cries and whatever the imagination was able to conjure, he dismissed the cry as purely unreal.

He grasped the shovel again, determined to release it from the death-grip of the grass.

"HELP ME!" The cry shattered the night air, exploding inside his ears.

Covering the sides of his head with his hands, Darren uttered a scream of his own, then fell to his knees.

The crickets had become silent.

Chapter 16

In a place that man had yet to venture, an evil presence grew angry. Again.

Since before the foolish prophets Christ and Mohammed had polluted the earth with their infantile beliefs of goodness, righteousness, and everlasting life, and willed countless numbers of people to follow blindly in their footsteps, it lived.

Before Neanderthals were able to place piles of stones upon the site of their dead as an offering to a mysterious creator, and before the Egyptians developed ways in which to crudely preserve their deceased, it breathed.

Before the Romans embraced the burning of those no longer breathing the air of life, and before Christianity declared everything pagan, it breathed again. And only watched, amused.

Waiting.

It sent the plague across Europe and all but destroyed it with furry little rodents that were never heeded as harbingers of death. So easy for them to scurry into the water supplies and dwellings, and multiply.

It observed man (such a fallacy of creation) with the fascination of a boy allowing a trail of ants to fall under the power of a magnifying glass in the afternoon sun. It studied, and let humankind begin to destroy itself. When it laughed, the earth trembled, at times ridding the surface of an entire, mindless race of skin and bones.

Cemeteries, the cities of the dead, sleeping places for countless numbers of rotting corpses, spread like wildfire. It seemed they had finally gotten a clue how to properly remember the dead. But that would soon change.

Cemeteries, once under the protection of the church's hallowed ground, began to crowd with the remains of the dead, becoming the foulest places of stench and rot one could imagine. There was no choice but to spread away from these protected centers and bury the dead in ground *it* controlled.

Now, two people in the world above had started taking what was rightfully its. Up until now, only few had crossed that line and discovered this other world existed. Of those few, none had lived to tell the tale. They were burning for eternity, forever paying for their sins.

But some had started disappearing from their stakes, removed from the punishment they deserved. It could only mean one thing: others had discovered its presence. Something had to be done. They would pay with their lives, their souls. Just like the others.

Since the beginning of time, this dark underworld was given to it as punishment. The souls that occupied this wretched place were all it had, its reason for existence. Most of them had enjoyed sinful lives as thieves, murderers, rapists, and sadists. They deserved to burn.

Eventually, the forgotten ones also came, screaming.

They were the souls no longer cared about, no longer lingering in the thoughts of the living. Souls with nowhere to go, unable to be remembered and allowed into the peaceful opposite of this underworld, easily sucked into this bottomless void. There would always be a place for these unwanted souls. It craved them.

Soon, it would present to the world its greatest creation and spread its wrath like a devastating, incurable disease.

Devastation. It loved the word, the concept.

The flavor.

It smiled.

Chapter 17

A steady drip fell into the tub, disturbing the smooth surface of the water with precision timing.

Andrea swirled the brownish water with her toes, concentrating on the way the water gathered repeatedly at the mouth of the faucet, swelled until it couldn't hold its weight, then fell. With each drop, her eyelids grew heavier. She was finally feeling relaxed. The tub seemed to do the trick, even with tainted water running between her toes.

She didn't care that the tub had cracks seeping water slowly onto the faded linoleum floor, or that the water was tinted with rust. She didn't care that the paint in the bathroom was puke green with pieces peeling away here and there, or that the bathroom held the scent of something horrid.

Maybe death smelled like this.

The only thing worth caring about was disappearing for a while, getting away from anything and everything.

Pushing away her surroundings, she closed her eyes and forced herself to find a perfect world that didn't really exist. A world full of harmony: no starving countries, no pollution, no hole in the ozone layer, no angry dictators trying to take over the world.

No forgotten souls.

She drifted into a lazy sleep in which this perfect world was able to develop, first with sparkling fields of green, then waves lapping against a desolate shore. The eerie cry of a loon penetrated her senses as it bobbed upon the water in a state of extreme relaxation, its wings fluttering as it crested on top of the wave passing underneath it.

The power of sleep silently pulled her from reality as the view of the sea bled into another part of her memory, and she was running through knee-high grass as a little girl. Ribbons in her hair flapped joyfully upon her head and flowers scraped comfortably against her small legs. Dandelions spread into the distance, knowing no boundaries. She ran and ran, tiny feet seeming to float above the sea of yellow, feeling unstoppable, indestructible.

In her dream, she stopped with a silent, jarring halt and looked at her feet. Between each sandaled foot, something in the grass protruded like a lonely, rotten tooth. Something she couldn't ignore, like the pain she used to purposely inflict upon herself at the first sign she was about to lose one of her teeth. Pulling, twisting. Hating the pain but doing it, anyway. Pulling and twisting until it came away in a nervous hand for closer inspection.

In the tub, the corners of her mouth jumped up and down in sporadic jerks.

The image became more defined as she moved closer. The rotten tooth appeared in the shape of a headstone with a name barely etched and unreadable upon its surface. Green mildew decorated the base of the stone like an abscess.

She was reaching to twist it from the ground and examine its roots, when a crying scream for help echoed in her ears. The stone exploded into a shower of fragments and the dandelions wilted on their stems, yellow halos becoming brown with decay, with death.

Andrea jumped in the tub, water splashing from the violent interruption of its calmness. She looked around, not knowing where she was and frightened by the ugliness of the room she was in. Eyes wide, she pushed her wet hair back from her forehead. At last, but taking longer than she would have liked, recent events came back to her and she gently slid back into the comfort of the water, which was growing cold too fast. Ripples faded and became a smooth pane of dirty glass, revealing the reflection of a light bulb with not enough wattage.

She felt herself drifting off again before she recalled why she had awakened in the first place. Had she actually heard a scream for help or was it just part of her dream left unfinished?

The quiet sobbing came again, of a woman she thought, now muffled and almost nonexistent. Andrea opened her eyes and knew the mildew appearing between flayed seams of old wallpaper was not the figment of a dream.

A trick she had learned years ago surfaced into her memory and she knew it was the proper time to use it.

First, you had to know who it was.

She didn't know how old this person was at the time of her death, so she rattled off names that were of more recent times, a slight pause after each. Stephanie . . . Lisa . . . Kristin were the first she thought of.

The sobbing continued, getting louder, then fading into almost inaudible inflections, as though a fitful slice of wind were cutting into her cries. Andrea tried to think of names that had been around for a while. Cecilia, Lucille, Bella . . . Still the crying continued. The name of the motel she and Darren were staying at came to mind.

Velora.

At once, as if the cries of despair had found an outlet for the pain, the crying came to a stop, taking Andrea by surprise. The steady drip coming from the faucet now seemed to drop into the water with unbridled fury, the silence around it that deafening. Making the connection to Velora, secrets immediately began being revealed to Andrea in complete trust, masking nothing.

Andrea saw Velora's toes (her toes) poking out of a steamy bath of clear water. She must have been a small woman, as her feet didn't even reach the mechanism in the shape of a hideous erection that plugged the drain. The walls now contained fresh coats of pastel-colored paint of a fashion shunned by today's generations.

From the murky mists of her dream state, a shadow appeared.

A man emerged and kneeled at her side, arm resting on the sparkling porcelain of the tub with a glass of wine in hand. Another full glass appeared from behind as he brought his other arm around. From a face devoid of any wrinkles, his mouth was moving, but no sound came forth. Red-rimmed eyes seemed to be looking in two separate directions and complemented the rosy glow of his face. His breaths were shallow, as if his lungs couldn't reach their desired capacity.

Reality and the dream started to blend together, as Andrea reached for the glass of red wine. She could almost smell it, taste it, as she brought the glass to her lips and let the crimson liquid warm her insides. Through the rippled features of the glass, she watched the man's hand slide from the edge of the tub and into the water, fingers creating separate wakes as he ran them just below the surface.

His knuckles dipped even farther below the surface and found her knee. A fluttering of emotions tickled her as he brought his hand up the inside of her leg, stopping at the point where her two legs joined, burying the tips of his fingers in her hair. The wine accelerated the warmness between her legs.

A low, satisfying moan escaped her lips as he found her

swollen nub of flesh and rubbed gently. The water provided just the right amount of lubrication to enhance her pleasure as he applied small, circular motions. Her body trembled, and just when her body wanted to release all of its pent-up energy, his hand glided up her waist, pausing before finding and squeezing a breast.

A finger soon traced her lips and slid down her chin. She looked toward the ceiling to let him continue the path to the hollow of her neck. He paused again, but not for long.

The single tip of his finger turned into many that surrounded the base of her throat. And squeezed.

She couldn't breathe!

Her eyes felt like they were about to fly out of their sockets as her windpipe was crushed inward under his grip. She heard it crunch, but wasn't allowed the chance to revel in the pain as her head was pushed underwater. Involuntary bubbles of air left her nostrils and the corners of her mouth as her body demanded to exhale. She resisted the urge to draw any type of breath into her lungs, instead trying to kick at her assailant, but found his weight heavy upon her thighs. She wanted to claw his crooked eyes from his head, but his free hand held her tiny wrists.

The pain in her throat began to diminish, instantly being replaced by an explosion of fire within her chest. The distorted shape above mocked her with blurred facial expressions one would use on an infant—cheeks puffed out, holding air. Much-needed air!

The foggy substance of unconsciousness started to consume the pastel walls as it waited to be invited in. She tried to slam the door shut on its milky grin, but her eyes began to droop as though someone were pulling the shades closed for her.

The need for air and the requirement to exit the dream

state Andrea now occupied twisted into a binding sense of panic. She pushed with all the strength she had left in her weary body, prying herself from the inevitable death trying to crawl inside of her.

A drop of cold water fell onto the top of her foot and her toes curled as they still rested on the tub's edge, near the spout. Her body released an involuntary shudder and she at once felt the coldness of the bathwater surrounding her. She drew in several deep breaths until her lungs almost burst in expansion, relishing the taste of fresh air mixed with a hint of mildew. She opened her eyes to the dull glow of the single light bulb and peeling wallpaper. Her teeth began to chatter.

The comfort of a tattered towel hanging from the back of the door seemed pleasant compared to the chill that kept rippling through her.

As she readied herself to get out of the tub, something cold grasped one foot, then the other, and pulled with strength that terrified her. Before she had a chance to inhale a last breath, before she had a chance to scream for help, she was underwater. The brownish gloom lurked above, as if she were at the bottom of a murky swamp. Her hair floated around her head like hundreds of tiny serpents. A steady hammering pounded between her temples and seemed magnified by the blanket of water surrounding her.

Andrea struggled to get to the surface, but something prevented her with an invisible weight upon her chest, trying to forcibly squeeze the air out of her lungs. The pain in her chest got stronger as she held her breath, and all too familiar.

The world above was changing, getting darker.

Minutes ticked by as she listened to the loud splash of water that fell from the spout in steady drops. Shadows fleeted around the poorly lit room above her, somewhere, and seemed to gather into a singular mass.

The shape of another person loomed over her.

This is the end, she thought.

Her world got darker still, almost black now.

Andrea opened her mouth and inhaled to relieve the burning in her chest.

Chapter 18

In San Francisco, California, an elderly woman clung to life by the only threads the machines let her have.

Machines let her breathe in rhythmic cycles and allowed her heart to beat faintly, but steadily. She even had a machine that let her go to the bathroom without having to worry about cleaning it up. Even at the very end, life could still have its pleasantries. She only listened as her body sucked at the artificial juices of these mechanical tethers. They were the last connections to a life already lived, to memories long since created, and a life spent remembering the dead she would no doubt become a part of in the near future. The tethers could snap at any moment, preventing any rebound. She knew this, and had to be careful.

Faye Clark couldn't see, at least not the world directly around her, but she could hear the faint bells and whistles of the machines that let her live, the machines that gave her a new breath on each waking day. Her body would not let her do things she used to do, but her mind still raged with the vivacity of her youth.

She knew when there were people in the room: she could feel the vibrations of their voices upon her skin. She knew when she was alone in the dark of night: she always felt someone pull the sheets over her toes before leaving only silence for her to contemplate. Faye only wished that person saw the faint wiggle of her baby toe, a small signal to leave her plugged in for just a while longer.

Faye couldn't die—not yet, at least. She had a job to do.

Doctors and nurses were her family for the time being

and she distinguished each by the intensity of their vibrations. All she could do was pray they let her stay alive, let her beep and whistle in conversation until her job was finished.

So far, her prayers had been answered.

She dreaded the day this would be taken away, yet yearned to welcome death. They were waiting for her.

But first, two people needed her guidance. The dead had told her so.

Faye just needed to find a way in.

Chapter 19

Darren knocked, more than once. She had been in there for over an hour. He just thought he'd check in on her, see if she needed anything.

He knocked again. Silence, save for an occasional drip of water he heard even through the door, seeming to bounce off the walls of the tiny bathroom and find a way through the spaces where the door didn't quite fit the frame.

"Andrea?" He still felt uncomfortable calling her by her first name.

Nothing. Instinct told him to barge right in, while common sense nagged at him to give her the privacy she sought. His hand fluttered around the doorknob while his feet wanted to pull him away.

A twinge of something unpleasant sprinkled his stomach like a spray of acid, and he opened the door without giving it another thought. He went into the bathroom with eyes almost closed, cast toward the floor, sure he was going to be embarrassed at the sight of Andrea in the tub.

By the time the door could finish its small arc before banging against the toilet, his heart skipped a beat as the remnants of a shadow were sucked into the darkest corners of the walls where the mildew was most prevalent. Maybe it was only the bad lighting or he was jumping at his own shadow, but whatever it was, it was gone now.

There was no curtain hanging from the bent rod, so he let his eyes travel to the corner of the tub and to her feet. He started to say something to wake her from a nap if she was sleeping, but ate his words when he saw her legs.

They were floating!

The rest of Andrea's naked body was partly suspended on the surface, eyes open, remote in their focus. A single bubble left her open mouth and burst on the surface. The sound it created seemed to accentuate the final breath that was able to escape her lungs.

A conglomeration of words and feelings of hysteria came from his quivering lips in the form of a struggled cry. He knew he had to get her out of the water and do something, anything, but found that his legs wouldn't move.

Panic. His body trembled to the core, hands smacked at the sides of his legs.

A flood of different emotions took over.

Adrenaline managed to move that first step, then the next. He reached for her arm and paid close attention to her eyes, hoping to see some sort of movement, but more because he thought she might see him looking at the rest of her.

Turning her with the pull of her arm, Darren reached from behind, tucked his arms under hers, and pulled her out of the tub while calling her name with the high-pitched voice of a child. He cradled her upper body as her legs followed and fell limply to the floor with two solid slaps. Her eyes remained glued open. Her skin was already starting to develop a faint shade of blue, her lips purple.

Darren watched droplets of water roll off her temples as he fought to remember the ABC's of lifesaving he had learned in a course that was right up there with details of his Ancient Civilization class.

He didn't know if he was supposed to, but turned Andrea's head, anyway. A small gush of dirty water found its way out of her mouth and disappeared beneath the cracks in the linoleum.

Tilting her head back to establish an airway in a way he thought was right, he placed his ear next to Andrea's mouth to check for breathing. He noticed her breasts while he looked toward her feet, each slick with water and hanging slightly at the sides of her chest, but all he wanted them to do at this point was rise a few inches.

They didn't.

What to do, what to do? Slowly, so damn slowly, instructions were coming back to him with the guise of fragmented lesson plans.

He checked for a pulse on her carotid artery. A slow heartbeat was there, barely noticeable, like the last spasm of a dying animal.

Darren placed the palm of his left hand on Andrea's forehead and guided her head back slowly. With the thumb and forefinger of the same hand he plugged her nose, then pulled her chin down with his other hand and placed his mouth over hers.

Her lips were ice cold.

He gave two rescue breaths, saw her chest rise with each, then fall flat, deflated.

"Come on! Come on! Andrea!" His eyes were starting to burn.

He gave one more breath, but pulled back quickly as her chest heaved suddenly and she coughed out more dirty water. She immediately rolled to her side, gulping at the air like a fish out of water, spit, then struggled to sit up. Darren held her down.

Andrea's color came back in a rush. She started to shake, almost uncontrollably. Tears began their painful, yet joyful ride down her face.

Darren held her as tight as he could, placing her head underneath his chin, against his neck, cradling her, wanting to give her comfort, warming her. She was going to be fine. He would ask later what had happened; right now he just wanted to hold her. Her body seemed so cold, and it trembled as she cried. Her breasts jiggled with each convulsion. Darren closed his eyes.

Andrea finally managed to slow down her crying and shivering. Minutes passed in complete silence, each holding the other.

She began to kiss Darren's neck tenderly, lovingly.

His eyes flew open.

It was Darren's turn to start shaking.

He didn't know if he should tell her to stop—it felt too good. Maybe it was only a weird sort of way to thank him. After all, he had never saved anyone's life before. His mind immediately traveled to the first time he looked down her shirt. Now, she was here, sans clothes, within his very arms!

As her kisses made their way slowly up his neck, leaving a welcome wetness with her tongue, he knew she wasn't just saying thanks. A burning sensation filled his groin. He was suddenly glad he still had his pants on to conceal his growth.

The wetness traced upward from the nape of his neck to his left cheek, until their mouths met. Andrea's tongue glided over his lips, awaiting entry. His lips were quivering. The only way to stop them was to open his mouth, which he did eagerly. Their tongues did a slow, tentative waltz until they were both dancing wildly in and out of each other's mouths.

Darren's hand was within easy reach and began to caress Andrea's right breast with a shaky touch. The slickness of her skin allowed his hand to glide smoothly over her nipple, making it erect. He repeated the motion over her left nipple, and gently squeezed her breast in full.

125

Andrea guided his hand to her soft mound of pubic hair, then her clitoris, letting his fingers rub back and forth over her swollen gland. Darren could hear and feel the vibrations as she moaned in his mouth. He heard a steady thumping in his ears.

Her fingers began to pull at the buttons of his jeans.

Between her legs, Darren felt the wetness the water had produced. Slow trickles of it moved from her pubic hair through his nervous fingers. But as he ventured lower, searching every part of Andrea, he felt the moisture that she alone produced. He imagined tasting it.

She was tugging at the tee shirt that clung to his body. Darren couldn't get the shirt off fast enough. As he pulled the shirt over his mid-section, Andrea licked and kissed his abdomen, tasting the saltiness of his sweat. She helped him with his jeans and boxer shorts in one sweep. He already had his shoes kicked off—his socks could stay on as far as he was concerned.

Finally free from the restraint of his clothes, Darren placed himself upon Andrea, kissing her neck and nibbling on her ear. He was taller than Andrea and his penis received a shock of its own as it touched the cold linoleum between Andrea's legs. The damp texture of her pubic hair tickled his stomach.

He wanted to taste every inch of Andrea—her breasts, her belly. Her womanhood. But he couldn't take the suspense any longer. He wanted to be inside her, *now*. As if reading his mind, she grasped his penis firmly and guided it to her opening. She placed her free hand on his right buttock and all but shoved him inside of her, her juices allowing him to slide in easily. She moaned deeply as Darren felt her body grow momentarily tense and then relax as he made slow, easy thrusts.

They continued like this, loving each other, letting go of each other's tension as one, loving the release as much as the loving. They continued until each was spent, sweaty, and drained of all the energy they had possessed.

They held each other for the longest time afterward, lying right there on the cracked bathroom floor, not wanting to let go, not wanting to let the moment die. Darren thought Heaven had just opened its pearly gates and allowed him to take a glimpse inside.

Andrea's head, hair mussed and drenched with sweat, lay on Darren's chest. Her eyes were closed, one leg spread over both of Darren's, resting. One arm covered his waist while her other hand curled his hair around her fingers. Whatever had happened earlier in the tub seemed ages ago, and he was in no rush to stamp it into his memories.

He wasn't sure how much of what she did was pure impulse, but he enjoyed every bit of it.

And welcomed it.

Chapter 20

Losing his virginity that night was like nothing he could have ever imagined.

He had come so close, so many times before, that it hurt—typically in the form of the nastiest shade of blue balls. He had gone steady with a few different girls in high school, had many hidden adventures in the pantry, garage, or wherever events had placed them, had done everything . . . except that. And for the first time in his life, he was glad he had waited.

He had thought making love involved some secret code discovered only through experience. How wrong he was—in his case, at least. He was amazed at what could happen once human instinct took over, once the body knew it needed something and acquired it.

Finally, he thought.

They didn't talk much after they had left the bathroom. Darren cast an occasional nervous glance at Andrea in her bed. Hair still wet from the shower they had shared, she was on her back, staring at the ceiling. An erection started forming again as he noticed how beautiful she looked in just her Bugs Bunny nightshirt, pink panties hinting from where the shirt pulled up. He wondered what she was thinking, but more so, if they would ever do it again.

As much as he had enjoyed it (Andrea, too, as far as he could tell), he still couldn't help wondering if it was the right thing to do. Maybe they both needed each other at that particular time in their lives. Emotions had been high. Andrea had almost died.

The thought hit Darren like a closed fist to the gut.

Why? Why had Andrea almost died?

The question rolled around in his head, as if upon a disturbed sea of thoughts, only to crash against a rocky coast of uncertainty. Andrea hadn't said a word yet about what had happened before he had pulled her out of the tub. He had to know.

The soft chirping of the crickets and the ticking of a moth against the lampshade on the nightstand—the only sounds amid the silence—started to make him feel uncomfortable.

"What happened in there, Andrea?" Darren asked, his sudden question causing her to jump and her shirt to pull up just a bit more. "I mean . . . before I came in," he said, blushing.

"God, you scared me," Andrea said, rubbing her eyes as she let out a muffled noise Darren couldn't quite make out. He thought it sounded like a small chuckle, and that made him blush even more.

"Well . . ." Andrea started. "I think I know what happened. But then again, I'm not so sure." She went on to tell him about the dream she was having, the cries for help, then being pulled under. The memory of looking up from the bottom of a swamp made her shiver. "I was beginning to black out and all I could see was a shadow. I think it was . . . Velora's husband."

"Who?" Darren couldn't place the name at first. "Oh, you mean . . . but you've never met the man."

"That's the thing. Velora showed me through her memories. I'm sure I'd recognize him if I were face to face with him. I saw him . . . Oh, those eyes, looking in two different directions," Andrea said, covering her mouth as she gasped, eyes immediately beginning to water. "What do we do?"

"About what?" It was the first thing he thought to say, as

he swallowed a lump in his throat at realizing whom Andrea was describing.

"He killed her, Darren. Drowned her while she was taking a bath." A visible chill rippled through her and she pulled the blanket up to her chin. She drew a deep breath, wiped at a premature tear with a pinky.

"And then buried her by the tree in the back," Darren finished for her, knowing he had found the final piece to this puzzle while he was outside. He briefly described what had happened to him and still found it hard to believe.

"But what do we do?" Andrea asked again.

"I say call the police. The guy's a murderer." The last word felt harsh as it left Darren's mouth, something he only heard in movies. He couldn't picture the small, helpless man that he had met killing anything, let alone another person.

"No, not yet," Andrea replied. His eyebrows rose at her comment. "First, show me where she's buried." She looked at her watch. "It's close to midnight already. We'll do it first thing in the morning. I'd like to at least try and get some sleep."

Darren agreed, but wondered how in the world he would be able to. He turned on his side, heard the click of the light switch near Andrea's side of the room, and stared through the darkness. And into the pale blue glow of moonlight coming through a crack in the curtains, filtered by dirt and grime, and entering the room in soft, scattered rays.

In light of recent events, a pleasant numbness tingled his body and, when combined with the soothing chirping of the crickets, allowed the fingers of sleep to pull him into the darkness.

Darren breathed in the morning air, noticed a spider's dewy web glimmering in the morning mist, and gazed to the endless reaches of the earth where the sun was climbing into a cloudless morning sky. It would have been a beautiful morning if he didn't know there was a rotting corpse below his feet.

He stood below the aging willow, which he felt had lost its beauty now that he knew Velora was somewhere below the ground in front of it. He imagined reaching just below the surface and grasping Velora's skeletal hand. If he could only pull out a flesh-covered, living body from the ground below.

The sun rose steadily behind the lone tree, producing a thick shadow upon the surface facing Darren. The shadow grew as the sun made its ascent and Darren unconsciously stepped away. The tree's once-beautiful limbs now appeared to be long, scraggly branches lacking life, in the shape of skinless bones.

He breathed a sigh, of mourning perhaps, knowing that he could do nothing to bring Velora back. Her screams still echoed in the recesses of his mind and all he had the power to do was remember her. He hoped it would be enough to release her, enough to place her into the world he only knew as Heaven.

Another sigh expanded his chest as he braved all evils and stepped into the shadow of the tree, turning away and leaning back against its rough surface. Slowly, he slid to the ground, edges of bark catching on his tee shirt and pulling it upward.

He survived. The tree hadn't opened up and swallowed him whole, and a decayed hand had not reached up from the ground to pull him under. Instead, the shadow seemed to caress him, love him, and protect him from the heat of the rising sun, from the world. He felt the sun's rays touching his arms and almost setting his elbows on fire in contrast to the rest of his body. He pulled them into the shadow.

This was where he would finally start his journal.

The smell of ammonia jolted her awake like a whiff of milk gone sour and she gagged against the harsh odor. In the second it took to register, the space of time between sleep and wakefulness confused and indiscernible, it was gone, the smell dispersed like the scattering of leaves on an autumn day.

A beam of sunlight fell across her squinting, sleepy eyes. Andrea pushed her hair away from her forehead and her fingers came away damp. Her entire body felt covered in a clammy stickiness as she pulled the sheets down with her feet. They seemed to peel away from her body like dressings from a gaping wound.

Her eyes adjusted to the change of light, pupils shrinking in a stinging instant. She looked over to Darren's bed. Empty. Her heart skipped a beat, fluttering like the wings of a dying sparrow, but settled when she saw a scribbled note on the nightstand. He was at the willow tree and didn't want to wake her.

She stared at the door that led to the bathroom and didn't know what to feel. Behind this door, something wonderful had happened, but something terrible, as well. It was this last thought that kept her from immediately opening the door to take a shower.

She thought about just putting on some clothes and running a quick brush through her hair, but took a quick glance at herself in a cracked mirror leaning against the wall. A half-grin, half-frown formed on her face as she looked at her hair sticking up, at the small pouches formed under her eyes—things a brush couldn't fix.

She opened the door.

Words didn't come easily. Everything he wanted to write was there within reach, but what he wanted to say appeared to him as images instead of words.

He imagined meeting a person who couldn't speak his language, each drawing pictures (probably pathetic little cartoon illustrations) until it was clear what the other was trying to say. It would probably take forever.

He thought hard, searching for a beginning, the end of his pen beginning to warp between the grinding of his teeth. He turned past the page containing his doodles and placed the date in the left margin of the page that would be his second entry.

Finally, he began, but didn't produce much:

Day three of the journey . . . where will it take us?

Darren tapped the pen on the page. A drop of spittle escaped from its end and produced a small streak as it ran across the fresh ink.

I still don't understand everything about what Andrea and I are setting out to accomplish, but even for just the few days we've been traveling, I feel the answers to my questions starting to come, sometimes all at once.

Darren's images suddenly became words, as if he had found an interpreter somewhere within his head. He tried his best at starting from the beginning—his beginning anyway, when he had agreed to be Andrea's partner.

He watched the tip of the pen in amazement as it glided across the page, creating words that couldn't keep up with his brain. He didn't want to stop. Afraid that if he stopped, even to stretch his cramping hand, the words would once again turn into indecipherable images.

He didn't stop.

His hand became a machine, producing words and filling pages with amazing ease. As though dissociated from the words his hand produced, Darren's eyes were blank, lost somewhere as they developed the events of the last few days. Somewhere in-between was the interpreter.

The warbles of distant birds and rattle of the branches above him fell under an invisible blanket, only able to manifest themselves as whispers to his ears. As though he were falling into himself, gathering into a darkened corner of his mind as something else took over.

At last, his hand came to a stop.

Darren shook his head as if waking from a taunting dream. He looked down at the notebook on his lap, stared in disbelief at the amount of information contained within the pages. He couldn't remember writing down anything past the first few paragraphs.

He tried to let the pen drop to the notebook, but his twisted hand wouldn't allow it. He pried his fingers from the pen, one at a time.

Cold drops came in intermittent spurts of torrent, but she welcomed them as she felt her body awaken from its slumber. She kept her eyes open, refusing to let her indulgence go further than necessary, and searched the corners of the bathroom for any growing shadows. They didn't come. She was out in record time and glad it was the last time she would see the inside of this particular bathroom. Before she even wrapped the towel around her dripping body, she slammed the door behind her, feeling a moment of joy as the wood threatened to splinter. "Take that!" she mumbled.

She dressed quickly, afraid of being alone in the room for any longer than necessary, and opened the door in search of Darren.

It didn't take long.

She leaned against the back corner of the motel and watched Darren with curiosity. He was bathed in the shadow of the tree, but she could tell he was writing. His head hung low, unmoving. He seemed to be totally involved, unaware of his surroundings. His hand moved quickly across the page, and every few minutes he would turn a page with his free hand to continue the process. Andrea watched him turn at least five pages before he finally stopped and forced the release of the pen from his grip.

She waited another minute or so before walking toward him, not wanting to startle him. She wanted to make sure he saw her approach, in case he was writing something private. She walked with heavy steps, trying not to be too obvious. This would give him plenty of time to put it away.

Darren's eyes didn't leave the notebook still splayed open upon his knees. One hand was rubbing the other. He didn't notice Andrea until she came to a halt directly in front of him. A glassy stare met Andrea and registered no surprise at her being there.

After a short string of silence, he said, "You're not going to believe this."

"Believe what?" Andrea asked, then pointed to the notebook. "What's that you're working on? Anything interesting?"

"Take a look for yourself." He gave the notebook to Andrea. She took it with slight caution and a questioning look. She didn't actually think he'd let her look at it. "I was going to start a journal and keep track of what we're doing, and all of a sudden I guess I went into sort of a trance and wrote this. It doesn't even look like my handwriting, except for the first few paragraphs."

Andrea leafed through the pages, amazed. "You did all this while you were sitting here?"

"Yeah," Darren said and looked at his watch. "I have

only been here for . . . oh man, twenty minutes. How could I—"

"I don't know, but it seems you've completely described the last few days in great detail. And then some," Andrea said, pausing here and there to read certain passages. "Unreal. And whose initials are these at the very end . . . V. H.?"

"I don't know; at first I thought of Velora. But we don't know her last name. I bet it's her, though."

"Bet you're right," Andrea said. "C'mon, let's go inside and get a closer look at this."

Once inside, Andrea set herself upon the only chair in the room and it seemed to have its own voice of squeaks and groans. The notebook was open on the table in front of her. Darren looked over her shoulder.

They both read slowly, carefully. Intently. Their disbelief increased with each turn of a page. What they were reading was an accurate account of each soul they had remembered. Each soul they had saved from purgatorial boredom or the heated depths of Hell itself.

The first passage after Darren's personal introduction had been about Albert: his life, his death, and his remembrance by Darren and Andrea. At the end of the passage were his initials: A. F.—Albert Fontaine. Andrea skimmed over the passages following Albert's. At the end of each passage were initials, all different.

"I can't believe it," Andrea said. "Each of these descriptions belongs to a different person. All of these next to Albert's must be the rest of the people buried in the same cemetery." Andrea continued to examine the pages, more carefully now.

"I don't understand how—" Darren started.

"Look, look," Andrea said, pointing with a shaky finger. "Even the handwriting is different for each one. This is amazing, Darren. Somehow, they used you as a medium to tell their tale. Every one of them."

Darren took the notebook from Andrea, prying it from her fingers. "There's got to be some reason they're doing this. I mean, I don't even remember a damn thing. People don't get taken over by spirits or whatever, for nothing," Darren said, disbelief and skepticism still occasionally hinting around his words.

"It's starting, Darren, it's starting," Andrea said, barely able to conceal her excitement, now up and pacing back and forth in short, hurried steps, fingers to her temples. "Well, I guess we'll have to see for sure. Every couple of days we'll have you sit down and do the same thing, or at least try to."

"I don't know. I feel kind of strange letting things take over my body, you know?"

Andrea wasn't expecting that, and felt a bit defeated, like she had just received a small punch to the gut. She turned away quietly, but he must have noticed her disappointment, as he quickly looked at the notebook, pointed to it with his chin, and said, "I think I may need more paper."

They stared at each other in silence for an awkward moment before bursting into twin fits of nervous laughter.

Their diminishing chuckles were completely strangled as a shadow crossed the threshold and grew into the room. It was Darren who noticed it first, turning to see the door he had left open. Andrea noticed the shadow soon after she heard Darren mutter a soft, "Oh, shit."

Though neither Darren nor Andrea could make out the features of the person hiding within the shadow, they both knew to whom it belonged.

The shadow was holding a shovel. The same shovel Darren had grabbed earlier.

The same shovel used to bury Velora.

The man stepped into the room, at last revealing his withered features. Darren recognized him as the man he had met the night before: slow moving, fragile. Even so, Darren saw a different man in the room with them, a man who caused the hairs on his arms to rise in sweeping currents and riddle his body with stinging pinpricks.

Eyes ablaze, chest inhaling and exhaling rapidly, the man seemed to be possessed by an entirely new life force. He seemed larger, stronger. Darren could practically hear the man's heartbeat as it flooded the room, blood pumping violently through the man's veins. Darren watched the hand holding the shovel open and close upon the wooden handle, at times sounding like the wood was about to split in two. The man stepped closer, closing the distance between Darren and himself, not viewing Darren as a threat, though Darren stood at least two feet above him.

The man's eyes locked onto Darren's in a defiant stare. Darren stared back, trying to anticipate the man's next move. He didn't dare drop his gaze for fear of being caught by surprise. Eyes glued to those of the intruder's, Darren slowly made his way in front of Andrea, telling her to move back with a wave of his hand. She did so.

"Leave my wife alone. She deserves to be where she's at," said the intruder, his voice coming in harsh, hoarse gasps. "Now I'll have to put the both of you right beside her. You can talk to her on the other side."

"Mister, how could you know anything about us?" Darren asked, slowly backing as the man approached, almost tripping over the chair. A forefinger picked at the skin of his thumb's cuticle. "Just put down the shovel and we can talk—"

"I'm to tell you that you will end your journey here,

now," the man said, almost wheezing. "NOW!"

The strike of the shovel broke Darren's gaze from the man's wild, frantic eyes. He was quick enough to miss the blow, pushing Andrea out of the way as the shovel came into contact with the wall. The blade carved into the plaster and knocked a picture frame to the floor.

"Get out, NOW," Darren hissed to Andrea.

"Darren, look out!"

Her warning didn't come quick enough. Darren fell to his knees, hugging the ribs at his side, panting for air, groaning.

The man stood above Darren triumphantly, crazed eyes pushed almost completely out of his skull, ready to wield another blow. His chest heaved, throat rattling, as chunks of phlegm broke free from somewhere deep within his chest.

"Come on, you old fart, show me what you've got," Andrea taunted. "What's the matter? I *know* you're not afraid to clock a defenseless woman."

She must have struck a nerve. The man's energy all but collapsed around his skeletal frame, his skin sucked into a horrid outline of every bone. Eyebrows raised in confusion, wrinkles of his forehead bunched into liver-spotted canyons, a childlike whimper escaped from a mouth that didn't seem to know whether to stay open or close. But only momentarily, as Mr. Hyde soon took over and stepped forward, shovel raised, jaws wide as though ready to take a bite out of anyone who got close enough.

Andrea brought her arms up to shield herself from the blow.

That never happened.

With a scissor-like grip Darren was able to weave quickly around the old man's legs with his own, Darren knocked

139

him off-balance. Twisted and rolled until the man's skinny legs couldn't brace themselves against the pressure, and he fell. Hard.

Seizing the opportunity, Darren clambered to his feet, wrenched the shovel from the man's grip, and pressed the blade against his throat.

He wanted to shove the blade through the man's neck until it met the floor, but couldn't. He wanted to see the blood fountain like Old Faithful as he sliced through the man's jugular, but whatever power had previously radiated from the man's eyes quickly receded into his dilated pupils.

All the fight now appeared to be drained from the old man as he lay beneath the shovel. What was now lying on the floor was the harmless old man Darren had first met in the lobby. The man's breathing now seemed to be normal, if labored, and he looked utterly exhausted. Sweat rained down the sides of his face and onto the floor. He looked up at Darren with eyes that didn't seem to understand.

"Go ahead and get our stuff in the car while I watch him," Darren told Andrea, still holding the shovel in place.

"Okay," Andrea said. "I'll have the car running in a minute."

They left in a hurry, adrenaline boiling and then slowly subsiding to a lull in the bottom-most part of their stomachs as they drove onto the interstate.

The day moved ahead around them. It was almost noon. The windows were down and damn, if her car only had air conditioning.

After what seemed to be a safe distance away from the motel, Andrea let off the accelerator and slowly brought the car to the appropriate speed limit. As her foot released its pressure, she slumped in her seat, demanding her body to slow down as well.

She looked at Darren. He bit at his fingernails and rapidly brought his leg up and down on the ball of his foot. One arm hugged the left side of his chest. He continued to stare ahead as she watched a small bead of sweat leave his temple and slowly form a path to the base of his neck for others to follow. She patted him on the shoulder.

"You . . ." She cleared her throat. "You okay?"

There was a moment of silence before Darren could pull his eyes away from the road to answer.

"I think so . . . ribs still hurt though," Darren said.

"You took a hell of a thunk. You sure none are broken?"

Darren winced as he pressed against his side. "Bruised probably, but not broken."

Andrea replied with a soft, "Ummm," as she concentrated on her driving. The dotted white lines that separated the two lanes of the interstate whisked by. Thick woods pushed against the interstate with occasional clearings that revealed farmers' crops with huge, dinosaur-like machines hibernating in the distance.

They didn't need to ask each other why they didn't kill the old man in self-defense or even call the police to put him away. From what they had witnessed, the man's life on earth was far worse than anything they could have done to him or anyplace the authorities could have put him.

He was paying for his sins with each waking day.

Chapter 21

Frank Carlson awoke angry.

Just like he had for the last day, month . . . year? He couldn't remember exactly how long he had felt this way—his entire life, he supposed. It was an ugly feeling, akin to depression, that made his stomach curl into a tight ball of nerves while an invisible weight pushed down on his scalp, forcing him to close his eyes in hopes that the world would go away when he opened them, that his decisions would be made for him in the time it took to blink.

The light coming through the small, rectangular windows at eye-level—his only visible access to the day outside—reflected the way he felt: dreary, depressed, angry. The dank smell that came with living in the basement also greeted him. Something he had yet to get used to.

The sky was overcast, the morning chilled and bitter in the basement until the sun brought its heat through the windows of the foundation. During the winter, he could even see his breath, the heat never seeming to penetrate this part of the house.

He groaned, shivered as he threw back the covers, and sat up on the bed to wake up, but wondered if he really wanted to. The fact that the sun was coming up meant he had another day to get through in his miserable life.

His parents had moved him into the basement when he had quit high school, saying he could use it while he figured out what he wanted to do with his life. Frank knew better—knew that his parents were ashamed and thought, by moving him into the basement, that he wasn't really living at home. A way to pretend to any visitors that might come, even if few ever did, that their son was finally about to leave the nest and start his own life. Any day now, in fact . . . yeah, right.

Much like Darren Jacobs, who didn't know what he wanted to do with the rest of his life, which career path to take, Frank Carlson *still* didn't know after more than eight years since dropping out. As a further act of rebellion, he had waited to quit school until only three months remained before graduation, something he wasn't proud of, although he would never admit that. As a result, Frank was probably the oldest man in Durbin still living with his parents.

He was from a long line of factory workers. The many "shoe shops" of southern Maine had provided a meager living for his entire family, so why should he do anything different? Still, like all his relatives who worked there, he had hated it. Despised working long hours and nothing to show for it. Coming home each night with his fingers raw, their tips cracked and bleeding from working the machinery. He wasn't even making enough money to get his own apartment, so he quit a few weeks ago without even a second guess as to whether or not he was making the right decision. He just didn't give a shit either way.

His parents were starting to get onto him again about establishing a living and moving on in life (more to get him the hell out of their hair, was Frank's assumption). They didn't know where they had gone wrong in raising Francis Carlson. They were beginning to worry that he would achieve nothing, amount to nothing. Be nothing. He was beginning to think they were right.

Dinners at night were met with silence once Frank took his seat at the table. Conversation began again as he emptied his plate into the trash, placed it into the dishwasher,

and limped back into the basement. The silent treatment—
supposedly to make him understand where he was heading,
but it only stoked the fire already ablaze in Frank. And
lately, he was full of a boiling hatred, had even gone to the
point of permanently borrowing a 9mm pistol from a friend
in hopes that he might some day have the guts to put it to
his head and pull the trigger.

With another groan, this one of disgust, he looked
around his so-called room. The walls were the beautiful
cement-colored design that only a basement could provide.
On their rough surfaces, rock posters barely hung by pieces
of duct tape curling at the edges. Shelves, originally meant
for an assortment of tools, were filled with music CDs and
Penthouse magazines. Tucked behind a stack of the latter
rested a hash pipe that might still have enough resin on the
screen to catch a buzz later.

He thought about what he would do for the rest of the
day and found it didn't take very long to come up with a
satisfactory answer. Simply assuming a horizontal position,
he pulled the covers over his head and fell back asleep.
Maybe when he woke next time, he would have something
to live for.

A reason to crawl from the basement and let the world
know he existed.

A purpose.

He dreamed with a smile on his face and a swelling in his
underwear.

Andrea Varney straddled his pillow and beckoned him
toward his bed, a single finger pulling him forward from underneath a lace kerchief. Words didn't tumble from her glistening lips, but he could understand exactly what they were
saying. Could read the "oohs" and "aahs" that accompa-

nied the slow gyrations of her midsection against his pillow. About to grasp her with eager arms, wanting her, craving her, so close to finally having her, she began to fade.

And was replaced by money. Lots of it. Hundreds of bills fell from the ceiling, swirled where Andrea's nude silhouette still lingered as a seductive wraith. The smell of fresh ink filled his nose, enlivened his senses. He bathed in it, made love to it. Worshipped it.

Moaning with satisfaction, eyelids fluttering in exquisite ecstasy, a state of euphoria left him utterly defenseless.

A pleasant fire roared within his abdomen and spread with molten emotion. When his insides begged for release, his chest thrust forward with a sudden painful snap he felt for only an instant and, in fact, wouldn't remember. His back arched and cracked among the segments of vertebra, sending nerve endings screaming throughout his body. But still, he smiled.

And collapsed to the bed, bathed in a sickly sweat.

Frank Carlson slept on.

Chapter 22

So close.

Beads of sweat gathered in the wrinkled shell containing the remnants of her being. Then fell down the sides of her chest with an agonizing slowness that teetered on the brink of driving her insane. Similar to an itch she couldn't find and scratch with a brittle nail, each tracing drop a tormenting reminder of her condition.

The beeps and whistles that kept Faye alive were fading. Fast.

She had traveled the highways of another existence, using the knowledge she had gained over the years to project herself elsewhere, searching for a certain pattern of colors and intersecting lines: a colorful grid marking the essence of Andrea Varney.

And she had found it!

But she was only able to observe Andrea with the likeness of a lone patron at a movie theater as she urged Andrea to wake, to push against the force that held her underwater. Frustration raged inside of her at being unable to reach into the screen of Andrea's projection.

She was running out of time—the machines let her know with each irritating twitter. If she weren't careful, she and Andrea would meet on the other side without accomplishing anything.

And right now, Andrea needed to get out of the water!

She observed with pained emotions as Darren pulled Andrea out of the tub, feeling as helpless as he did. With imaginary fingers, Faye clutched to the fraying thread of energy connecting herself to Andrea. Until, at last, the first splashes of water were spat from Andrea's lungs.

Andrea would be all right.

She heard a crackling, as if she had just pulled a wool blanket over her frail body. Small flashes of electricity danced around her as the image of Darren cradling Andrea's trembling body began to flicker.

Faye pulled back, let her energy slowly subside, felt herself being drawn heavily into the husk that still let her cling to the material world. Gravity seemed to push on her every limb, pressing the shape of her body into the cool hospital sheets she had become accustomed to. Exhaustion presented a weight of its own, allowing her to use the morbid melody of the machines as a lullaby.

She had knocked down one obstacle—the most difficult—and slept peacefully, proud of her accomplishment. Yet a fearful twinge kept picking at her, as she would the dried scab of a healing wound. She knew the presence was beginning to move its pieces quickly into place, readying itself for another attack. She needed to hurry.

Morning woke her with a ray of sunshine seeming to set her little toe on fire. A faint wiggle tried to cool it off.

Faye went to work at once, dreading any waste of valuable time, concentrating all of her energy into again seeking contact with Andrea, almost depleting it as she heard the distant sounds in the background getting even slower. One mistake and all would be lost.

Imagining herself as cool breeze of wind, she gently traveled the expanse of a separate world and wafted toward the mind she now instantly recognized, caressing Andrea's senses while seeking entry. When Andrea coughed in her sleep, Faye pulled back again as if adjusting the volume of a stereo, turning it down.

Almost . . .

Andrea was almost ready to accept her.

Faye tried to control her breathing, but found it much like concealing the excitement of the birth of a child, if she'd ever had any. A smile threatened to pull at the corners of her lips, but did not develop.

She watched as Andrea shifted to the "D" on her steering column, saw Andrea's eyes in the rearview mirror: bright, green, and beautiful. Her head turned and Faye could see Darren—eyes wide, smiling. His mouth opened and closed, but words couldn't reach her ears. Only a muffled buzz, as though she forgot to firmly seat a headphone jack into place. Then he was laughing, face turning red, eyes seeping small tears out of their corners. How nice it would be to hear him laughing.

Almost . . .

Faye pushed with a sudden surge of energy, perhaps a bit too much.

With each hiccup of air as he struggled not to laugh, Darren groaned in pain. Tears fell—from pain or laughter, she couldn't distinguish.

Andrea joined in the laughter, but soon heard her own chuckles diminish into mere echoes, as though belonging to someone else entirely. A peculiar smell entered her nostrils, almost driving directly into her brain, making her nauseous, dizzy.

Her grip slipped upon the wheel as jagged strands of darkness stabbed at the edges of her vision. She struggled to push them away.

The car began to drift.

Andrea fought to bring the car straight and level and forced her eyes open to keep her vision focused on the road ahead. She was about to gag. The smell was familiar, but she couldn't place it. It smelled almost like an antiseptic of some kind—a sickly smell, yet there was cleanliness associated with it, a sterile smell . . .

And then it was gone.

She breathed deeply, tasting antiseptic at the back of her throat. Shook her head as if clearing dreadful thoughts from her mind. Gathering as much phlegm as possible into her mouth with a forceful grunt any man would have been proud to hear, she unrolled the window and propelled a runny conglomeration of spit and snot far enough into the wind that the mass avoided splattering the side of her car. The taste lingered a bit, but not as potently. She rubbed her tongue against the roof of her mouth, trying to suck the remaining bitterness away with loud, smacking noises.

"I couldn't have done it better myself," Darren said, smiling. "Feel better?"

"No. I . . . uh . . . well, I don't know," Andrea started. "I just had this weird smell and then it was gone. Got kind of dizzy, but I'm fine now . . . yes, even feel better than I did before. Weird."

But she didn't feel the same.

"All right, but if you want a break, I can drive for awhile. You've been driving since we left home."

"Thanks, but that's okay," Andrea said, wondering if she actually *should* be driving. She really did think she was fine . . . for now. But if anything like that happened again, she promised herself to let Darren have the controls. Or maybe they just wouldn't go that far today.

She heard the constant grumbling coming from her stomach and knew it was almost time for dinner—a reminder that neither of them had eaten anything today. They were too busy fearing for their lives earlier to worry about such mundane things as getting something to eat. And Darren hadn't said a word about being hungry. He must be starved.

Ronald Grenier, a male nurse just returning from a late dinner with his newest girlfriend, heard the unmistakable sound coming from Faye Clark's room. Immediately, thoughts of the fine dinner, the first kiss, and what might happen if he got off work early, were dispelled into the dark world of the subconscious—for now, anyway.

He had a flat-line.

The hallways were dark and deserted in the intensive care unit, harboring a quiet he would always associate with the devious passing of death. All the same he yelled, "FLAT-LINE!" the words still echoing through the halls as he ran to begin resuscitation.

A cold wash of moonlight came through the window, blanketing the woman's face in a bluish halo. How much of her appearance was due to lack of oxygen, he didn't know. No sparkles of moisture were shining on the inside of the clear plastic mask that covered her nose and mouth.

He got as far as the first compression before the hallway came alive with feet squeaking against the floor and orders being yelled in various directions as the hospital staff appeared from nowhere. Hurried footsteps neared the outside of Faye's room. He didn't look up.

White coats slapped the sides of the doorway as they burst into the room. A doctor followed three other nurses from the night shift on duty. He looked as if he had been sleeping, hair standing like drunken sentries around his head, eyes red—the infamous signs of an all-nighter.

The doctor pushed his way through and replaced him. Following each compression he applied to Faye's chest, he winced as ribs started to give way under pressure. Hair danced on the top of his head while perspiration built on his forehead, an occasional drop falling onto the exposed chest of Faye Clark.

"Come on . . . come on."

Two minutes passed and a feeling of hopelessness saturated the room.

Ronald squeezed through those gathered around Faye with a paddle in each hand and a machine close behind. Nobody knew he had left the tight circle formed around the hospital bed.

On instinct, the doctor grabbed the paddles and rubbed them together in one motion, his eyes never leaving the monitors.

"Clear!" the doctor said before placing the paddles on her chest.

Faye's body jerked violently then fell limp to the bed. The sound of the flat-line seemed to grow louder with each passing second.

"Come on, beep, you fucking machine!" Beads of sweat turned into heavy drops that fell over the wrinkled creases in the doctor's brow, unnoticed even as they burned his eyes.

The machine charged up and he went through the same procedure.

"Clear!" Again Faye's body fell lifeless to the bed.

"Come on! Goddammit! Clear!"

Faye's body fell a third time, accompanied by the constant high-pitched drone of death claiming another soul.

As the doctor took a deep breath and stared at the others in the room, their eyes never able to meet his, the first beep came from the monitor. All eyes immediately looked to the machine for confirmation. The green line moved along the screen with the slight curve of a feeble heartbeat and disappeared to the left.

Eternity couldn't describe the time it took for the next heartbeat to appear on the screen—a curve a little larger and sharper than the first. Within a few minutes the peaks and dips registering on the monitor increased in strength and interval until a regular, if weak, heartbeat was present.

Silent thanks were acknowledged with a unified exhale from all those present, each wanting to smile but not being able to.

Faye Clark was still in a coma.

Chapter 23

French accents flowed among disjointed clips of conversation inside the Houlton Truck Stop, were almost hushed by thick aromas of burgers, grease, and liver and onions. Drivers talked to their suppliers near a section of CB radios and die-cast miniatures of the same trucks that they drove. Around them, travelers from both sides of the border hustled for snacks on the road or sat down to a meal almost meeting the description of home-cooked.

Darren filled out a postcard addressed to his parents, letting them know all was well and an explanation would follow in detail upon his return. It was much easier than a phone call.

Before grabbing a booth by the window, Andrea grabbed the local paper, separating the first section and leaving the rest folded neatly on the table.

The obituaries barely fit on one page. Mostly elderly people occupied the inside cover of the paper, but also a few of middle age resulting from automobile accidents or work-related injuries. Surprised at the number of people displayed for such a small area, it still proved exactly what she was looking for. Of all the obituaries listed, at least half of the deceased were going to be buried at different cemeteries.

"Anything good?" Andrea asked, feeling and hearing her own stomach beg her attention as she looked at the backside of Darren's menu. She folded the obituaries and fit them into her purse.

"The burgers look good. I'm sure they'd beat a Whopper any day."

Food ordered and delivered by an elderly woman who acted as if they were grandchildren she hadn't seen in many years, they ate greedily and in silence, only listening to the conversations around them as grease dripped down their chins.

Typical conversations about the weather or the potato crops dominated the atmosphere, but an occasional few stood out. One couple discussed their marital troubles, while a younger couple, seated upon barstools and smoking as if they never left the place, revealed their dreams of the future. It was a third conversation that piqued Andrea's interest, along with the muddied feet of one of the two involved. She casually looked in their direction while Darren dipped gigantic steak fries into a mixture of ketchup and mustard.

"What?" Darren asked, speaking around the fries.

Andrea only shook her head, listening intently, dabbing at the grease on the corner of her mouth with a napkin. The conversation seemed to be purposely kept quiet, demanding only the two involved hear the details. By the way the eyes of the other customers darted around the heated conversation, Andrea thought they were doing a terrible job of it.

With an understanding nod, Darren listened as well.

Their quibbling took place only a few feet away from Darren and Andrea's booth, near the entrance of the truck stop, while the taller of the two nervously plucked at his wallet and waited in line to pay for a gas purchase. A torn and dirt-stained flannel shirt with a checkerboard pattern barely clung to him. One button was missing and another hung by only a thread. He occasionally looked around, never letting his eyes linger on another's.

"I told you this deal would go bad. We should've waited.

Oh God, we should have waited." The taller one paused, taking a few deep breaths. "Goddammit, I can't believe you *did* that!"

The other participant of the conversation was getting red in the face, the cords of his neck straining as he attempted to keep his voice down. His clothes were neither dirty nor stained.

"It's done, over with, forget about it." The shorter one spoke low, seething. "He wasn't gonna pay up and he pissed me off. Bastard deserved it."

"But it was only for fucking cigarettes! We could've gotten another customer across the border with only a few more calls!"

"Hush your fucking mouth! Nobody's going to look for him at Evergreen."

The taller one turned away, ending the conversation. His shorter friend grunted and stormed outside, clawing for a pack of smokes in his left breast pocket.

Most of the argument had come across as mumbled expletives, but the mention of Evergreen immediately caught Darren's interest. Almost choking on a bite of burger in mid-swallow, he spat its remnants into a napkin and quickly reached for a drink.

"What's wrong?" Andrea asked.

"Wait a few minutes and I'll tell you," Darren whispered, glancing toward the checkout counter. The man was placing his wallet into his back pocket, too preoccupied to notice.

They heard the door close and turned to watch the customer join his friend waiting on the trunk of a rusted blue Nova. Pushing away a pointing finger and turning away from a slap that wasn't able to reach his face, the taller man climbed into the driver's seat and almost sped away before his friend could open the passenger's door. Squealing tires and a plume of purple smoke headed towards I-95 and an unknown destination.

"Evergreen," Darren said, wanting to say too much too quickly and not knowing where to begin.

"What about it?"

"Let me see the paper you put in your purse. The obituaries, wasn't it?"

"Yeah, so . . ."

"Let me see it and I think I'll know what to say next."

Andrea opened her purse and reached inside. "They killed someone, didn't they?"

"I hope not. Maybe they only hurt someone," Darren said, at once feeling the weight of falsity in his words. "Either way, Evergreen is all too familiar and someone might need some help."

Andrea unfolded the obituaries and faced them toward Darren on the table.

He briefly glanced at the bottom of each obituary. Evergreen did not appear as he'd expected. After a second run through the page, Darren spotted the name quietly nestled between two other listed deaths. Even though he knew he'd find it there, it still sent a chill through his body at its significance.

According to the *Houlton Pioneer Times*, Rosemary Ouellette was buried at Evergreen Cemetery yesterday. She had lived a long life, dying of natural causes at the healthy age of ninety-two.

Darren placed his finger on the obituary and turned the paper for Andrea to see.

"Wow." She was impressed. "How did you know?"

He briefly explained the conversation with his father the first night they were on the road.

"Well, I guess we know where our next stop is," she said after scanning the obituary.

Darren agreed with a nod, stared out the window, and wondered about everything. His eyebrows almost touched in concentration and puzzlement. They performed a nervous twitch and then relaxed.

He continued to wonder.

Chapter 24

An entire day later, Frank Carlson awoke feeling refreshed, rejuvenated, and strangely full of energy. As if he had crawled out of an old skin and climbed into another, like a rare clean pair of underwear. Everything around him seemed the same, yet different. The air was cold and clean and he took a deep breath of it. Something brewed in the pit of his stomach—a burning that made him shiver with excitement and anticipation that today would bring pleasant surprises. He was sporting the morning wood and silently touched himself. He felt good. Ready to take on the world.

Instincts told him it was time to rise and be counted.

Without thinking, he dug out an old suitcase and backpack from a cluttered closet whose organization and style only he could appreciate. He packed a sleeping bag and what few clothes he owned, and took one last look around his cave dwelling before turning to go.

As he crested the basement stairs, the sounds of pages turning and spoons clinking off the insides of cups welcomed him, and nothing more. His parents didn't look up from their morning coffee and newspaper to notice Frank walk past them, didn't feel the force of the suitcase as it banged against the backs of their chairs.

Stopping at the front door, Frank placed the suitcase at his feet and turned around. Still holding onto the backpack, he waited for any sort of acknowledgement from his parents—the raising of an eyebrow over the top of the newspaper or the standard, "Where you off to today?" from the back of the sports page.

And waited.

His pulse beat a steady rhythm in his ears. Not too heavy, yet heavy enough to allow him the proof that blood still pumped in his heart. That he was actually standing there. That he did exist as a part of their miserable lives and not a part of someone's cruel imagination.

Frank watched his father place the newspaper onto the table and reach for his coffee. Even between sips, his father's eyes were glued to a meaningless headline or the announcement of a summer sale at Sears. As his father picked the newspaper back up, his mother repeated the same procedure, looking like they were a pair of circus monkeys playing Simon Says.

Sliding a hand inside the backpack, knowing exactly where to reach inside the bottom fold of fabric, Frank pulled out his "borrowed" 9mm pistol. And raised it toward the kitchen table.

"Simon says, you're fucked," Frank whispered.

It was his father's turn to drop the paper and take a sip of coffee. He didn't make it to the sip before the back of his head exploded onto lace curtains and the sliding glass door that led to the backyard. A hairy piece of scalp stuck to the glass and began to slide down, looking like one of the gray spiders Frank used to step on as a child.

That got his mother's attention.

A senseless mutter of hysteria sprayed from her lips as she jumped from her chair and sought protection behind it. Foolish woman. The bullet took off her upper lip and half of her face before the rest of her knew what had happened. Her mouth was still trying to offer bubbly, unintelligible words as her knees buckled and the rest of her followed, tipping over the chair and falling to the kitchen tile in a lifeless heap. A few involuntary spasms and she was still, silent.

He paused to lock the door behind him before welcoming the soft warble of a robin, the warming rays of sunshine upon his face, and the stir of a gentle breeze. Had he noticed these things before?

Frank Carlson never looked back, nor would he ever return. The only direction he knew now was forward, with no stopping and no connection to his former self: a weak and pitiful man.

After placing the backpack under the front passenger's seat of the rusting heap of the Camaro, he pushed in a heat-distorted tape of Slayer while waiting for the initial backfire from the exhaust. When it didn't come, he turned down the radio to be sure the car was running.

It purred as though a new engine lived under the hood.

The wheels of the Camaro turned when they needed to, stopped when required. Frank was only along for the ride, at ease not having to make any decisions. Somewhere in the back of his mind, curiosity was frantically at work trying to understand what was happening, but was being battled down by pure instinctive energy.

He was free.

As he drove the car (or, more accurately, the car drove him), Frank relaxed his grip on the wheel and enjoyed the ride. He found himself along the back roads of town, riddled with potholes and cracks created from frost heaves, but the ride was smooth.

The car turned left onto a gravel road, then right onto a rotary before coming to a stop at an intersection. Straight ahead was Interstate 95, the lifeline to all of Maine, branching off in two directions. Frank paused to read a sign telling him that to go left would be to travel south and to turn right, north.

The car turned right.

The long stretch of interstate that rarely curved more than a few degrees gave Frank plenty of time to think and ponder about things. Why was he here? Where was he going? Who was he going to meet along the way? Did it really matter?

The questions seemed endless and the answers that much further out of reach. Even at a loss for explanations, Frank felt a certain inner peace he had never experienced before. Wherever he was going, whatever he was about to do, he was on the right path toward self-fulfillment. He placed his faith in this and the questions were instantly removed.

Everything felt so . . . perfect.

He didn't know how far a quarter tank of gas would take him, but he'd worry about that later, when the time was right. Right now, it was unnecessary, trivial. He didn't even have the money to pay for it. He only placed his foot steadily upon the accelerator and left himself open to what things might happen, leaving the past to the past and the future to unravel.

The sun shone brightly between scattered clouds. From the tops of trees paralleling the highway, Frank knew the wind was nonexistent. He unrolled his window to let in some fresh air.

Raking fingers through his hair, he looked into the rearview mirror and into the eyes of a very different Francis Carlson. One he admired.

A Frank Carlson with a purpose.

A twinkle in his eyes and a smile upon his face, he forged ahead.

Into a new beginning.

Chapter 25

With the aid of a map and the advice of a few locals, Darren occupied the driver's seat as they traveled toward Evergreen Cemetery, a few miles outside of Fort Kent, close to the Canadian border.

Stomachs filled and the kind of numbness that comes from driving long distances at bay for the moment, they traveled north on Route 1 towards Presque Isle, Caribou, and Limestone. A sign still stood claiming Limestone as the home of Loring Air Force Base, housing KC-135 tankers and B-52 bombers. The base had not survived the first round of closures by the first Bush Administration, and the sign was now part of Limestone's history. Reaching Caribou, they branched off on a northwesterly route on Route 161 that would eventually lead directly into Fort Kent.

They didn't speak much, possibly from exhaustion, but mostly from observing the surroundings of a new area. Even inside the confines of the car, the difference of being this far north was evident in the chill coming in conjunction with the setting sun. They rolled their windows up and Andrea placed the heater of the Plymouth on low. Only a few hours of daylight remained and both had agreed to stop before reaching Fort Kent.

Aside from a farm truck pulling a trailer full of dairy cows, this lonely stretch of road was uninhabited. They passed the truck and wrinkled their noses at a putrid stench that seemed to be breathed in through the grill and exhaled into the car.

A few local cemeteries were cut into the timber at infrequent intervals, stones already casting long shadows, but these would have to settle for a silent, passing acknowledgement.

"Getting late, hope we see something soon," Darren mumbled, arching his back and shifting his position to relieve some discomfort. He didn't like the idea of camping out on the side of the road with only the blanket of the surrounding darkness as protection. He reached up to adjust the mirror, if only to keep busy.

"I know what you mean," Andrea said, words barely reaching a pitch above a monotone, emotionless. "I've never been up this far before. Looks like I didn't miss much." Her head lay back against the headrest, hair bunched up at angles from slouching, and it took a visible effort for her to look from side to side.

Darren looked over and chuckled. Even after an entire day of driving, he still found her attractive.

"What?" Andrea said, herself smiling . . . sort of.

"Nothing," he chuckled. "Nothing." He exaggerated the effect of her punch to his shoulder.

Miles clicked by with slow turns of the odometer, and Darren struggled to keep his eyes open. A few looks over at Andrea had him envious of her ability to let the rumble of the car relax her and add invisible weights to her eyelids, easily succumbing to exhaustion and closing her eyes. Something he couldn't do without getting carsick.

Dusk quickly approached. Dotted yellow lines swept past the driver's side, consumed by the enveloping thickness of nightfall. The only light in view was a blurred neon sign ahead, marking the presence of some sort of establishment, visible only as the car came upon an elevated part of the road.

As the car slowed, Andrea brought herself upright

with an incoherent mumble.

Darren pulled into the parking lot of the *Pine Lodge Motel*, its pink neon sign claiming that there was indeed a vacancy. With the number of cars in the lot, the sign was unnecessary. The scene strangely resembled another motel they had recently visited—he tried to push this thought away.

After clearing his throat, he spoke. "Well, at least the road is paved."

And felt the humor melt away in seconds.

"I just hope Norman Bates isn't behind the counter."

Darren pulled into the first parking space near the main office and they sat in silence with the car running for a few minutes as though contemplating the decision to go inside or speed away, but knowing there was no questioning another five back-aching, back-sweating, suffocating minutes in the car.

He opened the office door and paused. Received the nod of approval from Andrea as she drew a deep breath close behind him, hands lightly holding onto the back of his shirt.

They were welcomed by the scent of fresh roses and an electronic chime above their heads. Soft music played in the background. A fresh pot of coffee brewed in a coffee maker. A middle-aged, overweight woman dressed for business came bustling to the front desk. Her cheeks seemed to be on fire and a lock of hair wouldn't stay out of her eyes after each passing of a finger.

"Welcome to *Pine Lodge.* Can I get you a room for the evening?" Her smile and soothing French accent immediately cut through an almost tangible tension that had entered the office right behind them. Darren felt an increase in slack from the back of his shirt.

They paid in advance and rushed to their room.

The scent of wood polish emanated from each piece of furniture and clean bath towels hung above a sparkling and well-lit vanity. Two beds waited anxiously for weary occupants and displayed a small piece of chocolate mint on each pillow. Darren turned on the television and collapsed onto one of the beds as the picture tube immediately came to life.

Andrea immediately went to the bathroom.

After completing a cursory look through some television channels, Darren brought in two suitcases and placed his notebook onto the small desk by the window. As he did so, he could already hear the faint running of water as Andrea prepared another bath. He only hoped previous events wouldn't replay themselves—or at least some of them. There were some things he wouldn't mind having happen a few hundred times over.

He kicked off his sneakers, sat in the chair neatly accompanying the desk, and reached for the television remote. He clicked past two French-speaking channels and a dozen infomercials before settling on MTV 2. As he fumbled with the pages of his notebook and No Doubt sang about dancing in spider webs, he leaned back against the chair and tried to relax. Before long, his head bobbed lightly, then came to rest on his chest as he breathed slowly in sleep.

His fingers twitched upon the notebook in front of him.

The hot water made her insides tingle and her outsides melt. She breathed in the steam, allowing it to cleanse her, opening all of her pores. As the water reached maximum capacity above her breasts, she turned the water off with her feet and sank deeper into the water, her body an imagined melting slab of jelly.

A drop without the tint of rust came from the spigot and created a ripple in the water that bounced comfortably against her chin before returning to the opposite side of the tub. She heard a small murmur coming from the television, but it soon disappeared. Her nose again began to itch, but she left it alone and let herself be pulled into sleep. Strangely, there was someone calling to her from the encroaching shadows of a dream. A smell she at first dismissed as cleaning disinfectant in the spotless bathroom seemed to get stronger as her name became louder.

Chapter 26

Almost there!

Excited, Faye's breathing began to increase—she couldn't help it. She didn't have to hear the amplified activity of the machines to know she was entering a dangerous realm: a fragile line between a world she had known and a world she was only beginning to really understand.

She had reached another level, as though she had crawled inside Andrea's mindprint of lines and colors, and was gliding slowly through a haze. She could almost feel the moisture of an enveloping fog wrapping her within itself. So comforting she almost believed she was on a casual, early-morning stroll through a San Francisco park that she enjoyed. Except on this stroll, her feet never touched the ground, no dogs barked, and the bickering of seagulls was eerily absent.

She need only think which direction she wanted to travel and she would move.

A small glow began to emanate from the region ahead of her, eliminating some of the shadows, providing her a path to follow. Somewhere, Andrea was unknowingly waiting for a special visitor. But would she willingly accept her?

"Andrea," she called softly, fearful of destroying the silence.

No answer, nor was she expecting one. Was she even close? She continued forward, the shadows and fog parting the way for her. She moved quicker as she became more comfortable with her surroundings, anxious to finally meet Andrea. Her breathing finally began to slow, but her heart was still beating double-time.

And it beat faster still as shadows began to shape them-selves into human forms. Hands appeared at the sides of her, reaching from the shadows, then faces. Faces that she instantly knew from years of helping people along in their deaths. They were not reaching for her, but motioning to her, guiding her as she once did for them, pointing in the direction of the light ahead, into the projection she longed to become a part of.

"Andrea," she called in the utterance of a shaky whisper.

Faye almost screamed her excitement as she heard mum-bling ahead of her, as if someone were being stirred by a dream.

She *had* to be close.

Sensuous warmth suddenly coursed through Faye's body, comforting her, easing the pain she had in her joints. She seemed to be in another body altogether, separate from her earthly form. She felt lighter, couldn't even feel her heartbeat anymore, that steady if feeble thumping that had kept her a part of the material world for so long.

The air stirred with electricity as the path became brighter, wisps of fog now sparkling with white shards of light against a milky background.

The faint humming of a television pricked at her ears.

When she reached an edge of light marking the way into another region, Faye forced herself to stop. By crossing this border, she knew everything was about to change.

She quickly looked back on what she had accomplished in life, possibly searching for worth in all she'd done. She had no regrets, wasn't sorry for anything, and was proud of her achievements, though it had been a very lonely life.

Satisfied, knowing that she was ready, Faye took the step that would be the most important thing she would ever do.

Andrea attempted to respond to the greeting, but couldn't find the energy—she was much too relaxed. What came from her throat was a weak grumble, words masked beneath her slumber. Occasionally, she opened her eyes just enough to peer through the slits of her eyes at the wallowing pillows of steam coming from the water. They seemed to have a life of their own, constantly changing shape . . .

Her eyes soon closed completely. Andrea tried to focus on who was calling her name, but the trailing echoes of the voice dissipated before she could pinpoint a direction to turn toward. The smell continued to get stronger, intoxicating.

Then her name was whispered into her ear.

Bath water splashed into her eyes as she sat up violently, feet slipping on the bottom of the tub. It wasn't only a whisper. The breath in her ear tickled, her own name resounding as if someone were there beside her. She pushed herself over to one side of the tub and strained to take in her surroundings within the swirling clouds of steam, blowing at them, waving her hand through them, anything that might let her see through their milky centers.

Silence. She was alone. She'd been sleeping, dreaming— hadn't really heard anything. Her pulse slowed . . . eventually. Andrea placed a warm washcloth over her eyes and slowly descended into the bath to relieve a sudden chill.

It was then that she felt the touch on her arm. A gentle touch—soft. She removed the washcloth expecting to see Darren at her side. Almost hoped for it.

Only steam surrounded her. She looked at her arm in disbelief, at the hairs standing erect atop bumps of flesh. Something was happening.

The steam took shape, condensing.

"Andrea, please don't be afraid."

Another gentle touch to her arm, but she still couldn't see anyone. Andrea was startled, but the voice sounded so soft, so motherly; there was no way she could be afraid of this presence.

"Hello?" It seemed the obvious thing to say.

The steam continued to pull at its outer edges and develop, but not into a complete substance. She could still see the toilet through the curtain of grays and whites. But it was solid enough for Andrea to see an elderly woman kneeling beside the tub and smiling—the biggest smile she had ever seen.

Andrea smiled in return.

In California, the steady flat-line from the monitors signified the end for Faye Clark.

In one world.

Chapter 27

Darren snored softly as drool seeped out of the corner of his mouth.

Under the glow of a crescent moon, luminescent spider webs entered his dream and weaved a threaded nightmare. Each web, wrapped tightly around a glowing sphere of light, pulsed from the soul it held captive and threatened to snap. Silken threads began to rip and tear as glowing rays of light grew with intensity and fought to be set free.

Voices rang throughout the scene, begging for help, blindly searching for a way out. The screaming of a young girl caught his attention and almost brought him to tears. Terror-stricken, she was crying for her father, pleading to be let out of the darkness she so feared—a darkness beginning to suffocate her. The voices called for him by name from all directions—screaming wails of agony, each begging to be the one he turned to next. Even as he watched, the webs were growing, spreading rapidly with groping filaments as more souls were captured and the cries of the newly deceased questioned their new existence, not quite understanding what was happening. Darren attempted to call out to them, give them encouragement—a sense of direction to aim for, *something*, but had no voice.

Before his feet, a new web began to appear, sprouting from nothingness. He imagined stepping back, not wanting to become entangled, and the web receded only to sprout more tiny filaments, apparently not wanting him. Yet.

Instead it sprouted like a plant on a warm sunny day, its flower that of a forgotten soul. A glowing sphere appeared as the web came to completeness and a low, humming noise pulsed concurrently with a beam of light. Darren thought it was similar to a heartbeat, a sign of life on the other side.

As the humming and light accelerated with intensity, the sphere looked as if it were about to crack. It shuddered beneath the grip of the web, almost like it was being crushed, but the force of the cracking was coming from within the sphere itself, like it was about to explode. Darren gazed upon the sphere in fascination, attempting to justify what was happening before him, but was only able to look on, anxiously awaiting . . . something.

More light pulsed rhythmically from within the sphere's shell as the cracks grew in number and size. Whatever was inside was eager to reveal itself—to be free. The tangled webs surrounding the sphere began to weaken and fray from the strength trapped within the glowing ball of light.

Darren was shocked when he heard a muffled voice call his name weakly from inside the sphere. Then it got louder as fragments of the sphere's outer shell chipped and fell, destroying the strands of web they came in contact with.

In a sudden, brilliant flash of light, the sphere exploded.

Darren closed his eyes, or at least imagined he did so to shield them, and debated whether or not he should open them again.

"Darren, it's been so long," a voice said, directly in front of him. It belonged to an elderly man unable to disguise the slight tremor of age in his voice.

Darren had no choice but to open his eyes.

And remember the wrinkled, sad face from pictures in old photo albums. He was dressed in the same suit and tie Darren supposed he was buried in. The man's nose was aged and somewhat misshapen (a chance meeting with the Royal Canadian Mounted Police, if the story proved cor-

rect), but it resembled a small, sharp nose that now belonged to him. Darren believed he had even bounced on
this person's knee, once upon a time.

Grandpa Reginald W. Jacobs stood before Darren, fidg-
eting and looking frantically from side to side, but striving
to pay total attention to Darren. He brushed at his arms,
ridding himself of the remaining strands of web in disgust.
He looked worried.

"Darren, you have to hurry," Grandpa said quietly,
warily casting a nervous glance behind him. "We're running
out of time."

"Grandpa?" Darren said, unsure if he was heard. In his
mind at least, his voice was also shaking. "Running out of
time?"

"It's trying to build . . ." his grandfather began before di-
recting another glance over his shoulder. He turned back
around, eyes darting about.

"Build what?"

Grandpa Jacobs started to fade. His eyes searched for
understanding and filled with glistening tears as he brought
up a hand in a sign of farewell. A deafening, ripping sound
permeated the air as freshly spun webs stretched to gain the
purchase of his grandfather and pull him down . . . down.

"Hurrrrry . . ." His grandfather was cut short as strands
of web covered his legs, chest, and face—the panicked
whites of his eyes were the last to disappear. They crushed
and squeezed the image of his grandfather until it was once
again a sphere, now glowing weakly, trapped within the
web's unyielding filaments.

"Noooooo!" Awakened by his own scream, Darren almost fell over backward in his chair. His heart added an
extra beat as his body went into the spread-eagle formation
to catch his balance.

He wasn't certain if Andrea heard him or not, didn't know how long he had been asleep. Water splashed from behind the closed bathroom door, so he figured he must not have been dozing for very long. Though his body, exhausted as if it had just been through a workout, and the stiffness of his neck, tried to prove otherwise. And his right hand, numb and curled with a cramp, sent small pains to his shoulder with each thump of his pulse.

He wiped at the clammy wetness at the corner of his mouth and looked around the room. Same as it had been when he had fallen asleep.

Except for the notebook.

It lay on the table, open and pages crinkled. What was left of a pencil, its tip ground to the yellow paint and particles of graphite surrounding it, was still rolling on an open page. He must have dropped it there when he had awoken. He didn't remember taking out the pencil—presumably from the small drawer in the desk—but he knew what was scrawled on the pages without looking. He decided to wait for Andrea before daring to examine the contents of what he had written. *Or what someone had helped him write.* He didn't want to be alone to find out where this new door, just opened enough to peek inside, was going to lead them.

Darren turned as he heard the remnants of bath water gurgling down the drain. Andrea appeared from the bathroom wearing a complimentary robe.

She looked . . . different.

She also felt different.

The pleasant conversation she had with Faye had given her a sense of fresh courage, another reason to move on. And quickly. Something was building—they had to work fast. She could have talked with Faye forever, but the conversation was hurried, fragmented, with Faye trying to convey as much information as possible.

As she spoke, Faye's form had become more solid, her features more distinguishable. Her eyes were pale blue and full of determination. The wrinkles at the corners of her mouth and eyes only provided a mystery as to what she had experienced over the years. All the while, she had held Andrea's hand, gently rubbing the back of it with her thumb, caressing.

Andrea had felt Faye's grip tighten as her image became undefined at the edges, incomplete. Faye had become silent, but still smiled as her body became transparent, then disappeared altogether.

"I'll be in touch." Faye's whisper had faded along with her apparition into the dissipating clouds of steam, leaving Andrea in a numb state of wonder.

Andrea was amazed at how much their lives paralleled each other's. In the short amount of time they had spoken, Andrea knew Faye like a friend she had known for years. That they were finally able to make contact with each other opened so many possibilities. They had each other, and together they could continue the journey that each had started separately.

Andrea had left the tub refreshed, relaxed, and anxious to inform her *living* partner of the new alliance they had to assist them.

As she patted at her hair with a towel and was about to explain what had occurred to Darren, she noticed as he turned around, that something wasn't right. He didn't appear scared, only confused, as though he were sleepwalking. A dazed expression left his eyes droopy, his jaw slack. He was slowly wringing his right hand with the left.

"What's the matt . . . ?" she began.

He pointed to his notebook with both hands.

She thought she understood.

For the next few hours, they learned about the past and the questionable futures of the souls that had visited in Darren's dream. In-between pages, Andrea told Darren what had taken place in the bathroom (of all places to have another episode), and he shared the mysterious vision of his grandfather. Neither was surprised.

Dozens of souls had briefly recorded their histories in the notebook and were all buried at Evergreen Cemetery. A different hand had scribbled each entry into the notebook, but they did have one thing in common: they were all written in a rush, as though there wasn't enough time to re-veal anything but the important facts. Some of the entries were mere scrawls, barely legible, a lot of the paragraphs cut off in mid-sentence before the start of another.

A common theme also presented itself within the passages: each individual wanted their relatives to know that they still existed, albeit in a different sense or a different world, even. Some were screaming from the pages for their living relatives to visit them, to release them. Others only wanted messages passed on, accepting their current state as punishment for things they might have done.

But they all wanted to be remembered.

And were all scared of something that kept pulling at them.

Chapter 28

Night moved in quickly, bringing with it a sense of victory at devouring the daylight in its continuous cycle.

Frank enjoyed the crisp air wafting through the car, letting the chill enter his bones. He savored the deep breaths he pulled in, allowing each to cleanse him before its release. The Camaro's headlights were the only beams parting the darkness in either direction, giving him a feeling of ownership. All was his, and his to be had.

Amazed that the quarter-tank of gas he had left home with still remained, he tapped at the glass protecting the gauge, but the needle didn't move. Still believing the gauge to be faulty, he knew he had to stop for gas soon. And food, though he wasn't even hungry.

When he walked into the Houlton Truck Stop, heads turned, mouths stopped chewing, and cash stopped changing hands.

Frank felt the despising, insulting looks immediately. Had felt them many times before, but the looks he saw upon these faces also held another quality. He found it in the way they averted their eyes as he tried to make eye contact. The way they quickly went back to what they were doing, but sneaked a peek at him when they felt brave enough to do so.

They were fearful of him.

And he liked it.

Fuck you all, he thought, casually smiling at the feeling of power he had over them. Someday, they would all be eating out of the palm of his hand—if he let them.

As he walked toward the checkout to pay for his gas, his stride was longer, his shoulders a little straighter. He brought out his wallet while thinking of ways to explain the absence of money. If he showed the cashier an empty wallet, he might get her to believe he was robbed, but that was doubtful. A man in front of him finished his business and left the line.

Frank opened his mouth to hear what excuse would finally come forth, but snapped it shut as he looked into his wallet, mesmerized. One-hundred-dollar bills were all but falling out, so much so that he would have a hard time folding it again to place it in his back pocket. He pulled one out and watched the bill flutter within his trembling fingers as he gave it to the cashier.

She eyed him carefully, then held the bill to the light, flipping it over twice. Undeterred, she grasped a counterfeit detector pen from the cash register drawer and, making the obligatory mark on the corner of the bill, grunted in amazement. Satisfied, she placed the bill into the register and returned Frank's change with a forced smile, almost a grimace.

He was too preoccupied to even care what kind of looks she gave him. Otherwise, he probably would have punched her in the face.

Right now, he was still trying to figure out how in the hell all that money got into his wallet.

Everything can be mine.

Why had he thought of that?

No idea, but he loved the sound of it.

"Could you step out of the line, *sir?*"

"Fuck you," he replied and was pleased to see the look of surprise upon the cashier's face. He folded his wallet with some effort and shoved it into his back pocket. And didn't even glance at the food being served or notice the aromas in the air before strutting out of the truck stop. He felt as if he had just eaten a four-course meal.

The needle read full on the gas gauge and went unnoticed. Frank sped off and continued on a northwesterly heading like a seasonal waterfowl following its inner compass, finding its way home.

Its true home.

Chapter 29

His mind raced and he didn't try to slow it down.

Instead, he enjoyed the loud rumble of the engine and watched the speedometer sail past eighty miles per hour, only slowing when the car wanted to turn. And acquired a thirst that could only be filled by an ice-cold beer and the means to spend some of the money that kept growing inside of his wallet. A wallet he now had to place in the inside pocket of his leather jacket, where it would fit.

A hole-in-the-wall bar, nothing more than a converted doublewide mobile home, appeared on cue and the Camaro slowed, turned.

Smoke hung thick in the air, giving overhead lamps a ghastly glow around them, while a jukebox skipped through some oldies. Muffled conversations took place beneath the clamor of clinking glasses and pool balls crashing together. An ancient bartender wiped the bar near the beer taps as automatically as taking another breath. Frank imagined each wrinkle in the bartender's face containing a thousand wipes of that same surface. A surface probably as smooth as the amber bottle he now craved, in contrast to the chipped and scratched surface that no doubt existed along the remaining length of the bar.

The instant he walked in, Frank knew he was an outsider and didn't belong. Thick, flannel, checkerboard shirts that doubled as jackets seemed to dominate the room, worn by men as well as women.

Strike one.

Frank shrank inside his leather jacket. He noticed their

stained and heavy work boots next, the kind that laced up and occasionally came with a steel toe.

Strike two.

He scuffed the heel of his cowboy boot against the floor as he chose a place to sit. He found an empty table in the darkest part of the bar and sat down with his back to the wall. He could hide here for a while.

A barmaid made her way slowly around unbalanced customers to his table. He saw a smirk on her face as she looked at the other customers, as if to serve him was a flaw in her perfect life. Silence pervaded the smoky air as they all watched eagerly, waiting to see what would happen, anxious to begin a new chapter in their lives.

"Can I help you, sir?" She barely stifled a giggle. Frank thought about telling her to go fuck herself, but thought better of it as he noticed the size of a few of the customers, every one of them staring at him.

"Can I get a beer?" He kept his voice barely above a whisper, but it proved ineffective.

The entire bar started laughing. Instead of hearing the usual Yankee twang, they noticed he didn't have one, or barely a hint of one. They heard him pronounce the "R" and couldn't contain themselves. To everyone else in this part of the state, *beer* was pronounced *beeyah*.

Strike three.

Instead of being out with strike three, he was *in* with style when the barmaid saw him pull out his wallet. That shut the bitch up. The rest of the bar as well, as Frank heard a collective gasp and conversations began anew.

"Bud Light please, and hurry." He tried to keep his voice down, and managed to keep his anger under control, but still directed a wary eye over the rest of the customers, not in the mood for any trouble.

She was still spellbound at the sight of the money coming out of his wallet. "Y-y-yes, sir." As she walked away, she made a motion of fanning herself below her chin to all of the customers and received a few wary chuckles, noticeably quieter than the previous laughter.

After a few beers and a dozen cigarettes, he went all but unnoticed in his own dark corner of the bar. The beers kept coming and he kept pushing more money away from him on the table. Getting a buzz seemed to be taking too long, and he soon graduated to Long Island iced teas to quicken the pace. His face began to flush with color and his eyes became a bit glossy, lids a bit heavy. The world instantly became a better place.

The music he had heard before now seemed muted, as if his head were under a pillow. He had to keep one eye closed to keep the bar, a few feet in front of him, in focus.

"You enjoying my money?"

Frank's head wobbled slowly upon his shoulders as he tried to find the source of the question. The voice was clear in his head, painful to his ears, and heavy with authority. He hadn't noticed anyone sitting next to him the entire evening. The customers of this fine establishment seemed to avoid him like an infectious disease. So where did this idiot come from? And where was he?

He felt a hand placed on top of his—ice cold. He tried to yank his hand away, but felt the strength of the grip increase promptly. And painfully. He'd better not. He kept one eye closed as he looked to his left, at a man sitting next to him.

The man was smiling. Frank was suddenly nauseous.

His appearance reflected the power Frank had just felt. He wore a black suit with a starkly contrasting white turtleneck underneath. Hair, the color of midnight and slicked back with every hair precisely in place, sat atop a pale face. Two symmetrical curls of hair were tucked in behind each ear. A goatee surrounded a mouth that produced gleaming teeth behind thin, red lips. Frank felt as though the man's black eyes could stare through him, enter his mind, and devour it with a single glance.

Afraid to look away, both eyes now open, he took the chance to glance down at the hand still on top of his. Pale as his face, even his hand looked strong, each fingertip displaying a finely manicured and lengthened nail. Frank slowly pulled his hand away and was permitted to do so. His body still swayed with the effects of the alcohol, but his mind suddenly felt clear—sober.

"Do you like what you see?" A hand casually stroked at his goatee while a slithering tongue licked at his lips.

Frank was speechless, only managed to let out a thin line of air.

"I'll take that as a compliment," said the man, grinning as his eyes met Frank's, causing Frank to immediately drop his gaze. The man moved in a head-spinning blur, silently, and took the place opposite Frank, placing his elbows on the table and rubbing both hands together slowly, admiring his fingernails. "Now, let's talk business."

Frank still didn't know what to make of the man, but felt a strange attraction to him all the same. The man exuded complete power and authority. He could imagine nobody, including him, who would be able to stand up to him. To do so could only mean instant pain and suffering.

He looked about the bar, wondering why there wasn't a single customer eyeing this new arrival. Surely, he was out of place, even more so than he was. The barmaid returned to ask if he wanted another round, taking not a single glimpse at the stranger sitting across from him. Looking between the barmaid and his new acquaintance, he wished her away with a wave of his hand.

Maybe he was still drunk. Passed out and dreaming, more like it.

Another look into those black, powerful eyes said otherwise. He tried to see his reflection within those eyes, but found none. As if he were swallowed within, chewed up, and spat out. He tried to make out pupils, but saw only a darkness so deep it made him queasy.

He looked away.

Feeling the pull of the man's power, Frank was forced to look back. He focused on the man's forehead, noticing skin so smooth it shone, and determined not to let his gaze fall even a fraction of an inch.

"There's plenty of more money where that came from; all you have to do is want it. And I know you do," he said, the words entering Frank's ears as a hypnotic melody.

Frank remained silent, in hope that more beautiful words would follow, and enjoyed a numbness beginning to spread throughout his body. He was no longer in a bar somewhere in the northern part of Maine. The music, the people, and the smoky atmosphere seemed to be pulled from conscious thought. His world now only consisted of the mysterious stranger in front of him.

Frank stole a few furtive glances below the man's brow and slowly found himself drawn into his eyes again, no longer such a threat. They pulled at him like a diamond to a thief. Frank's stare began to spread across man's entire face and he noticed the man's good looks, his stature, his poise. He wished he could be like him.

As though poisoned by the man's beauty, admiration filling his every pore, Francis Carlson wanted to *be* him.

"You could be like me," the man said. "Have anything

you desire, and then some. The rewards would be many, the satisfaction immeasurable. It would only be the beginning."

The words hummed pleasantly, creating a comfortable thud within Frank's head. If these words were drugs, he would shoot them up. If they took the form of alcohol, he would drink every last drop and lick the glass dry that they poured from.

Frank looked deep into the man's cavernous eyes and remembered his life . . .

He didn't see the ocean until he was in high school. Living only thirty minutes away from the waterfront, his parents had never even thought to bring him to the Atlantic along the Maine coast. His friends had talked about it often enough, especially on those hot, humid days. To him, it was like describing a cold glass of water to someone beaten, naked, and stranded in a desert. He had attempted to hide his shame.

His friends tried to relay in words what it was like to let the icy water chill your bones as you decided whether to jump right in or walk in gradually. Either way, they said, your balls shriveled and it hurt like hell the first few minutes. It was the only time in his life that he had wished for the opportunity to feel his balls hurt—anything to see the ocean. He finally did experience the pain after almost begging his way into a trip with some friends. Something he would never forget.

When he got his own car, the Camaro he still owned (paid for by many hours of washing dishes at a local restaurant), he went to the ocean on every chance, wanting to escape everything around him and stare beyond the endless froth of turbulent waters. The feeling of his balls stuck between the crushing grip of ice cubes—strong enough to push them into his throat—he could do without . . . on most occasions.

He was never close to his parents. They were always too busy to deal with him, no matter how menial the task. He knew not to ask for anything at an early age.

Frank was never allowed the luxury of hand-me-downs from an older sibling, let alone a new shirt. He only wore clothes that his mother managed to buy at yard sales, mostly pinstriped or button-up. Years of stinging remarks by everyone in school, with even his friends having to get their two cents in. He tried to laugh along with them, but inside, he hurt. Birthdays were depressing, Christmas always a disaster. Both were yearly reminders that he shouldn't be here on this earth—a mistake that wasn't supposed to leak from the end of daddy's dick.

"Of course, there's a price," the man said, but the words fell silent. Frank only nodded when he knew it was time to agree.

"We're closing up for the evening sir, you're gonna have to leave."

The change in voices was brain-rattling. Frank was now looking into the faded eyes of the bartender sitting directly across from him. Behind him, the perky barmaid eyed Frank like an odd circus attraction, pretending to wipe down a table. The remainder of the bar was empty, chairs lying on their respective tables, upside down, legs in the air like dead bugs.

Frank's head produced spikes of pain from within, like a jagged piece of metal trying to force its way out with violent surges. He remembered speaking to a total stranger, but vaguely, as if he were trying to hold onto fragments of an old memory. He stood up, lost his balance, fell. An exhalation of disgust came from the bartender.

Frank refused the hand offered to him and, with two, staggering footsteps, managed to hold himself upright with the aid of a nearby table. Avoiding the stares of both, he fumbled with his wallet and placed a hundred-dollar bill on the table still littered with bottles, glasses, and an overflowing ashtray. At the sight of the bill, a spark of recognition came to him, but immediately escaped.

He flipped the bird to the perky barmaid and left, welcoming the cool night air.

His car was the lone inhabitant of the lot except for two he assumed belonged to the bartender and Miss Smart-Ass. As he weaved the short distance to the Camaro, he dug the keys out of his jeans, dropped them.

"Sonofabitch," he slurred, fixing a one-eyed stare upon the key to unlock the door.

Several attempts finally allowed him entry into the car where he sat, wondering just what the hell to do. He didn't know where to go. Had the money to get the finest hotel room in the state, but didn't want to even consider seeing any human beings until he was feeling better.

As he put the car in gear and left the parking lot, his car drove a straight path onto the northbound lane of Route 161. Frank decided to drive (ride), until he found something interesting and then sleep under the stars, away from anyone.

The darkened stretch of highway unraveled in front of him. The forest seemed to threaten to intrude upon him with heavy, towering pine branches, but was kept at bay by the two beams of light from the Camaro. A thin sliver of moon shone from above, but not enough to alleviate the darkness.

Frank drove with bleary, reddened eyes and a headache that could kill a man. His thoughts kept going back to the bar, but everything was a blur. *Better to be forgotten,* he thought. To forget would cause the least amount of pain. He pulled himself upright with the aid of the steering wheel and hoped he would find something soon, so he wouldn't fall asleep at the wheel. However, a part of him knew it wouldn't matter. Somehow, his car would bring him where he needed to go.

He rubbed at his eyes with one hand while keeping a light grip on the wheel with the other. *That's the last time I mix fucking drinks,* he thought. He unrolled his windows, hoping the air would clear his head.

As the headlights revealed a turn in the road ahead, an opening in the thick wall of trees also exposed a dirt road leading . . . somewhere. As he got closer, an iron entranceway that looked as if it had seen better days stood above the road. Frank slowed and turned into the opening, rocks crunching beneath the tires. He stopped far enough away to read the sign above. Large letters barely hung on to the structure and one letter was missing, another upside down. He was still able to read what it was meant to say: Guerette Heights Cemetery.

He placed the car in gear and popped the clutch, causing a shower of dirt to shoot from the rear of his car. Following the road, he drove around to the back of the cemetery as gravestones began to peek from hidden paths. It made him think of a joke he once heard: *Why is the cemetery so popular? People are always dying to get in!*

He laughed to himself at the stupidity of the joke, his head throbbing in reply. Years ago, he had thought it was the funniest thing he had ever heard. Idiot.

He followed a turn to the right at the farthest reaches of the small cemetery and listened to the overgrown center of the road brush against the undercarriage of the Camaro. He was now parallel with the highway and knew he wouldn't be seen.

He grabbed his sleeping bag—the mummy type used by soldiers in the field—and looked for a large enough stone to hide behind.

Found one.

The air was clean and crisp, a slight scent of ozone filling the atmosphere like a dash of spice. His breath formed in front him, lingered as if in thought, then dwindled into nothing. Only taking his boots off, Frank unrolled and crawled into the sleeping bag, his head pushed against the backside of the headstone. He rolled his eyes toward it from the ground and realized that's why he didn't see a name engraved.

Frank imagined it could very well be his own. He grinned.

The view of the sky past anything farther than the tops of the trees was blocked, but the stars shone through a creamy layer as clouds were beginning to gather. In answer, two drops splashed against his forehead, rolled down the sides of his nose, and trickled onto his lips.

Francis Carlson opened his mouth in hopes of devouring the universe.

Chapter 30

"I don't know," Darren mumbled, teeth beginning to chatter. He rolled on the balls of his feet, felt the dampness in his socks and the way they bunched uncomfortably between the cracks of his toes. "Maybe we should just leave," he said, and immediately regretted it, knew exactly what was going to come next.

"Too many people have already done that."

Darren looked down at his sneakers and felt the warm flush of embarrassment. "Sorry," was all that would come.

"Not necessary," Andrea said, giving him a friendly slug to the arm.

They stood before the gates of Evergreen Cemetery, marveling at a scene only age can provide over time. Heavy drizzle fell from the early morning sky, creating a chill in the air and dulling the scene before them, yet accentuating it within a shroud of mist.

Rusted gates were fastened with a lock long since broken, a passive attempt at preventing visitors from entering. From the look of things, Darren figured it wasn't doing a very good job. Behind these gates, lengthened grass inhabited the unkempt grounds surrounding each stone. A few paths were beaten down (presumably by staggering feet) and littered with beer cans, paper cups, and fluttering wisps of paper towels or toilet paper.

An older section of the cemetery lined the banks of the St. John River a short distance ahead, where gravestones protruded from the ground, each aiming at different points in the gray sky like a set of teeth badly in need of braces.

Most of these stones were weather-beaten, some even spray-painted, but a few were privileged enough to be decorated with dead flowers.

A small section nearest to them was freshly mown, the area around one stone showing signs of being newly erected, the ground freshly unearthed. Upon a small mound of dirt nearby, fresh flowers lay on their sides and separated as if thrown.

Darren thought of his grandfather and wished he remembered more of him. As a child, his family had visited this part of the state only a few times, usually around the holidays. When his grandfather passed away they stopped visiting completely, leaving what was left of him alone, underneath a rectangular patch of earth somewhere behind these very gates. Forgotten.

He gripped an iron rod of the gate, ignoring the slivers of rust that came away beneath his grasp. He brought his face close to the gate and stared into the cemetery as though he were a child again, visiting a museum and staring at an ancient beast that once walked the earth with magnificent strides. If only his parents had known a fraction of what Darren was learning now. If only they would understand him if he told them. If only . . . there were too many to list. All he could do now was continue forward and shed new light on a topic lost in the bustle of the twenty-first century.

He was too young to attend the funeral service and was therefore uncertain where exactly his grandfather was buried. But he knew he would somehow find the final resting-place of his grandfather before leaving, even if it took combing away grass and dirt with frozen fingers to reveal the headstone nestled in the ground like a solidified fossil. He would do this, if only to apologize for the years that had passed, years in which Darren let his grandfather's memory become a tiny speck of recognition and disappear deep into his subconscious.

With a mumble of unease, he lifted the broken lock from its clasp and gently pushed the gate open, wincing at the protests issued from neglected hinges. Placing his chilled hands into his pockets, he slowly walked among the stones and tried to concentrate.

Andrea blinked at the drizzle that had accumulated on her eyelids and tucked her chin against her chest, bringing the collar of her jacket almost up to her ears. She followed Darren, but allowed him his space and only watched from a distance as he began weaving in and out of the paths of those he had recently been introduced to.

As she made her own way through the cemetery, keeping Darren in view out of the corner of her eye, she knelt every so often and introduced herself. Her hands came away wet as she brushed each stone with her palms to better read the inscriptions. From the stones near the riverbank that allowed her the liberty, she removed a small piece of each and placed it into her jacket pocket.

She recognized a few of the names from Darren's entries, but many others were here that hadn't been allowed the chance to pass a message through him. These were the stones she paid particular attention to. In doing so, she shared the pleasant release of energy, the liberation of an immeasurable weight that pulled at the very core of their existence. They were remembered and set free.

Only when she removed her hands from each headstone did she feel the cold, the dampness, settling into her clothes, the draining of her own energy. She moved quickly, not allowing her mind to fixate on her own discomfort, only concentrating on reaching as many souls as possible.

In a deep corner of the lot, Andrea glimpsed what appeared to be a fence of some kind surrounding a certain headstone, seeming odd and out of place among the rest. As she moved closer to the stone, able to read the inscription, this small mystery began to unravel.

A chord of sorrow struck within the hollows of her chest.

She wasn't a mother herself, but longed to be. Her insides craved to bring a child into this world and experience the emotions, the love, and nurturing that came with raising a child. She was able to become part of children's lives by working at the library, but nothing came close to the cuddling of a baby, the nuzzling of her cheek against its cheek, or seeing that baby grow and develop into an adult. Andrea thought only few things could be worse than a woman unable to become a loving mother.

Of one she was certain: to bury that child prematurely.

Tears flowed and she made no attempt at concealing them.

She stared sadly—head cocked to one side as though trying to console a child—at what she thought was a fence, but was actually an aged, wooden crib built around the headstone of a child. A battered, stuffed rabbit, its fur dampened and an eye missing, lay on its side against a corner of the makeshift crib.

Andrea knelt on the outside of the crib and read the inscription:

SARAH JOSEPHINE PARKER

1964 – 1969

SHE WAS AN ANGEL AND WILL BE MISSED

Simple, yet monumental. She read the inscription again, allowing one more tear to fall before brushing at her cheeks.

She looked over her shoulder before lifting one leg over the crib. Darren was still wandering among the stones.

Her pant leg caught on a sliver of wood that had separated itself from one of the fence posts, but she managed to wriggle it free before losing her balance. Once both legs were over, she knelt before the stone on both knees, oblivious to the dampness of the ground. She simply stared, fixating on the inscription, reading it over and over. What or who could allow a child to die at such an early age?

She hesitated, then placed her hands on the stone and allowed the visions to fill her mind.

Darren wandered with feet that seemed to have a predetermined direction in mind and attempted to concentrate on the memory of his grandfather, or what little of it still remained. He wasn't sure what he was waiting for, his grandfather's voice perhaps, but thought he would know when it came. Until then, he grasped for the memory of the days when he would sit on top of Grandpa's knee and marvel at the sunset seen from his grandfather's back porch. The days when he would laugh hysterically as his Grandpa rubbed the palm of Darren's small hand against the hard gray stubble of his chin.

A grin formed upon Darren's face at this last memory and his feet suddenly stopped, finally receiving the message from his brain that they were going in circles.

Long blades of grass now lay on their sides like fallen soldiers. They formed a circle. A circle that was becoming well evidenced from the weight of Darren's steps. A circle that encompassed a single headstone.

Drizzle began to turn into rain and left Darren's hair flattened to his scalp and hanging in his eyes. He shivered from the damp cold that crept beneath his jean jacket and found its way into his bones, then shivered from the way the stone stared back at him, finding its way into his soul.

Darren looked down, startled as he felt jolts of electricity climb up and down his body and cause his hair to stand on end.

REGINALD W. JACOBS
1916 – 1984

He had died when Darren was only six years old. That would explain why only a few memories were available. He felt somewhat better at the thought.

Darren touched the top of the gravestone with his fingers, letting them linger lightly. He was unsure of what to do, or say, or think. He was here and didn't know how to proceed, almost as if he had just been asked to give a speech on thermodynamics and the world was waiting.

"I'm sorry, Grandpa," he began, causing himself to jump, unaware he had spoken aloud.

The ice was broken and he felt as if he could continue. He talked to his grandfather, trying to describe every moment he remembered of their times together, not wanting to leave anything out. The rain continued to fall around him, but went unnoticed.

If they only would have known.

Satisfied he had told all he could remember, it was time to let his grandfather speak to him in the way Andrea had shown him. Though still new at the procedure, and still uncomfortable at doing so, he knew it would work.

He closed his eyes, placed his hands upon the cold gravestone to let his grandfather into his mind, and . . .

His grandfather was waiting anxiously, almost knocking Darren over as he made his bold entry.

A forced breath, like he had just gotten punched, jumped from Darren's throat as he was bombarded by visions of his grandfather. His eyes squeezed shut as he tried to rid himself of a sudden headache. He pleaded with his grandfather to slow down, there was still time, and was almost forced to take his hands away from the stone.

As though sensing the impending release of Darren's hands, the images in his mind slowed, took shape, began to come into focus.

IT'S BUILDING AN ARMY! His grandfather's voice screamed within his head.

Andrea longingly observed Sarah on the day of her death.

Beginning with Sarah getting up in the morning, brushing her teeth, and getting dressed in a beautiful pink dress for kindergarten—she was a big girl now. Andrea watched as though it were a dream, with herself as the girl's mother. And she very well could have been. Her feelings were stirring, what she thought would be the same emotions a real mother would have.

She was excited on this first day of school for her daughter, not wanting it to end, not wanting her daughter to leave the kitchen table and begin another segment of her life—without her.

Pieces of cereal spilled out of Sarah's mouth as she quickly tried to force in another spoonful. A drop of milk fell from her chin and back into the bowl. Andrea knew what she was feeling: she didn't want to be late for the bus—especially on the first day!

"Careful, or you're going to choke."

Sarah's eyes gleamed with excitement as her feet tried to frantically tap at the floor from the height of the chair, but struck only air. Her cheeks were rosy with color, dots of red held in sharp relief against the creamy color of her skin. The sun illuminated her blonde hair with rays of sunshine coming through the kitchen window behind her, making her head appear surrounded by a golden halo.

The Big Kid bus. Brakes squealed as it stopped a couple of streets away. Soon, it would be picking up Sarah for the very first time. She bounced eagerly on her toes and delivered a high-pitched giggle of excitement that pierced the already-frenzied atmosphere of the kitchen.

"Mommy! Mommy, it's almost here!"

Mother hurriedly put a coat on Sarah and zipped up a new backpack filled with required school supplies, then used some of her infamous spit to clean away a dried patch of milk from the corner of her daughter's mouth. A squeeze to her cheek, a soft pat on the behind, and a final look-over; it was now time for the tears to gather.

Mother opened the kitchen door and watched Sarah prance down the walk to the bus stop, hair bouncing happily off her shoulders.

Sarah made sure Mother stayed indoors. She was a big girl now and could walk the short distance to the stop all by herself!

Sarah skipped along the small paved path to the bus stop, all smiles. She heard the bus getting closer. Saw it turning onto her street out of the corner of her eye. She kept glancing over her shoulder to be sure Mother was watching. She was. Mother was waving and wiping at the corner of her eye.

She looked back again and wondered why Mother was pointing—of course she knew where to go. Still skipping along, she noticed the bus getting closer. She wished it would hurry up—she wanted to get to school!

Sensing her time as a little girl drawing to a close, Sarah turned her proud, beaming face toward the front door and saw her mother's mouth open and eyes widen like never before.

The screen door started to open.

Raising her hand for a final wave, Sarah didn't see the edge of the curb until she felt it with her shoe. Her feet entangled each other and she fell forward, but tried to regain her balance without tripping and looking silly on this first day of school.

From the corner of her eye she watched as Mother tried to run to her. Mother was trying to tell her something, but her voice wasn't able to rise above the screeching brakes of the school bus.

His grandfather held nothing back.

Images swept through Darren's mind, hazy at first, but gaining clarity as he focused his energy, clearer than he would have liked.

Transparent beings were herded together near the base of a towering stake, flames beginning to reach from beneath a pile of kindling that looked all too much like human hair.

They stood with distant stares, more puppets tethered to a master's ancient fingers than souls deciding their fates. But choose they were able to: a path of torches to a spot beneath the throne of an unseen presence, or to the stake that stood before them in anxious solitude. To join the others in kneeling at the throne, accepting their duty as servants—or burn in an eternal fire.

Those who refused to serve were fastened crudely to the stake, rusted nails hammered into overlapping, screaming apparitions that struggled against one another. Between the arms and legs of some, faces of others could be seen, eyes bulging, begging for release. Beneath the screams, a faint chanting emulated from hooded figures in a low-lying drone, making Darren pause and determine if he had heard correctly. It sounded familiar, like reading the same book many years later, a pinprick of familiarity in the back of his mind.

He cringed as the screaming in his head became unbearable. In a matter of seconds, the fire encompassed the single stake and ignited the squirming beings, creating a melded form of transparent flesh. Limbs and torsos attempted to break free of the nails that held them, some partly succeeding before being consumed within the flames, their screams now merely echoes to fall upon a barren and unforgiving land.

Soon, only small signs of movement twitched upon the stake and another group of apparitions stared up from the base, contemplating their decision.

Darren's vision shifted to the throne, giving him a chance to catch his mental and physical breath, and ready himself for whatever would come next.

"Please help us, Darren," came his grandfather's voice, pleading. "They are trying to gather all of us. We can feel it pulling at us. It will be here, soon."

"But . . ." he began.

"Just watch for now."

Darren did, but wished he hadn't.

Symmetrical rows of hooded figures rested on their knees before the throne, backs rising with each unified breath. Darren felt a tension in the air, heard an electrical buzz that sent vibrations into his bones as the figures waited for a single command.

And then it came, but not by voice.

Darren was one of them now, or as close as he would ever want to be. And, like an alcoholic that couldn't resist the act of his arm reaching for a drink, the command came as an automatic bodily reaction rather than heard, their bodies being told to disrobe with no choice but to obey.

The buzz within his head was replaced with the sound of flesh tearing away from muscle and bone. And pain. His entire body burned, as the protective shell of his skin seemed to leave his body with one swift pull, skinned alive. He tried to squeeze his eyes shut and seal away the pain, but his eyelids had been pulled away with the rest of his skin and he was forced to watch for a little while longer.

Stripped of all flesh, all identity, those that had chosen the throne and knelt before it quivered like frightened sheep. The bare muscles of each shone beneath the light of dripping torches. Their heads hung from glistening torsos as though waiting for the blade of an executioner, foreheads touching the ground. Their robes were at their sides, steaming from the contents within.

Darren stared ahead and watched as a figure appeared. A black shape of a being, a shadow more or less, took shape upon the throne. It was too difficult to discern whether it appeared to be a man or a woman—the vague outlines the shape presented could have belonged to either. In some weird way, Darren thought that was the point. Evil possessed no sex, though it could probably choose to, if it so desired—an entity in and of itself, left to the interpretation of the individual bearing witness to its power.

In its left hand, it held a golden staff. Crudely pushed onto its tip was the head of someone who had made the wrong decision.

As if all were being pulled simultaneously, the heads of the skinless bodies snapped to the sound of the staff hitting the ground. A thunderous echo reverberated, then slowly ceased.

The soldiers awaited their orders.

With another loud crash of the golden staff, the kneeling sheep of an army looked back at Darren. Faces lacking any flesh, eyes devoid of all but one emotion, fixated on him as if *he* were the enemy.

They had received their first lesson.

Hate burned in their lidless eyes.

"There's a—"

But he couldn't let his grandfather finish. He had seen enough.

Darren gasped, then released his grandfather's stone.

They had to hurry.

Darren was on his knees before his grandfather's gravestone, his body shivering.

Andrea gently tapped him on the shoulder. He looked up into her eyes and she knew he had traveled along a similar journey of visions, that they wouldn't be released from his memory anytime soon. A frown pulled at the corners of his mouth. Droplets of water fell from the ends of hair flattened to the sides of his head.

They would share their experiences, but later.

Andrea offered Darren a hand to bring him upright. When he stood, he ran a hand through his hair, slicking it back at odd angles, water dripping down his arm as he did so. His body still trembled.

Andrea placed an arm around Darren's waist as they began to walk toward the entrance. She did this not as a lover, and not in a motherly gesture, but as a friend . . . a partner.

They were nearing the gates when Andrea noticed the

fresh mound of dirt, now muddy.

Totally consumed by the events they had witnessed, emotions running in high gear and minds filled with questions, they had almost done what they were out to avoid. They had almost forgotten to remember one of the dead. The two men at the truck stop were buried deep within their subconscious minds, seemingly nonexistent. Andrea didn't know if there was indeed another body buried in the fresh grave, but needed to know for sure.

She went to the mound of now liquid dirt and closed her eyes, then placed her fingertips beneath the surface of Rosemary Ouellette's fresh grave.

A second presence emerged, like the gentle fluttering of a moth against a light fixture, hovering at the edges of her mind. As though the deceased didn't know or understand that he was dead. Andrea felt his confusion, his apprehension. He knew someone was there, but didn't have the nerve to come forward. He was scared.

She tried to comfort him, explaining what she had learned from the others. That there was something better out there, and there were others on his side that would show him the way. She also warned him about a presence that would try to use him, and that he needed to join in their resistance.

Slowly, the darkness within her mind began to dissolve and the face of the victim appeared.

Andrea witnessed the meeting of the three individuals, the argument, and the gun that the shorter man produced. She saw him fire, felt the burning of the bullet wound in the center of her chest, the life leave the body of the victim. It had all happened within a matter of seconds and the victim still didn't know exactly what had transpired after the argument.

He opened himself up to Andrea.

Donald Levesque, Canadian native, making money on the side by buying cigarettes in the States and selling them for double the value in his country. A common practice these days, but this time he didn't have the money to pay. And a promise fell short of protecting him.

She rose from her crouched position, rubbed her hands together to rid them of dirt and warm them. While happy she had found him, sadness still lurked unbidden. She could only hope that justice would be dealt and those who loved Donald would remember him.

It was a sad world in which they lived.

She took Darren's hand in her own and, with a final look around, acknowledging the forgotten one more time, they made to exit the cemetery. As they passed through the entrance, the temperature changed. They could feel the sudden warmth, though slight, and welcomed it.

From inside the car, they saw the change in the air. A slight mist formed at the base of all the headstones and rose above them. Sunlight broke through cloud layers and caused the mist to assume shapes.

Hundreds of them.

In front of them all, three distinct shapes formed behind the gate. Two were approximately the same size, the other quite a bit smaller.

Three figures raised their hands in thanks. Standing this close together, they could have belonged to the same family—the little girl, the middle-aged father, and the grandfather. The little girl mouthed the word, "Mommy," and Andrea felt her insides begin to twist.

Andrea and Darren waved in return, but still shook their heads in disbelief. Other shapes were joining them—gathering behind the gates like forces coming together. Though transparent, the sheer number of them blocked out the rest of the cemetery, as if they were becoming one, coalescing into a solid being.

With another break in the clouds and sunlight beaming down unimpeded, the shapes dissolved as they rose to a better place. Darren watched his grandfather's form dissipate, but knew he would talk to him again soon.

His grandfather had more to tell.

Chapter 31

It owned him.

The vulnerable ones were always the easiest. They hated their lives, the world, themselves. Any way they could strike back at the God-fearing world in which they lived was well worth it. Chances to redeem themselves in their own eyes and gather a few worthy prizes along the way seemed like a bargain.

They loved money the most and it was easy to flaunt before them. They would grab for it like homeless men scrambling for loose change thrown at their feet. They couldn't resist. Mention a price for revenge and wealth, and their heads nodded without thinking—at least not until it was too late. Only then would they beg and plead, only to be awarded its painful laughter within their ears.

Frank Carlson was no exception. Like so many others, he was easy to manipulate, to pull in any direction and have him accomplish its will without resistance, without realizing the consequences, or caring.

Occasionally, a few would make an attempt to resist. This usually happened after the money, the gifts, and the feelings of power had lost their marvel, like new toys would eventually bore a child. Then they would pay—like the others.

And burn.

It had yet to see if Frank could produce—God help him if he didn't. He was a new pawn in an ongoing cycle that had odds against it, but progress had been made in recent years. These days, once people were buried, that was it.

Relatives moved on with their own lives after only a short period of grieving, thinking the occasional memory of a lost loved one would suffice.

It was becoming relatively easy to take the forgotten ones prisoners and give them a choice, though the end result was the same. The man upstairs seemed to be getting a bit lazy. Were his creations losing their newness? Was he becoming *bored?*

Mr. Carlson wasn't alone. Other pawns were strategically placed about the world, tearing down the remaining obstacles that needed to be removed. The time was near and it wondered if the being viewed as God was toying with it by sending the boy and the woman in the way of its path, like irritating bugs needing to be squashed. And a newly-deceased who thought she was smarter than she actually was, having prepared before she made the crossover to the other side. They were becoming a nuisance, almost a handicap.

The chess game of the universe could indeed be enjoyable at times.

It thought about its next move.

It laughed, and the Earth trembled.

Chapter 32

Still getting used to her surroundings, Faye found guidance from those she had once remembered. To not be attached to the body she once inhabited was different and disquieting. She was no longer restricted inside a husk, limited in abilities. The freedom she felt was unbounded, beautiful.

She had seen no pearly gates, no angels with wings. Only the glowing spirits of souls she had remembered, and she had been remembered by others. Some had waited many years for her arrival. Could this be the proverbial Heaven? Perhaps. Could there be more? Perhaps.

Could it all disappear, destroyed by the evil presence they were fighting? Perhaps.

The crossover had been better than any sort of reunion she could have imagined. They welcomed her eagerly, were waiting for her to lead them into the fight against a presence that was finding new ways to pull at them, claiming them as its own.

With Faye and the few other people that were undertaking similar journeys around the world, the bond was getting stronger, almost enough to prevent its uprising once again.

Faye had looked on as Darren received a hard lesson from his grandfather and Andrea met a little girl named Sarah. If Faye could have cried, she would have, but tears were part of that other world she recently belonged to and was no longer a part of. The world she was trying to save. She welcomed the new arrivals that Darren and Andrea had released from Evergreen Cemetery. Some were confused, but all were happy.

Faye felt the frustration that ate at Darren's grandfather, had experienced it recently herself. There was so much information that he wanted to give to Darren and no time to do it. She tried to comfort him, thanking him for doing his part. She knew he held a link that she couldn't tap into just yet.

Time was closing in on them to thwart its plan, but she was confident that their combined efforts would do just that.

Chapter 33

They left Evergreen with weary bodies, wet clothes, hair weighed down upon their shoulders, and more questions, but a wonderful sense of accomplishment leveled the scale. A scale beginning to tip in their direction, giving them the strength and reason they needed to continue.

The day surrounding them reflected their accomplishments, as did their drained, but smiling faces, and hopeful eyes that had somehow developed blackened half-moons beneath them. The comforting and powerful rays of a rising sun into a clear sky had eliminated a drizzly, overcast day. The sun had yet to reach its zenith.

It was almost eleven o'clock.

The St. John River flowed peacefully beneath a bridge that led to Canada, while the border patrols checked vehicles as they came and went. Sunlight reflected off the roofs of vehicles. Seagulls flew majestically above, beneath, and around the structure and Andrea absently wondered why seagulls were present when there wasn't even an ocean for them to flock to.

They ate at a mom and pop restaurant on the small main street of Fort Kent, neighbored by only one gas station, a music shop, and a ski shop, and by the very hand of God himself, seemingly blessed with a grocery and thrift store. A billboard pointing to a drive-in theater—amazingly still operational—told them it was only one mile ahead. Now playing: *The Goonies*. It had been playing for quite some time.

Before entering the restaurant, Andrea made an anonymous phone call to the police station, probably only blocks away from where she stood on the street corner. An officer answered the call with a thick French accent and took down the information she provided: that two men were messing around the gravesite of Rosemary Ouellette, and they had shovels—this, a day after her burial. She gave a description of the men and their vehicle and quickly hung up, afraid of being traced, though she doubted if the station even had the technology to do so.

Darren could only describe the bodies, souls, or whatever they were, as peeled tomatoes—just like a dream he'd had as a child—with only the top layer of skin removed, exposing muscles and veins.

"And they were looking at me . . ." He trailed off, imagining the scene all over again, remembering the dream. An icy chill touched the base of his spine and spread, finally coming to rest on his neck, hovering for a few seconds, but seeming like a lifetime. Darren shivered the feeling away.

Andrea nodded, letting him finish the telling of his second meeting with his grandfather.

"He wanted to tell me something else, tell me more, but . . . but I just couldn't hang on." He dropped his eyes as if admitting to a mistake, ashamed. "It scared me," he finished, looking away, his voice just a bit lower. He drew circles in the egg yolk on his plate with a fork.

Andrea nodded, slowly chewing on a piece of toast. She took his hand in her own and gave it a small squeeze.

"It's okay Darren, we'll do the right thing, I promise. And we are. I can feel it," Andrea said. "In here," she finished, placing a hand over the center of her chest.

"I just—" Darren began, but Andrea held up her hand, showing him her palm. He waited.

She took a sip of her coffee and cleared her throat, wiping crumbs off the corners of her mouth with a napkin. A waitress came and filled her cup.

It was her turn to tell.

She told him of her own feelings of despair at not being able to save the little girl. Even though she wasn't the girl's mother, for a short time she indeed was, and the loss she felt was just as intense, just as real. She also described what had happened to Donald Levesque. Though what he was doing was wrong and he may have had good reasons for his crime—mouths to feed, bills to pay—he still didn't deserve what had befallen him.

"We have to hurry," Darren said once she was finished.

"I know," she said. "I know." She took a deep breath, as if readying herself for another eventful day.

Andrea paid the bill and left three dollars folded under her coffee cup.

The car bounced violently as they entered a vintage Texaco station, the frame of the Duster protesting as the tires rolled across an outcropping of pavement caused by the bitter winters, first once, then again as the rear tires found the same spot. Their heads almost struck against the roof of the car.

Darren pumped the gas while Andrea went through her purse.

The station contained only two pumps, each with dialog-type numbers that rolled backward. Parts of vehicles and old tires surrounded the entrance to the store portion of the station. A dog, thankfully tied to a metal chain, barked, snarled, stubby tail pointed to the sky, as Andrea found her way inside to pay. She kept the dog in view until she was well within the protection of the small building.

A bald man, head as round as his mid-section, greeted her from behind a tabloid. He chomped on a cigar and eyed Andrea up and down, up and down. She tried not to look at him as she gathered a few items they could snack on, dreaded going to the register.

"Howdy," he said. His name was Norm, as she saw stitched on his grease-stained shirt. "What's a pretty lady like you doing up heeyah?"

Like she hadn't heard that one before.

"Just passing through," Andrea forced herself to reply, biting her tongue.

She wrinkled her nose at the smell of the place and tried to ignore him, wanting to be on her way as quickly as possible. He took the money she gave him slowly, letting the bill linger between both of their grips. Andrea's skin crawled and she immediately let go of her end. She tapped her foot on the floor, impatiently waiting for her change.

Rolling her eyes at Darren as she exited, she jumped as the dog barked at her yet again. She picked up her pace and slammed the door once she was inside the safety of her car.

"I think he liked you," Darren said between chuckles.

"Who, the man or the dog?"

"Both."

She laughed, then slapped him on his thigh.

They took a left and then a right onto Route 161 southbound, toward Caribou. They passed a small number of homes as they climbed up a small hill, some still having plastic nailed or stapled to the outsides of windows to keep the cold air out. Once they crested the hill, only a long stretch of road greeted them, homes nowhere to be seen. With a gradual decline in the highway, the temperature dropped as they were swallowed by the shadows of tall pines and birches, guarding against any intrusion of sunlight. They climbed another small hill and the sun was able to peer at them. Briefly.

Darren squinted his eyes against the sudden change in lighting, feeling the first pangs of a headache right smack in the middle of his forehead. He pressed down on the bridge of his nose with both fingers, but it didn't help.

He laid his head back, scooted lower in the passenger's seat, and kept his eyes closed. He listened to the hum of the tires on the pavement, the wind captured by the open window, and the fading signals of a music station. It relaxed him, but his headache remained. Soon, although he never thought he'd be able to without vomiting all over himself, he drifted into a nap.

And was welcomed into a daymare . . .

Peeled tomatoes with bulbous, glaring eyes and no lids peered at him, the surfaces containing swollen veins that pumped a bluish fluid so fast as to almost burst. They were still attached to their stalks, but were struggling to be set free, making them look as if they were dancing a comical, yet horrid, jig. He tried to scream . . . or laugh, but couldn't.

Some managed to break free of their stalks and come forward, but not before they assumed the shapes of humans and slithered upon their chests in his direction. Teeth, absent of any lips, threatened him with a bone-rattling chatter. Yellowed claws reached for him.

His name was being called from somewhere in the distance, the blackness. He didn't know which was worse: the peeled tomato bodies or what could possibly exist in the void beyond.

The skinless bodies now crawled away from him and formed a circle, their heads joined together at the center, oozing into one. Shoulders, arms, and torsos soon followed suit and began to rise, until a crude stake of muscle, sinew, and organs grew from their mass.

Hooded figures brought a body (one that still had its flesh) toward the living, breathing stake. Darren heard his name now with the distinct clarity of a scream. And recognized the body thrashing violently beneath the hold of these hooded figures.

They tossed his grandfather upward in a one-two-three gesture that would have been comical at any other time. Hands took shape and protruded from the stake. They held fast to the body thrown to them. Reginald looked down at Darren with terrified eyes and was trying to say something.

"There's a—" A hand appeared, tendons and muscle glowing, and covered his mouth. His grandfather took a bite of one finger and shook his head from side to side in a desperate snarl.

"There's a portal where they'll rise from the depths of Hell!" he screamed, determined to get this message to Darren. And with this he was satisfied, disappearing within the stake of flesh, consumed.

The scene changed and Darren now stared from the edge of a blackened hole in the ground. He was on all fours and felt the moist earth beneath his palms. He was fearful of falling in, but needed to get closer, to see what was at the bottom. He inched closer on his knees, allowing his head to descend partly into the hole, but only lambent light danced below, like a match in a giant cave. A caustic odor set his nose on fire, made his eyes water. He gagged.

His forehead touched something, something sticky, but the darkness only allowed his imagination to think of the possibilities. However, even his imagination couldn't invoke the tongue of the fleshless beast that licked at his eyes.

Andrea looked over, startled by the small whimper. From deep within his dream, Darren was trying to push something away.

Another whimper, an incoherent murmur to someone or something, and Darren sat up in a hurry, staring outside the windshield as if dazed.

"I know where we need to go," Darren said. He turned to look at her with a look of stunning realization.

"Huh?" She eyed him carefully, unsure if he was still dreaming.

"We have to go home, back to an area I used to hang out in. I think I know where this . . . this presence is going to try and surprise the world." His words all but tripped over each other.

"Hold on, hold on," Andrea said, trying to calm him. "Let's start at the beginning. Were you dreaming?"

"Yeah, but everything was connected: my grandfather, hooded figures, and a dark pit. I know where this pit is."

Andrea's ears perked up at the mention of hooded figures. A distant memory clawed its way to her consciousness and made her stomach suddenly tighten.

"Tell me about the dream. Everything." A small stutter punctuated her words.

And he did. The words came out hurriedly as he tried to recall every detail. Afterwards, out of breath, he sat back into the passenger's seat, deflated. He unscrewed the cap off a bottle of Pepsi and took several long, hard swallows.

Andrea tried to envision in her own mind what he had seen. She kept going back to the hooded figures and the dark pit, which had to be the tunnel she had traveled the very first day she had met him. The similarities were too exact to be simply a coincidence.

Her fingers drummed on the steering wheel and she chewed on her bottom lip as she played out recent events in her mind, trying to determine what should be the next course of action. They needed a strategy, some semblance of a plan to enact when they did finally reach this pit, if there really was one. They needed many forgotten souls on their side before doing so, and were at least three hundred miles away from home.

Home.

She had to laugh at this. The source of the trouble that might come was right under their feet the entire time. Literally.

Of course, if they hadn't done what they had already accomplished, they wouldn't have met Darren's grandfather—clearly a key player. Or saved a little girl from a hell she didn't deserve, or uncovered the malice of a few criminals. The path they had chosen, she believed, had already been chosen for them. They had only had to walk it.

There had to be another way to remember the forgotten ones without actually visiting each cemetery. Had to be. They only had to find it, and promptly.

Darren rested his elbow on the armrest of the passenger's door, holding his chin in the palm of his hand as he watched the trees diminish and give way to farm fields. He knew exactly where this pit was—underneath an old warehouse. He and his friends had run from it as kids and now he was about revisit it again, hopefully for the last time. They had to close this portal . . . somehow.

While grim thoughts of what might unfold coursed through him with unsettling concoctions of every boyhood nightmare he could imagine, he was still happy—happy to be going home. Just to be able to sleep in his bed again would be worth whatever they had to do. The thought of seeing his parents again comforted him. They must be worried sick, and he wouldn't be surprised if they had the Maine State Police looking for them. But he hoped they had taken him seriously and knew he had to do this, even though they might not understand why. He never wanted to let them down, only wanted to find his purpose in life. And believed he had found it, however ridiculous it might seem. He would tell them everything, but not before he and Andrea finished what they had started.

Darren felt his chin slide forward beneath his palm at the sudden deceleration of the vehicle. Andrea turned left onto a dirt road and under the entrance of another cemetery. The same cemetery they had made a passing greeting to on the way to Fort Kent. It was a larger cemetery, considering the size of the surrounding communities.

He was suddenly uneasy.

Chapter 34

They stepped out of the vehicle.

The air was different, and their surroundings quiet, as though waiting in anticipation. Though the back part of the cemetery was the beginning of a patch of woods, they heard no birds, no chattering chipmunks, no wind soughing through the branches. When they closed the car doors, two small explosions seemed to shatter the silence with shrapnel.

A dirt road encompassed the entire cemetery. Toward the rear, the stones appeared to be cracked and bleeding, while some had toppled over. In the front, newer stones marked the sites of the most recent burials. Only a few of these held the remnants of a recent visit: a single flower or an empty vase. In the center of a group of three stones, a used six-pack of beer bottles remained, with many cigarette butts around and inside them.

Afraid to announce their arrival and break the eerie silence, they remained quiet and proceeded to the first row of headstones, unaware that they were staying close together, keeping each other in close contact.

Andrea looked into the forest beyond the cemetery, imagined hundreds of eyes peering at them, recording their every move.

As quietly as possible, like kids afraid they would get caught, they greeted more forgotten souls.

Grass and weeds, resembling yellowed, tangled hair throughout most of the area, caused her to almost stumble on more than one occasion as they tugged at her feet. She used high steps, as if she were sneaking up on an unseen prey hiding in the lengthened blades, her breathing getting more labored with each step. Darren waded through his own river of weeds in front of her, forcing his legs to push through the stilled current. After a few minutes at each stone with feeling hands and closed eyes, they continued their trek through the cemetery.

Minutes seemed like hours as they slowly made progress and finally reached the rear section of the cemetery. They had to stop more than once to catch their breath, chests heaving.

"Wow, didn't think it would be this physical," Andrea said between breaths, noticing Darren breathing hard, but not *as* hard. "Promise me you'll exercise often after you reach thirty."

"Promise."

Realizing it was the first time they had spoken since entering the cemetery, Andrea looked around, half expecting the sky to fall. Instead, she caught the glint of sunlight reflecting off a metal object at the rear of the cemetery, then a glimpse of movement.

Only one pair of eyes had been recording their every move, filled with the burning fire of hatred.

He had awakened to the sound of birds chirping and a slight breeze. A chill had managed to find a way in, leaving his feet cold, even though they still had socks on them. He had curled into a ball during the night, trying to stave off a nasty chill, his head buried beneath the protection of the sleeping bag.

The night prior was only a blur in his memory, leaving no clues as to what he did besides walking into a hick bar and meeting a prissy waitress. He did remember the money in his wallet and quickly reached behind to feel the familiar bulge—still there. He knew he had drunk a lot, but couldn't tell by the way he was feeling. He didn't have the pulsing migraine or the fuzzy head.

He felt good.

For a while he just stayed where he was, letting the rising sun warm him and remove the small puddle of water that covered his sleeping bag.

Without warning, the world around him became silent and the wind ceased. Perspiration beaded on his upper lip and his pulse began to increase, while small tremors started coursing through his body. He no longer felt so good.

Two car doors being shut got his heart racing. He jumped out of the sleeping bag and frantically searched for his boots, his mind reeling for possibilities of who had just arrived. Someone must have seen his car and informed the local police. Probably two officers ready to question him and take him away.

He quickly rolled up his sleeping bag, remaining behind the headstone he had chosen for cover, shoulders hunched, knees bent. With curiosity eating at his mind, he slowly rose from his crouched position and peered over the top of the headstone, expecting to be told to come out with his hands placed behind his head and to turn around slowly, then get on his knees. He had done the same a few times before.

Two individuals had indeed arrived at the cemetery, but he was sure they weren't looking for him. Instead, they were trying to make their way through lengthened grass, having a tough time doing so, and stopping here and there to touch the stones. He had no idea what they were doing or why, but was glad they weren't the police. At first, he watched them move throughout the cemetery, more for amusement than anything else.

The woman was beautiful, but her hair looked as if she had just come out of a shower and had forgotten to comb it. The younger man was dressed in jeans and a jean jacket to match—how cute—and was taller than the woman, bigger than him. Frank couldn't tell if they were boyfriend and girlfriend, brother and sister, or any other combination. He kept looking back to the woman, drawn to her, and started to get hard.

As they got closer, a flame of hatred began to lick at the pit of his stomach.

They seemed to come from a distant past that Frank once remembered, looking familiar but not being able to be placed within his memory. Unable to arrive at any logical explanation for why he almost recognized people in a place he had never been, he watched more intently, lured by the excitement of being a predator. Like a cat on the prowl, he studied their every move, allowing only his eyes to move within their sockets, the hairs on his body standing upright, heart thudding rapidly behind his ribcage.

Hatred. Instinctive hatred.

He licked his lips and waited patiently.

As he observed them still meandering among the headstones, the flame within his gut developed into a small fire, then a raging inferno, engulfing his entire body. Like a thirst that needed to be quenched, he would only become satisfied when the two people he was watching died by his hand.

With each passing second, he was finding it more difficult to contain himself, to harness the fury, to avoid announcing his presence too early. Had to wait. Had to wait.

The woman was lost in concentration for the moment, eyes closed, kneeling before a stone with her hands resting on top of it. Frank undressed her in his mind. Put her clothes back on, then undressed her again, this time more slowly. With each piece of clothing removed, he got harder, relishing the feel of his pulse down there. He shifted his position to give himself more room to grow.

As he watched the younger man imitate the same ritual as the woman, Frank realized he did so with the same conviction, but with a bit of uncertainty. He kept looking over at the woman, as though seeing if what he was doing was correct, never closing his eyes for long. Or was it just to be sure they were alone? Maybe he had sensed another presence. At this particular thought, Frank lowered his position, so his view contained half of the headstone he was behind.

Slowly, steadily, they walked toward Frank, so far appearing oblivious to his company.

Almost time.

Hatred.

They had to die and it was a shame. He wouldn't have any time to play with the woman. Or make them play with each other as he watched. A grin quivered on his lips.

Closer, closer.

His nerves were on edge—his body shook with delight.

Closer.

It was time to pounce.

From behind a tall, weather-beaten gravestone, Frank Carlson jumped into their lives.

Andrea noticed at the last second, with only enough time to take a step backward and utter a small shriek; but it was enough to avoid being trampled on by this intruder. Seemingly out of nowhere, this person appeared, obviously without any intention of saying hello. A second later, Darren was in front of her and she had to peer over his shoulder to see who had surprised them.

And a surprise it was.

Unable to convey what she was thinking, her mouth dropped open behind Darren's shoulder, allowing only her enlarged eyes to be seen. She didn't believe whom she was seeing.

All three of them stood their ground as if evaluating each other and waiting to see who would make the next move. The only sound present was coming from the heaving chest of their new arrival, bringing forth a guttural noise with each quick breath, almost animal-like—a dying animal at that.

"Frank?" Andrea asked, stepping out from behind Darren. Darren put an arm out to prevent her from going any farther, casting a questioning glance at Andrea while keeping Frank within view, but she pushed it aside gently. She kept her eyes focused on Frank's, still not believing who was in front of her. She stated his name in the form of a question, because the man standing in front of them was barely a semblance of the Frank Carlson she knew.

Hollowed, crazed, bloodshot eyes stared at them, dark shadows hanging from each. Sparsely decorated with un-shaven lengths of hair, his face was dominated by an evil grin revealing teeth that hadn't been brushed in quite some time. A length of drool shook from his lower lip. His clothes seemed to hang on him like they were two sizes too big—his pants were fastened with a leather belt drawn so tightly around his waist that the end of the belt stuck out at least six inches from the buckle.

At the mention of his name, he tilted his head, appearing confused and disoriented, and that grin never left his face. He flexed the fingers of his right hand, knuckles popping, while his eyes darted back and forth and his shirt fluttered over his quivering chest.

As feeble as he appeared, Frank still delivered a quick and powerful blow to Darren's mid-section with a closed fist.

"Darren!" Andrea screamed.

Darren doubled over and fell to his hands and knees in the tall grass, gasping for air.

The phlegm-congested breaths of Frank were increasing. He seemed to be readying himself for another blow, presumably at her this time. She heard Darren begin to dry heave; then spit at the ground before starting to rise.

Frank's crazed eyes now fixated on Andrea as he moved toward her with short, tentative steps. He licked at his lips and what sounded like a moan rose from deep within his chest. His shaking hands attempted to unbuckle his belt as he took another step forward.

Andrea responded in kind, taking a step backward. She would have taken more had it not been for a marble headstone now pressing against the backs of her legs.

"Frank, please," she said, trying to prolong the inevitable, whatever it might be. The only response from the man in front of her was another lick of his lips. She cringed.

She could smell him now, and would rather have slid a piece of glass under her fingernail. A lump formed in her throat and she almost vomited. She dared not move a muscle as Frank reached out and grabbed her breast, giving it a painful squeeze. She winced, turned her head away in disgust and shame, and leaned back, almost lying on top of the headstone.

Where was Darren?

In answer, a wad of phlegm left Frank's congested chest with a forced blow. His eyes widened and saliva sprayed from between his teeth.

Feet flying through the air, Darren completed the full

tackle and crushed Frank beneath him, muffling the chilling crack of bone.

"Who the hell do you think you are?" Darren screamed at him, getting to his feet. Face red, veins sticking out of his neck, he seemed ready to stomp the man in the face. A gurgle they couldn't understand was Frank's only reply as he crawled to his car. Yellow drool hung from his mouth and stretched into thick strings as it came in contact with the grass.

Darren turned to Andrea, fists still clenched at his sides. "You okay?"

"Yeah, I think so," Andrea said, rolling her shoulder and bringing the inside of her arm against her breast, attempting to massage it without being too obvious.

"Who *is* that?" Darren asked, watching Frank open his car door and lean inside.

"An old acquaintance."

"Looks like he's in bad shape."

She nodded, still watching her previous assailant. His door was still open and she could only see his back, pants hanging low around his waist. "I have no idea how he found us or why, but I think we should leave before he gets any more ingenious ideas."

"Fucking weirdo," Darren said, and Andrea had to look at him. It was the first time she ever heard him swear. She didn't know how to react to that, and felt her face redden. A motherly instinct had almost taken over, or rather the older librarian in her, and she felt ashamed.

Seeing her eyes drop and her feet shuffle nervously, Darren offered a quick apology.

"No, no, that's alright. Just never heard you get mad like that before." She looked him in the eyes and smiled.

"Well, he shouldn't have done that. That's bullsh . . . wrong."

They turned to leave quickly, still wondering what was taking Frank so long, doing whatever he was doing. As much as she hated him—she couldn't ever remember having a pleasant run-in with him—Andrea had to resist the urge to go see if he was okay. Frank needed help—that much was obvious. Who, if not her and Darren, would help a man in his condition? Why or how he had seemingly tracked them down she probably would never know, nor did she want to know.

Andrea stopped and cast another concerned look to the back of the cemetery. The driver's side door was still open. An air freshener of some naked lady spread in a compromising position gently twirled below the rearview mirror, but there was no sign of Frank. A tingle of fear crept through her. Maybe he had fallen down behind one of the gravestones and was gasping for a final breath of air.

She felt a tug on her jacket and turned away without knowing if she had just made the right decision to follow Darren.

The grass still pulled at their every step, but their pace quickened with the force of pure adrenaline still pulsing through them. They needed to get out of here.

Her Plymouth gradually came into view through the spaces between the headstones. The air still remained silent around them, creating doubts as to whether or not their visit to this cemetery was actually over. They picked up their pace, pushing through the grass.

Then stopped, frozen in their footsteps. Darren caught Andrea by the forearm to prevent her from stumbling as her feet became entangled.

A 9mm pistol stared at them, daring them to move just another inch. Behind it, Frank's shaking hands waited for a reason to allow a shaking index finger to pull the trigger. At a distance they probably could have chanced it, trusting that Frank's aim would fall short of his mark. However, he stood only a few feet away, leaving all the room for error he needed. The smile on his face confirmed that he, too, knew their odds—until it faltered.

The air seemed to crackle around them.

Invisible, yet completely audible, the atmosphere seemed to build its energy and was about to express it in the form of a massive bolt of lightning. The hair on all three of their heads began to rise, as if someone from above had their hair attached to invisible threads, gently pulling on each. In another situation, another day, this would have appeared to be a wonderful phenomenon of nature.

The barrel of the 9mm still stared at Darren and Andrea, shaking more than it was a second ago. A drop of sweat from the tip of Frank's nose fell and slid down the side of the barrel, creating an ominous, shiny path. Ignoring their floating hair, they stared at the trigger in return, concentrating on the index finger above it, which could end at least one of their lives with a sudden motion, a sudden change in pressure.

The fingertip, decorated with a dirt-blackened fingernail, hovered above the trigger, eager to be put to use. It appeared to shake with delight. As they watched, their hearts dropped when the fingertip came in contact with the trigger, shaking no more as the pressure applied to it increased. The 9mm happened to be set to double-action and they watched the hammer move away from its housing. Their eyes squinted in unison and thoughts of jumping, dropping, or rolling out of Frank's line of fire entered their minds.

As the hammer reached its apex, something happened so quickly they would forever wonder how.

In an instant, their rising hair fell heavily to their shoulders, a powerful scent of ozone filled their senses, and a white ball of electricity, crackling with intensity, sent Frank flying through the air. One moment he was there, the next, only the soles of his boots were seen following the rest of his body.

The ball of electricity missed Darren and Andrea, but the tips of their eyelashes and parts of their eyebrows were singed. They both stood in disbelief, unblinking.

"What the hell was *that?*" Andrea asked.

Darren had no idea—didn't offer any guesses, either. He resorted only to blinking his eyes and almost pinched himself to see if this was real. He looked around, seeing Frank's boots partly concealed by the thick grass. He quickly went for the 9mm that had fallen from Frank's grasp, wanting to be sure they had it before they even thought about checking on Frank.

He tentatively picked it up by the handgrip with his thumb and forefinger. He had never even shot a BB gun. The hammer was still cocked back just enough to frighten him. He gave it to Andrea in hopes that she knew what to do with it.

She grasped it confidently and Darren looked on with an open jaw as she slid the barrel back until it locked into place, turned over the weapon, and caught a single bullet in the palm of her hand. Then she pressed a button and the magazine fell to the ground. The gleaming brass she now held between two fingers was all they needed to know how close they had been to the other side.

Andrea picked up the magazine and pushed it back into place. Putting the gun into one of the deep pockets of her coat, she said, "In case we need it."

He nodded. He was just glad to be rid of it—manly thing to do or not.

From the woods behind them, the wind blew gently, sometimes accompanied by a sudden gust, as though cleansing itself. The sun warmed their cheeks. A brave bird offered a single chirp to hang in the air, testing the result. Satisfied, others soon joined in celebration.

"Guess whatever was going to happen, has," Darren said.

Andrea looked into the sun, closed her eyes. "I think you're right, but let's go check on Frank first."

He didn't like this idea, but followed behind her just the same. She had the gun, after all.

Frank had flown a distance of at least thirty feet and hit a headstone before coming to rest at its base. His boots were still the only part of him visible, until they were standing above him. Then they saw the nightmare of Darren's dreams lying in the grass and covered their noses against the stench.

A peeled tomato in human form was sprawled in the grass, a lump of glistening muscle that was once Frank Carlson. Steam was rising from all openings and crevices formed by the tangled mess of the body. His clothes had been taken away, along with his skin, leaving only his boots and small pieces of flesh hanging onto the tops of them. Eyes glared into nothingness, still looking crazed and terrified, prominently bulging without eyelids or flesh surrounding them. They appeared ready to fall out with the smallest breeze.

Andrea turned around, gagging, then fell to her knees and let her breakfast make another appearance in the world.

Darren gave Frank's boots a nudge with his own feet, proving to himself that Frank wouldn't be getting up anytime soon. He let Andrea finish her business as he turned away himself, facing the wind to allow the stench to be carried behind him. He peeked over at Andrea as she was wiping her mouth with the back of her sleeve.

"Ahh, that's better," she said. "We'd better get out of here."

"Thought you'd never say that. Let's go."

Neither Frank's car nor his body, separated by a few hundred feet, was visible from the cemetery entrance. Except for the faint paths through the overgrowth, the cemetery looked as sad as before—as if no one had even visited.

Her stare was vacant, half-moons a shade darker. Darren knew she wouldn't be able to drive. He held out his hand and she dug deep into her coat pockets, pulling out her keys and the gun.

Darren took the keys while she wiped the entire gun down with her shirt, emptied its bullets, then threw the gun, magazine, and brass in different directions. She made sure to throw the gun the farthest, into a thick copse of trees that no one would venture into for quite a while.

Darren jerked the Duster into reverse, got the car facing in the right direction, and left a plume of dirt twinkling in the car's wake.

Chapter 35

He held his foot firmly on the gas pedal, slowing only when the cemetery disappeared from the rearview mirror. So much had happened in the last couple of days, he didn't know if his head could keep anything straight. Of one thing, he was sure. He was going home, and just the thought of it unwound the first knot of a bundle that rested inside his stomach.

Andrea had forgotten to fasten her seatbelt, but did so as the car found a pothole and she rose a few inches off the passenger's seat. Sunlight came through her window, casting a pale shadow on the left side of her face. She looked exhausted.

Darren placed a hand on her knee, started rubbing it with his thumb. He felt the cold dampness of her hand as she casually pushed him away, and he immediately went to the radio, in search of a station. His face burned and he hoped Andrea wouldn't look at him. She didn't.

He settled on a soft rock station—the only station—and thought about his friends at home. No doubt, they were still getting together every night to talk about their big plans of leaving Maine in search of better futures.

Simon had turned out to be a decent guitar player and played weddings, clubs—anyplace that would let him play. He changed the spikes in his hair to braids, only letting his hair hang about his scalp naturally when he was playing weddings. He knew if he didn't leave Maine, his chances of hitting the big-time were nil, and was trying to save enough money to head to Los Angeles. Darren hoped he did.

Mark Wilson surprised everyone by being a master of the written word—over thirty of his short stories were published in various magazines by the time he was a senior. He was currently working on a novel and would stay locked in his room all day, coming out only after much coaxing from his friends.

A local restaurant had snared Craig Potvin as a dishwasher while he was a sophomore and slowly groomed him into head chef. He complained every night about how busy it was, never having time for a break, and constantly hearing the waitresses bitch and moan about who was in charge of what table. In reality, he loved it because the customers were coming in to eat his food, and did so regularly.

Darren's friends were all on their own paths, knowing (for the most part) what they wanted to do. And here he was, driving someone else's Plymouth, chasing down souls while warding off demons, ghouls, and whatever else might pop up. The world had a funny way of turning. He had to admit that he was actually enjoying the adventure, knowing that the work had meaning—a higher meaning—but wasn't sure what would happen next or how long it would last. What was he to do afterward?

They were nearing Houlton—from the other direction now—and Andrea felt better. She flipped down the visor and looked into the small mirror attached to it. Rubbed at the dark circles beneath her eyes, but was pleased they appeared to be fading. Her queasy stomach was gone, her mind becoming clear. She was busy trying to discover a way to reach so many souls in so little time. There had to be a way.

Her hands rested on her lap, fingertip to fingertip, using one fingernail to scrape beneath the nail of another, absently picking at the dirt that had gathered over the last few days. She hadn't had any time to worry about her nails, or her hair, which she usually brushed for at least thirty minutes each night. She ran a hand through it, grimacing as it got caught in tangles.

She took a deep breath and smelled a familiar scent—faint, but there.

She opened her mind and waited.

"The book," whispered a familiar voice. Andrea jumped.

She wasn't frightened by the voice of Faye, but welcomed it. The voice was quiet, yet had a strength within it that contained not a hint of fear or uncertainty. She chewed her bottom lip, waiting for more guidance.

None came.

Which left her to figure it out.

She looked around the inside of the car, as if she were searching for a lost pair of keys or a wallet, and ignored the confused stare Darren returned. Most of her books were still in the trunk of the car. The only other book she knew of was Darren's notebook full of entries. Full of . . . that's it!

It was sitting on the back car seat, partly hidden by Darren's coat that he'd thrown on top of it. Only the corner of it jutted out from beneath the coat, its used pages quickly outnumbering the blank ones, separating themselves from the compressed, unused pages. The cover of the notebook now held evidence of being bent on more than one occasion, leaving white cracks visible against the red surface. She found it amazing that something, which could be purchased at any drug store for under a dollar, could be worth so much more. As if it were a prize-winning novel, originally having its beginnings as a blank page, waiting to become a masterpiece.

She tossed his jacket aside and took out the notebook, dug through her purse, and found a pen, blood pumping with excitement.

The familiar blue and white sign, signifying a nearby rest area, swept past her window—the last before Interstate 95.

"Pull into the rest area!"

"Something wrong?" Darren asked.

"No, just pull over. I'll be driving for a while."

"That's fine. My bladder won't last much longer."

Darren slowed the car and turned into the rest area. As the car came to a stop, he quickly undid his seatbelt and half-walked, half-ran to the door marked for men. Andrea ran as well, more to get out of there as soon as possible than to relieve a swollen bladder.

They settled for some vending goodies with the spare change Andrea had in her purse—they could eat later. They listened to the clunks of soda cans, as they pressed the selections they wanted. Not much to choose from, since most of the choices had a red light illuminated above them—sold out.

They stretched, letting the blood flow to their extremities, and walked through an area sparsely filled with picnic tables and trashcans. A gentle breeze stirred the trees and the sun projected subtle warmth. Nearby, a poodle barked at the birds as an elderly couple talked quietly and waited for it to relieve itself. A younger couple enjoyed a picnic lunch at one of the tables.

Making sure they were out of hearing range of both couples, Andrea told Darren of Faye's whisper in her ear: suddenly there, then gone. "As we drive back, try to concentrate; let them find their way to you. The very first entries you put in there were done the same way, I'm sure of it. They were the first souls you ever remembered. They

234

were drawn to you. You may be able to feel them, or maybe not. Either way, be ready. You might want to flex your hand a bit—you may be writing for a while," Andrea said, finally pausing to take a breath, unable to hide a smile of growing excitement.

He did just that: opened and closed his hand multiple times, remembering the way his hand had cramped up before, the way it curled with a will of its own, refusing to reopen.

Andrea decided to trade in the car on their return. It had been a good trooper, but it wouldn't last much longer, nor could she imagine spending anymore time in it. She was practically living in it now. She patted the hood as she would a child for doing a good job, then climbed in, adjusted the seat for her shorter legs, and turned the key in the ignition.

It stalled.

She turned the key a second time, her pulse slowly increasing.

It caught, purring like a kitten.

The joke was on her.

Chapter 36

Within the shrinking confines of an aging Plymouth Duster, Andrea Varney and Darren Jacobs, partners in an unthinkable journey, turned onto Interstate 95, knowing where they were going, but not knowing what to expect. A local news segment crackled from the AM radio as both of them stared ahead. The chance for thunderstorms over the next few days was increasing, along with the humidity, which lurked, thick and clammy.

Darren's notebook lay open upon his lap as a pen twirled back and forth between his fingers. A bead of sweat fell from his chin and onto a blank page, causing the blue of an ink line to spread and darken. The paper dried quickly, buckling and changing shape. Darren shifted in the seat, pulled the damp shirt away from his back.

Andrea frowned and resumed her count of white center stripes and wiped at her upper lip. The humidity and the driving were making her edgy, impatient. She would be glad to trade in the vehicle for one with air conditioning. Thoughts of a cool bath were the only way to keep from stopping the car and screaming until her throat turned raw, just to relieve the tension. Darren still sat there, waiting for something to happen. Maybe she was wrong, had misunderstood what Faye had said.

The interstate began a slow decline, the long stretch of highway uncurling for miles before disappearing into the horizon. A lake to the east displayed boats that looked like toys stranded in a bathtub. Reflections on the water made the boats appear larger than they were. The sun had begun its descent, creating a yellowish glow upon the lake's surface and a glare on the windshield.

She was about to comment on the lake's glasslike stillness when a ripple in the water turned into a thousand wrinkles sweeping across the surface.

The ripple had originated from an end of the lake darkened by the start of evening shadows. An outcrop of land and trees created a gloomy cove at this end, obviously not to the liking of any real estate developers, as no camps or summer homes inhabited this part of the lake.

The disturbance crossed the lake and the boats stirred in the distance a fraction of an inch. As a party boat rocked from the effects, she wondered about the true size of the waves, as whitecaps now speckled the entire lake, eliminating the reflections.

Andrea looked to the sky, but the clouds had yet to gather, and the surrounding trees, for now, were still.

When a scratching sound cut through the thickened air, she turned toward Darren and had to resist the urge to leap for joy.

His head hung low, eyes closed. His hand was clamped to the pen, making the skin beneath the fingernail turn white from the pressure being applied. The paper occasionally ripped as words flowed with stunning speed.

Darren's mind had suddenly filled with visions and messages that arrived in stunning brilliance and clarity, enough to chill his body with icy tentacles despite the sweltering heat.

A small tremble had filled his body and he suddenly felt out of breath, anxious. He knew what was going to happen and prepared himself. A minute later, his hand had twitched and his mind went blank, filled with a sudden darkness.

Images pervaded the darkness with a feeling of hopelessness and a need to cry out, but being unable to, as though he were being suffocated, not allowed a single breath, buried beneath the corporeal weight of the images.

The pen made contact with the paper as the tale of another soul entered itself in the pages of Darren's notebook.

And his lungs began to burn.

Jerry Labonte started the day only wanting to drink a few beers, catch a few fish, and spend a few hours relaxing in the sun. Small quantities of each were plenty to relieve the tension of his hectic life.

He was the head of his own company—manufacturing pencils, of all things. But the pressures were still there to meet production quotas and deal with the tree huggers. His pencils were the traditional wood and graphite combinations and he was constantly pressured to conform to the advent of the mechanical pencil. Not a chance. The company had been passed down from his father and he wasn't about to give in.

A day on the lake was exactly what he needed. Just to get away—for a time, anyway.

He placed a twelve-pack into one end of the canoe—a traditional Old Town, straight from L.L.Bean in Freeport. The fishing gear followed, with two poles, a net, and tackle box. Then a cooler filled with a very light lunch.

Slacks rolled up to the mid-point of his calf, he pushed away from the shore of his summer camp and jumped into the canoe. Then paddled away.

A mist rose from the calm water as dawn made its silent entrance. Beneath its clear surface, boulders, once left by a melting glacier, littered the leafy bottom. The occasional shadow of a fish darted in and out of its natural shelter of waterlogged trees and nests of twisted branches.

In the distance, a water skier took advantage of the early morning water—plumes of white contrails followed closely behind.

Small bubbling noises erupted as Jerry brought the paddle through the water with soothing strokes. His favorite cove appeared around an outcropping of land a short time later, and his anxiety increased just knowing the success it had produced over the years.

Never a place to welcome direct sunlight, it seemed to harvest only the biggest of fish. The shadows touched his arms and sparked pleasant chills at the sudden change in temperature. The mouth of the cove emitted a boggy, almost unpleasant smell like a puff of bad breath. Not too bad once you got used to it, especially when there were monster bass lurking beneath the surface.

With the aid of an old paint can filled with concrete and a hundred feet of nylon rope, he set anchor.

One pole was fixed with a crank-bait, while the other was baited with a fat night crawler that still squirmed around the hook penetrating its segmented body. He cast the latter out first, letting it drop to the bottom and await any passing visitors. Before he used the crank-bait, he would have a beer . . . or three. It was hard to take sips of beer with constant casting. He would just sit back for a while and enjoy himself while keeping an eye out for the bending of the baited pole.

He purposely didn't eat anything before he started drinking; a quicker buzz meant a longer day of enjoying it. Six beers and no fish later, he felt just fine.

Time to start casting.

He brought his arm back and placed a precise cast to where the big ones always seemed to be. No luck on the first two casts (separated by another guzzle of beer), but the third changed his world.

The crank-bait landed near the shadowy presence of a stump. He let it sink below the surface and did a quick retrieve with the reel, jerking the end of the pole as he would a piece of yarn to a kitten.

BAM!

A quick splash of a tail and his pole was almost pulled from his hand. He immediately stood up in the canoe and yanked back to set the hook. Leaning too much to one side, water started pouring over the lip of the canoe. He countered his weight to prevent the canoe from flipping over, but only lost his balance. The combination of movements sent the canoe rocking and him falling backward.

As he fell, he realized what a stupid thing he had done. As his head struck the pointed edge of the canoe, he wondered why he had decided to go fishing. As he fell into the water, he tried to scream, but couldn't.

His lungs filled with water and two air bubbles floated past his vision to burst on the surface. The branch of a sunken tree caught his pant leg and wouldn't let go. In a sudden panic, he struggled to move, but other branches ensnared his free leg and both sleeves of his flannel shirt.

And held him prisoner with gnarled and twisted fingers.

Darren blinked his eyes, winced at the sudden brightness. His head felt a bit fuzzy. Oddly enough, he felt dehydrated and took a long swallow of his Pepsi, now warm. He wished he had some water, but feared that if he took a sip, he might taste the tangy substance of the lake water instead. Warm Pepsi was fine. He looked down at the pages open upon his lap and was impressed, but not completely surprised at the amount he had written.

"How long was I under?"

"Only about ten minutes," Andrea said. "You all right?"

Now he was surprised. "Yeah, I think so. Pretty intense though."

"I can imagine," Andrea said, having witnessed the speed of his writing and the constant flipping of pages. It was all she could do to concentrate on driving and not stare dumbfounded as Darren transcribed. More than once she had to take her foot off the gas pedal and slow down.

Darren released the pen, flexed his fingers, and cracked his knuckles. Rolled his neck and placed his head back against the headrest.

His hand twitched again.

"Already?" he asked.

Chapter 37

Nestled a few miles off the interstate within a jagged perimeter of peeling white birch trees, more than a few souls awaited the arrival of two important people. The pain that they had become numb to over time reached a new level, cut deeper into the thin layers of protection that had grown over old wounds. They screamed from the pain, screamed more from the torture of their souls. And screamed to be released.

They were anxious to join the mission caught among recent whispers, but knew each of their tales could not be told. Most were willing to settle for their names alone being placed as entries into the beautiful work in progress, and for most, this would be enough.

But there was one . . .

. . . a burning soul that refused to have only his name written between the entries. He needed his tale to be told, to be relieved of the guilt.

He had burned for far too long.

Burning, burning. Flesh melting, then reforming.

Darren saw a stake of flesh much like the one his grandfather had been attached to in his dream. Other souls in their human forms surrounded this one, hanging from stakes, forming a disjointed circle as though they were meant to see each other burning in a painful mirror-image of their own melting bodies. They screamed, veins bursting through weakened skin, bodies thrusting against restraints.

The stake in the middle held an occupant who had long since given up screaming, as though he had gotten used to the pain. His skin blistered and popped and yellow fluid drooled from open wounds without so much as a quiver of discomfort. His limbs hung loosely beneath their binds, unmoving. As the flesh disappeared, his blackened eyes hung from their sockets, then were sucked back into his newly formed face, only for it to happen again and again.

Arthur Hamilton constantly relived the nightmare that had delivered him to the bowels of the universe: a sinful night of passionate pleasures he was ready to confess to.

His wife had loved for him to tie her up while they were making love. Not too unusual in the present day. However, this was during the early 1900s before even bikinis were thought of, before infamous talk shows where it was common to openly discuss your sexual preferences or hidden desires in front of a camera as an entire nation watched. A time when to partake in this activity would surely buy a one-way ticket south of Heaven.

For the Hamiltons, Monday through Friday were always the same: work, sleep, work, and a little more sleep if the neighbor's dog quit his fucking barking before having to work again. Working their fingers to the bone just to have enough money to pay the mortgage. But when Saturday night came around, oh, the fun they had!

They enjoyed the tingling sensations they received from preparing to do something sinful and knowing they would not get caught. Feelings they welcomed as an erotic appetizer, allowing them to peruse the possibilities before assuming their various positions and activities.

The ritual began with slow music, as they occupied the dinner table decorated with the best dinnerware they could afford. After a few glasses of wine to get rid of the few inhibitions they had, they'd leave a trail of clothes into the bedroom, loins stirring.

Arthur would watch as Geraldine got on her knees and scooped out their favorite box from beneath the bed. She made a point to exaggerate her bending over by sticking her behind in the air and giving it a seductive wiggle, allowing Arthur to see her already wet crevice.

The box soon occupied the center of the bed, cover opened, two pairs of eager eyes peering inside, deciding which utensil to use. Crude instruments had been made from materials they had found around the house, all small enough for any type of insertion they were craving. Four pieces of nylon rope were also inside, but were hardly used. Instead, Mr. Hamilton liked to use the bed sheets for tying—they didn't leave a mark.

This particular Saturday night was unlike any of their previous experiences. It was the first time Geraldine requested a rope be placed around her neck. It was also the only time Arthur nearly balked at one of her ideas.

But didn't.

It wasn't long before he had both of her arms tightly secured to two bedposts, Geraldine facing away from him with a pillow placed on its side in front of her to prevent her head from striking the wooden headboard. He tied her ankles as well, but allowed enough play for her to move rhythmically on her knees the way he liked. To add an extra bit of flavor, he tied one of his shirts over her eyes.

He began the endeavor using the small utensils from the box, teasing her with quick, yet gentle insertions wherever he felt like it, then making her wait in anticipation. Soon becoming too much even for him, he eased his way inside her, enjoying the shiver that went through her body, the arching of her back, the soft moaning. Not wanting to ruin the event with an early release, he maintained a jittery, yet controlled pace.

When a seductive snarl erupted from Geraldine, he was unable to contain himself any longer. He reached inside the box while still applying gentle thrusts, and grabbed one piece of nylon rope. He almost came knowing what he was about to do with it. A few gentle whips upon her back let her know it was coming.

She moaned louder.

With shaking hands, he held both ends of the rope and tossed it over her head, letting it strike lightly against her breasts. He eased the rope back until it was at the base of her neck, then formed an "X" by crossing one end over the other.

She rolled her neck against the feel of the rope, hissed as though it burned her skin. A bead of sweat trickled from beneath the cover of her hair and continued between her shoulder blades as she tried to playfully pull against the restraints.

He pulled the ends of the rope away from each other and his pulse increased in conjunction with his thrusts.

He gave a gentle tug at first, not knowing what to expect. When she bucked, he was quick to apply another tug, more pressure this time. Random tugs with heavy thrusts in the interim provided the best results. She started to buck out of control as he pulled, released, pulled, released.

As he applied pressure for longer periods of time, Geraldine responded with gyrations that almost threw him off the bed. He couldn't believe how much she liked it and wondered how long he could actually hold the pressure, how long she wanted the pressure. He was building toward his own climax with small shudders. She was doing the same, but responded with only strangled grunts and violent bodily motions that were sending her limbs into frenzied spasms.

245

In the final moments of his orgasm, he imagined killing her, loved the sensation of power and the amount of fluids brewing that he'd ultimately spray into her from behind. He pumped harder, pulled the rope tighter, longer, and swooned in exquisite rapture.

As she fell limp, he exploded into her, livid with her for just falling on her stomach like that. Hadn't she enjoyed it?

Out of breath, he climbed around her and removed the blindfold, ready to yell at her for stopping just when he was coming. When he saw her eyes bulging out of her head, he reconsidered. His sweat suddenly turned cold. Sorrow came and went before an immeasurable hatred set in. He wanted her awake just for the opportunity to kill her again.

He knew he would spend the rest of his life in prison. No one would actually believe it was all her idea and was actually an accident, however bizarre. No woman of any integrity would allow herself into those situations, is what they would say.

Before they took him away, he would make most of his situation—she would have wanted him to. At the thought of it, his cock stood at attention.

He'd never been able to make love to a corpse.

Arthur Hamilton never made it to a trial. He opened the front door to get the morning newspaper and Geraldine's father met him with a double-barreled shotgun . . . and got away with it.

A tremor coursed through the macabre landscape as a piercing wail of agony erupted from Arthur's stake. At the sudden scream, silence saturated the air.

The binds securing him were severed with deafening snaps and Arthur peeled his skin away from the mass of flesh it had become a part of for so long. An enjoyable pain was exposed within eyes that had regained their focus and streamed with pent-up sorrow in the form of pure, cleansing tears.

Sins had been committed, confessed, and penance had been served.

Arthur Hamilton was forgiven.

Darren opened his eyes to another entry, another soul on their side among the other many names he had managed to scribble inside.

"What happened there?" asked Andrea, the hint of a grin barely masked.

"What? Why?" He sounded exhausted, his voice hoarse. He licked at dried, cracking lips.

"Sounded like you were getting a bit excited there for a minute."

"Oh," Darren said, scarlet decorating his face. "You wouldn't want to know." He turned away and stared out the passenger's window, flexing his hand.

She sensed his change in tone and decided not to press him any further. She meant to give him a friendly shake on the shoulder, but drew her hand back. Best to leave him alone for a while.

The sun was nearing the horizon, elongating shadows as clouds tried to build.

They would spend their final night on the road in Bangor to prepare themselves for the supposed portal that Darren had talked about. From Bangor, it was only two more hours to Durbin. If they started early, they would be able to face whatever was presented to them with plenty of daylight remaining.

The AM radio now picked up a fair number of stations. The weather didn't look good for the next few days. A small earthquake had registered at several geographic stations—

the chances for any aftershocks were extremely low. The Red Sox were actually in first place.

Andrea heard none of this, was only able to focus on the scratching of pen on paper.

Chapter 38

Like a swarm of worker bees flocking to the queen, hundreds of souls in the form of glowing spheres of light searched for the beacon of luminescence that was Faye Clark, seeking instructions. She welcomed them like the children she was never able to have, embracing each with brilliant waves of pulsating love.

They were testing their abilities with each passing second, preparing for an inevitable battle. More or less equal to the size of a dust particle, they seemed utterly harmless. But when joined together, were able to equal the force of a lightning bolt or a blast of pure invisible energy, powerful enough to strike down the Devil. Or those that thought they were the Devil . . . like Francis Carlson.

Movements were quick and exact, like the fluttering wings of insects, only taking the shape of their former selves when needed. Assuming a human shape required too much precious energy, causing movements to become slow and sluggish. They saved this for when the living needed the evidence or comfort of a tangible form. Or when they could pass easily through the gateway provided as the human mind dreamed, open to anything and unhindered. Or, as some had recently witnessed, when they were needed as guides, leading a remembered soul to the other side.

Though they were all bathed within a sphere of light, a different kind of existence, every one of them knew everything about the others: what they looked like, what they had done, where they had been. The only items in question were where they were all going, or if this was it. And could they stop what they were up against?

They could only gather as many souls as possible and attempt to destroy the presence consistently pulling at them. Fate would prove which way the scale would lean. It had been done before, but the presence hadn't been as strong. It had kept quiet for centuries, feeding and fueling itself on the forgotten ones, the numbers of which were much more prevalent than before. People were too wrapped up in their daily lives to remember those that had preceded them.

Faye watched those surrounding her in a buzzing fury fall ever so slightly in their hovering paths, struggling just a bit harder to remain at her side as it pulled from below. Had they noticed?

Faye knew about the tremor that shook the state of Maine and worried about what the results would be. She saw the earth split an existing opening a bit wider and a mist rise in thick milky curls from below, spreading as it reached the surface.

A skinless hand reached for the edge of the earth, found it, and pulled itself up.

Then another.

Chapter 39

Farming fields were dulled a deeper shade of yellow as the sun bid farewell to the western sky, then disappeared completely as civilization presented itself in Bangor in the shapes of bigger buildings, bigger cars . . . bigger everything. Sprinkles of rain fell from the sky and low rumbles of thunder rolled in from the direction of the Atlantic Ocean.

Neon lights burned in the early dusk and the highway suddenly seemed congested. *People obviously have plenty of things to do,* Andrea thought, *except to visit any type of resting place for the deceased.* There were too many new shirts to buy, too many movies to see, and way too many e-mailed chain letters to answer to worry about such things.

Soon, they would all know.

She pulled into a Super 8, hopefully the last of any such establishments they would see for a while.

When she approached the reception desk, ignoring the two steps away from her the clerk took (most likely from her appearance or smell—or both), Andrea was unsure of what was going to come out of her mouth until the words were spoken, unable to be retrieved.

"Two rooms please, non-smoking."

Andrea busied herself with taking money out of her purse. She heard Darren shuffle his feet behind her, thought she actually heard his shoulders slump. The glare she felt on the back of her neck could have burned clear through to the other side. As much as she followed her instincts as a child to visit the dead, she did now and knew it was something that needed to be done.

"Is that all right with you?" she asked with a quick glance, toward Darren, making sure the appropriate amount of money was in hand—three times. Her face burned with shame. Darren was staring beyond the window near the entrance and only gave her a courteous nod when he knew she was looking. He was deflated, and for that she was sorry.

They entered rooms that were side by side to each other. The day had left each of them with a coating of rain, sweat and adrenaline—a sticky film they could almost peel away from their skin and wanted to be rid of quickly.

Hearing Andrea's door shut, Darren locked his and got undressed. His clothes could almost stand up by themselves. He thought about placing a chair on top of them to prevent his pants from running away with his shirt. He laughed at this thought, a certification of the day being long and tiring. Or, more likely: a way to forget that Andrea had opted to have her own room. He remembered his father telling him to swallow his pride and move on, and thought he finally knew what it meant.

He looked into the mirror above the vanity and pulled back as someone else stared back at him. He was reassured when he realized he was probably the only one in the world having just three strands of hair sticking out from his chest.

But still, his face was gaunt, almost ghoulish, as if he had filled the bottom inch below his eyes with eyeliner. His cheeks looked hollow, like he had lost a few pounds in the last few days. His hair was dry and wiry. He brushed his teeth with his eyes closed, refusing to look at himself, and shaved by guiding the razor with his free hand.

He didn't bother wiping the shaving cream from his face. Letting water drip from his chin, Darren walked into the shower and slid the fiberglass door closed. From beyond the wall of the tiny bathroom, he already heard the pipes groaning as Andrea started her own shower in the next room. He still couldn't stop himself from thinking about steaming droplets cascading down her body as she ran fingers through her hair.

Under his own stream of hot water, images of Andrea faded as he concentrated on shedding an old skin. Face turned upward, eyelids being pummeled by the comfortable sting of water under pressure, he did nothing but enjoy the spraying jet of water before even deciding to wash his hair or find the bar of soap.

Once showered, he put on clothes he would have paid a million dollars for, even if they were over a year old. They were clean. He placed the small pile of things from his previous pair of pants deep into the pocket of his clean pair: loose change, a pocketknife, and the piece of Albert's tombstone he had almost forgotten about. A small wave of sadness swept through him.

He went outside to wait for Andrea, stood below the small balcony of the room above, enjoying the sound and smell of the falling rain. The streets shone in the surrounding darkness, while sporadic bolts of lightning flashed in the night sky. Peaceful.

She came out of her room only moments later, hair still wet and a glow about her face. Darren's stomach twisted with something he had never felt.

Rather than climbing into the car for another ride to find someplace to eat, they opted for a Denny's adjacent to the motel's parking lot, walking at a slow trot to avoid being soaked by the rain. They ate in comfortable silence, avoiding each other's swollen, baggy eyes.

Fresh, warm sheets beckoned them as they called it a

night before eight o'clock. Darren didn't bother flicking through the channels before climbing into bed. He lay beneath the sheets, enjoying the swollen comfort of a new pillow. He stared at the ceiling, arms behind his head. Even the thought of actually thinking about something tired him. Within minutes, he was under the spell of a dreamless sleep.

Light coming between the crack of two drapes touched his eyes. He stirred, squinted into the light, and brought the covers over his eyes. Within the darkness provided by the covers, he pushed the light button on his watch and read the display: 7:00 a.m. Rain still pattered on the pavement outside.

Amazed he had slept so long, he still didn't want to leave the bed. He rolled over and tried to prolong his sleep. No use. To prove the point, there was a knock at the door.

"Darren, you ready?" Andrea. Up already.

He muffled a groan in response and another knock came. "Coming, coming." He opened the door just enough to peek outside, bed sheets wrapped around his waist. "Time to go, already?"

"Daylight's burning, time to round up the cattle."

"Oh yeah, almost forgot."

"I'll pay for the rooms and meet you in the lobby. I could use some coffee."

"Be right there," Darren said, eyes finally able to stay open on their own. Coffee actually sounded good.

They were the only two customers taking advantage of the small assortment of muffins, toast, and fruit offered on a wheeled cart. They sat alone at a small table and talked about the possibilities of the day. At times, it was as if they were talking about a fairy tale, pretending they would be fighting an evil villain. And succeeding of course, because that was how fairy tales ended: happily ever after.

He told her about Jerry Labonte and his accident on the lake, but left out the story of Arthur and Geraldine. She could read it later, if she liked.

"Well, we'll see what happens today, once we get there. You sure you still know where this place is? We should be able to get there by ten o'clock," Andrea said, consulting the clock hanging behind the breakfast cart.

Darren nodded. He still remembered the chants coming from below the hole. How he ran with the others, vowing never to return. Something he could never forget, no matter how much he tried.

They placed their bags into the trunk as quickly as possible. Andrea shrank against the coldness of the raindrops landing heavily on the back of her neck.

The inside of the car smelled musty, old. Sweaty. A raindrop fell from her hair and found its way inside the front of her shirt and she shivered. She picked the ignition key from between many others and inserted it. Turned the key. No response, save the red check-engine light. Her heart crept into her throat and she forced herself to calm down.

"Come on Betsy, one more time."

She cranked again. The engine teased her with a taunting whir. She pumped the gas pedal a few times.

Nothing.

"Pop the hood," Darren said, opening and shutting the door behind him as fast as he could manage, eyes squinting against the rain.

She did so, still attempting to crank the engine.

Nothing.

As Darren looked beneath the hood, she rested her head

on her hands at the top of the steering wheel. Said a silent prayer.

"Try it again," Darren called, his voice almost drowned out by the rain and the beating of her heart.

She did.

Only sinister whirring and raindrops drumming on the roof of the Plymouth prevailed.

"Not today, not today," she prayed. "Goddammit!" She hit the steering wheel. Darren looked at her. She raised her hands and shrugged her shoulders.

Darren slammed the hood and ran into the car, sitting beside her once again. "Couldn't see anything unusual; maybe it's your starter."

"Whatever the hell that is. Dammit!"

"I can look again—" Darren started.

"No, never mind." She wiped at a tear. "Sorry, it just pisses me off."

They listened to the rain.

A quick tapping on the window made her jump. The look of the man peering inside made her back away from the window. He wore a full beard and flannel shirt that almost, but not quite, contained his round belly. A John Deere hat was perched, half-cocked, on his head. A dampened cigarette hung from his mouth. He spat it out when she opened the window just a crack.

"Where ya headed? I can probably give you a lift, if you're going south that is," he said as he pointed to the eighteen-wheeler behind him with his thumb. Rain dripped from the brim of his stained hat. "Been on the road for a while and wouldn't mind the company." His voice was deep, scratchy, probably on account of too many smokes on the road.

"I don't know, maybe we should—" Andrea began,

looking for help from Darren. He shrugged his shoulders.

"Wouldn't be any trouble, got plenty 'a room."

They took everything but their dirty clothes from the trunk of the car and didn't speak until they were well within the safety of the truck's cab, Darren in the middle and Andrea on the passenger's side.

Andrea tried to casually move the empty cigarette wrappers on the floor with her feet. The inside of the Duster smelled like a blossoming flower on a spring day compared to the inside of the cab. The ashtray was overflowing; remnants of chips and doughnuts littered the floor. Somewhere beneath the clutter, traces of a once-plush blue carpet tried to look at her from beneath the mess.

A CB set on channel 19 hung from the roof, with its mike dangling within easy reach of the driver. A clipboard filled with numbers and addresses on multicolored sheets lay on the dashboard. Taped to the center of the steering wheel was a picture of a woman and a young girl. Andrea perched herself on the edge of the large seat, hand well within reach of the door handle . . . just in case.

As opposed to Darren, who was anything but nervous about riding with a stranger, instead marveling like a child on how high they were above the road. Andrea watched as he all but drooled over the cord hanging from the ceiling of the cab. The cord that would produce the furious tone from an exhaust pipe that looked strangely like a teakettle. It was almost like seeing a child eye the special jar of the most expensive candy on the top shelf of a store. A shelf he could climb, if no one was looking.

"You can pull it if you like," the trucker said, giggling, then coughing. He finished making some entries on the clipboard and placed it back on the dash. Cleared his throat.

Darren couldn't resist any longer and pulled. The sound of the air horn was felt as well as heard. Andrea jumped in the seat beside him and signaled for him to let go with a wave of her hand. He let go, elated.

"Feel better?" Andrea asked, exaggerating the cleaning of her ear.

"Much," Darren answered, laughing.

The trucker keyed the ignition and the rumbling entered their bones and tickled their fannies. Andrea kept her eyes on her car as they left the parking lot, not helping the feeling of sadness that overcame her. For so many years she had driven that car, the only car she had ever owned. As mad as she was for it to break down at the most inopportune time, she was already missing it. She almost thought it was her own damn fault for even *thinking* about trading it in. Go figure. She would have to return and get it later.

The wipers moved with stunning speed.

"Name's Earle," the trucker said once they were on the highway. "Earle Dumaine." He offered a hand to Darren.

Darren took it. "Darren Jacobs. And this is my . . . friend, Andrea Varney."

Earle tipped his hat to her, being too far away to shake her hand.

"Nice to meet you," Andrea said, smiling, though she still felt uncomfortable.

"Don't mind the mess, I don't clean it till I'm done with the run. Then I make her shine until the next trip. My daughter loves to wash this thing, tells me to save it for us to do together." He tapped the picture as he said this, then went to his shirt pocket and dug out a cigarette, opening his corner window to let out the smoke.

Andrea sat farther back into her seat and let her shoulders drop a fraction of an inch, and saw Earle smile as he

noticed her relaxing . . . somewhat. She tried to return one of her own.

"What you got there?" Earle said, seeing Darren's hands toying with the edges of a new notebook. The older one was beneath it.

"Oh," Darren began, "a kind of diary, I guess. You probably wouldn't believe me if I told you the whole of it. Don't know if I do yet, either." Andrea nudged him with her knee gently below his calf. He looked back at her, trying to apologize without words.

"I'd probably believe a lot more than you think. Seen a lot, traveling these roads. Been doin' it most of my life. But, that's fine if you wanna keep it to yourself and all."

"How much does one of these big rigs carry?" Darren said instead, with a tone of genuine curiosity. Andrea tried her best to at least appear interested, but doubted she was able to.

"Well, under the hood of this beautiful Freightliner," Earle began, caressing the steering wheel, "is a turbo-charged Detroit diesel which allows me to take on loads of up to . . ."

Andrea closed her ears to the rest, well beyond the conversation by now, staring out the passenger's window, transfixed by a continuous rivulet of water that formed, traveled the length of the window, then disappeared at the window's edge. But she did remember to nod when she thought it was appropriate. Darren seemed to be enjoying his elevated view of the road and even the one-sided conversation he was having with Earle.

Earle lit another cigarette, either choosing to remain silent, concentrating on his smoking, or thinking about what to talk about next. It had probably been a while since someone had occupied the cab with him. Hank Williams Junior sang to them via cassette in the radio, the treble a little too harsh, the lyrics and music distorting every now and then. It had been played too many times in the radio, but Earle hummed to it anyway, sometimes knowing exactly when to distort the lyrics.

Earle stopped humming. Andrea felt him correct the rig a little to get it straightened out.

"Miss Varney . . . he okay?" His voice had a slight, childish edge to it—an edge that returned Andrea to the space of the cab.

"Oh—" Andrea didn't know how to continue. Darren was slumped forward. "Shit," she said.

"Is he retard—handicapped?"

"No." She chewed her lip.

"Do I need to wake him up or what?" His voice rose in pitch again, eyes darting back and forth between Darren and the road, an occasional glimpse toward Andrea.

"No!"

"Suit yourself." He tried hard to stare at the road ahead, hands attached to the steering wheel, but much like Andrea was doing, kept peeking at the words being scrawled upon the paper, at the names—so many names—at the pages turning. And turning.

"There's a cemetery nearby, that's where the names are coming from." Her voice had a comforting tone to it—intentional. But her breath wavered, her heart picked up an extra beat. "You probably wouldn't understand, but he'll be fine."

"If you say so." He swallowed hard.

Ten minutes later, Darren came to and sat upright.

He looked to Earle and said, "What's up?" a slight grin causing his cheeks to dimple. "Sorry about that," he continued. "It happens every now and then. It's like people forcing themselves into my head as if they're in a hurry to get to work and crowding into the only car of an already-packed subway train." He squeezed the bridge of his nose and looked at Andrea. She only stared ahead, mouth agape, doing her best to ignore what had just happened. Hoped Earle would do the same.

Earle shook his head, reached for another cigarette, smoked it down to the filter in rapid drags, then lit another. He turned up the radio and continued driving. They passed the exits for Waterville, then Augusta, twenty miles farther. Darren had one more episode in between, now almost becoming a normal activity within the truck. Earle only glanced at him curiously then smoked another cigarette at a relatively normal pace.

Even this far south, the rain continued unabated. Exit 13 to Lewiston, Maine was two miles ahead according to the sign, and couldn't have presented itself any sooner for all of them. Andrea and Darren were almost home and Earle Dumaine would be able to continue on with his route. Alone.

The remaining distance of highway whisked below them. Then began to tremble.

Chapter 40

At first, Earle thought it was the surface of the pavement causing the trembling sensation, knowing road construction to be going on this time of year. The roads were scraped, paved, and smoothed at feverish speeds while workers tried to complete as much resurfacing as possible before the winter freeze set into the ground, making it futile to even attempt to chip at the solidified earth. The work, though needed, had often caused Earle to barely meet the timing his route required. This length of interstate probably needed some work.

Then he thought it was a flat in one of the front tires, the vibration getting worse, but not quite feeling like the thumping of a sack of potatoes that usually accompanied the demise of a punctured tire. And he hadn't heard the shotgun blast of the tire blowing either, or any calls from truckers behind him. This vibration held an audible quality to it that no tire would ever produce had it gone flat, or even come apart. He began to slow the rig down anyway, unsure of what to expect. If something was going on with his rig, he didn't want to fight for control with so much weight going forward. To stop on a dime, he could not. If he tried, the rig would only jackknife.

And a jackknifing eighteen-wheeler could kill people.

"What's going on?" asked Andrea.

Earle said nothing. He didn't know.

The sound of the slowing rig rose above the increasing vibrations, almost comforting. There was a tension felt among all of them, as if they expected the truck to begin hydroplaning or skidding out of control.

One mile still remained until the exit.

The whir of the slowing tires on the pavement and sound of the air brakes filled the silence, familiar sounds calming his nerves for a time. A time cut short as the pavement in front of the rig began to separate.

The interstate split open in front of them as if north and south were fighting for control in a game of tug of war on a monstrous scale. The truck shook violently, with only the seat belts keeping them firmly seated inside. It tilted to one side, barely missing the crack nearest to them and seemed to be surfing on a giant swell of pavement.

A car on their left tried in vain, with smoking brakes and squealing tires, to avoid the gaping crack that was only getting bigger. They saw its hood disappear, then come to a jarring halt reminiscent of footage from San Francisco the entire world had seen.

Earthquake.

But Maine *never* had earthquakes! Not of this magnitude, anyway.

Andrea felt nauseous. She placed her arm on Darren's leg, searching for comfort. Feeling him gave her a sense of security, a sense that she wasn't alone in this. She looked out her window, unable to keep from wondering what fate the people in the car had just endured. And who was in it?

The six-foot drop-off into the ditch loomed to the side of her. On instinct, she leaned the other way, turning her face into Darren's shoulder, closing her eyes. It didn't matter. She could feel the truck getting unbalanced, teetering on the edge. She leaned as far into him as possible, hoped her body would be enough to act as a counterweight.

It wasn't.

A muffled scream came from Earle as he fought for control, but he finally faced the inevitable and threw his arms up in front of his face. Darren did the same, and not because he saw Earle doing it. The ditch was coming at them quickly as the truck succumbed to its own weight and tipped toward the passenger's window.

In the moments of the truck rolling onto its side, Andrea, Darren, and Earle communicated through the use of a short, simultaneous scream. It wasn't enough to block out the sounds coming at them from all directions. They still heard the windows breaking and the passenger's mirror being crushed beneath the awesome weight of the truck—merely an eggshell. The gray sky was now perpendicular to the windshield. The truck seemed to have a voice of its own, as a deep moan was heard from metal bending and breaking, as if it were a large dog rolling onto its back to have its belly scratched.

The slick surface of the ground allowed the rig to slide down the ditch instead of doing a complete roll. They were still moving, sliding. All eyes were closed until the truck came to a solid halt where the ground leveled out once again.

"Everybody okay?" Earle was the first to break the sudden quiet. He hung onto his armrest, keeping most of his weight off Darren. Darren seemed all right, hanging from his seat belt, resting on Andrea's side. A trace of blood flowed down the side of Andrea's head where she had hit the window.

"I think so," Andrea said, wiping at the wetness. She would live.

"Me too. The belt's cutting into my side, though. I can barely breathe. Andrea, you unbuckle first, then I'll try to stand up without falling on you," Darren said, surprisingly calm. He still clutched one of his notebooks. The other was next to Andrea's head, against the broken window, almost slipping through and becoming lost beneath the weight of the truck.

Andrea unbuckled, then managed to tuck her body underneath the dashboard. Darren unbuckled and placed his feet onto the passenger's window, careful of the broken shards. Grass and mud were poking through some of the cracks in the window. He stood up within the cab, reached down, and picked up the other notebook, brushing off some dirt.

"Let me try to climb out before I crush you both with my fat ass," Earle said, already unfastening his belt and unrolling the window. He pushed his pack of smokes deep into his flannel pocket—they had almost fallen out.

They welcomed Earle's humor and the picture they were provided while he climbed through his window, just able to see the crack of his behind, filling the space of the entire window frame. Andrea looked away, finding the floor of the truck—now at her side—suddenly interesting.

When she was sure only Earle's feet remained to go through the window, Andrea searched among her things thrown haphazardly within the cab. The clothes were left behind, but Andrea remembered her prized possession: the box of headstone pieces. Ensuring the lid was still securely in place, she passed them up to Earle, then followed. Getting a boost from Darren, still standing on the broken passenger's window, she reached for the driver's armrest, using it and the steering wheel as leverage, and pulled herself up. Earle was standing on the door on the outside, offering a very large hand. She jumped to the ground and immediately placed a hand over her mouth and nose.

Darren pulled himself out of the window next and soon

stood beside Earle, hanging onto the large mirror for balance, his face becoming a sudden shade of yellow. Only Earle failed to cover his mouth and nose. It seemed he had smelled far worse things in his travels. They all stood below the left front tire, still spinning upon the axle, and surveyed the destruction, or what they could see of it.

The rain continued as a low-lying fog spread from the crack in the interstate, carrying with it the stench of an unearthed sewer. The fog was thick, allowing only flashing hazard lights to be seen in circular pulses. Of the few cars near them, some were running, but remained in their spots, as if waiting for the pavement to knit itself back together so they could continue on their way. A small number of shapes were cutting their way through the fog in search of accidents, injuries. Fatalities.

The air contained a silence almost as thick as the fog. They stood in the recent aftermath, knowing it was too soon to hear any sirens, let alone people to know about what had just happened. How far the quake had reached outside of its epicenter was anyone's guess. These things just didn't happen in this part of the country.

A crying cut into the fog with the sharpness of a surgical instrument.

A baby.

Andrea swallowed hard, immediately moving toward the screaming. She knew where it was coming from, remembered the car being swallowed whole.

"Come on," she yelled, handing her box of stones to Earle, her words quieted by the thickening fog. Earle and Darren quickly followed as she disappeared into the gray matter in front of them.

She regretted running, as deep breaths of the smell were allowed deeper into her lungs. She slowed down, not only because of the stench, but also because the crack would appear out of nowhere if she went too fast. The baby continued its cries and Andrea used them to guide her along, waving a hand in front of her face to rid heavy tendrils of fog from her view. She almost fell into the crevice when her right foot came upon only air. She leaned back, catching herself. Darren bumped against her.

By the dull glow of the dome light, she saw the vague outline of a small car. The passenger's door was jarred open from the violence of the impact. Between the door and the frame of the car, a leg was twisted into an undefined shape. Blood saturated and stood out against a white stocking.

Andrea let her feet find the trunk of the car and slid down the passenger's side, hands against the car as she sidestepped to the door. The ear-shattering squeal produced as she opened the car door increased the volume and intensity of the baby's screams.

"I'm coming, baby, it's okay." She hoped her words sounded more comforting than she thought they were. It seemed to work as the baby quieted. Andrea heard quick draws of breath as she supposed it tried to determine who she was.

Her hand slipped off the handle and the door slammed against the twisted leg with a thump that made her cringe. The leg was almost severed at the kneecap.

The baby began screaming again.

"Hush, hush. It's going to be all right."

With the determination that existed in mothers or those who desperately wanted to be, Andrea climbed inside the car and onto the lap of a middle-aged woman. She stared into the woman's lifeless eyes and looked away when she felt tears begin to gather. Next to her was a man dressed in a suit, his head dented and leaking from the blow of the

267

steering wheel. A tooth hung from his chin, attached to something red and stringy. Small, congested breaths came from his chest as he tried hard to stay awake. His eyes closed every few seconds while his hands shook upon his lap. Andrea couldn't see his legs—they were underneath the tangled conglomeration of the steering wheel and dashboard.

"You need any help down there?" the heavy voice of Earle asked.

"We'll need some medical help here soon," Andrea said, leaning toward the door to avoid yelling into the baby's ears. "I think the baby's okay, just shaken up."

She avoided going into more detail as the father was barely hanging on, in and out of consciousness, gurgling sounds now evident with each shallow breath. Unsure of what he could hear or not, she played it safe and mentioned nothing about his or the mother's condition.

A boy. The baby produced a toothless grin as the buckle was undone from his car seat and he was swept within two loving arms. He had the hiccups.

"There, there, baby doll," Andrea said, holding him tight against her chest, trying to block the view of his parents. She wrapped him in a blanket decorated with smiling yellow ducks that was once folded neatly next to him.

She welcomed the smell of the baby and the softness of his sparsely populated head of hair under her chin. Taking a moment to herself, she gathered her senses. Weaving out from between the parents, daring not to hold the baby with anything less than two hands, she used only her elbows to push against the seats and the dashboard until she was pushing against the door. The rain seemed to have eliminated some of the smell and the distant wail of a siren was heard, along with the churning rotors of a helicopter.

She covered the baby's head against the rain and tucked the ends of the blanket back into place where it had come loose. She kissed the top of his head. Then used her butt to push against the side of the car and move forward until she was in a position to hand the baby to Earle.

"Hey there, little buddy," Earle said, already making googly eyes at him. Andrea was beginning to like Earle.

She took Darren's hand as he kneeled before the edge of the crevice and tried to walk up the short distance of jagged ground. Bits of rock and wet send fell into her shoes. When she tried to shake some of it loose, a cold hand grabbed her ankle.

Chapter 41

"Hurry up!" Darren shouted with three high-pitched squeals.

Andrea tried to pull against the sudden restraint, but it was too strong. A nail grazed the top of her ankle as she struggled. She wanted to look back, wanted to believe the father of the boy had come to and only wanted help before it was too late. But something inside her knew this wasn't true, knew that if she looked back she would be horrified.

And she was.

Lidless eyes glared into hers from beneath the car and would not allow her to pull away. They were powerful, emitting strength beyond measure—like the grip around her ankle. She imagined her flesh puffing grotesquely between its fingers, similar to a water balloon in the hands of a child.

Its arm stretched as she pulled, muscles twinkling with moisture, pulling her toward it. Bits of dirt were being soaked into the surface of its muscles. Illuminated by the glow of the dome light inside the car, it looked like some mutated night crawler that had fallen under the predatory beam of a child's flashlight searching for fishing bait. There were no lips to cover the serrated teeth, no cheeks to conceal the hollow of the cheekbones. A tongue slithered at her obscenely then shrank back into its throat with a disgusting slurp.

Andrea forced her eyes away from the hypnotic glare that beckoned her. Her grip slipped from Darren's hand and she shrieked. Kicked. It still pulled at her, the hand now at the calf of her leg. It was pulling itself out of the ground from below the car, piles of dirt forming at its waist where it was still partly below the surface. She didn't want to imagine what would happen if it did break free or what it would do to her.

"What the *fuck* is that?" Earle shouted his surprise, but did remember to place a hand over one of the baby's ears hidden beneath the blanket.

Darren was trying to reach into his pocket with his free hand. He kept his eyes locked onto hers. They got larger when her hand slid from his grasp another inch. He dug deeper into his jeans, one leg extended while he still kneeled on the other. Darren pulled a knife out of his pocket, almost losing it in his rain-slicked hand. He pulled at the single blade, with his bottom teeth catching on the edge usually meant for a fingernail, and pried it open until the blade snapped firmly in place. Reaching for it, Andrea prayed with silent mumbling that it wouldn't get lost in the exchange.

Her fist closed upon the knife with a speed that brought Darren's hand back in a hurry. Pulling against the gruesome hand that still held fast, she plunged the three-inch blade into a spot just above the wrist. If it bled, she couldn't tell. Its muscular covering matched any color of blood that she had ever seen. All she cared about was that it let her go.

A guttural combination of a scream and a snarl roared from its chest, but its grip only tightened. Her calf burned as a lengthened nail sank easily through her pants and into her muscle, slowly slicing her open with a downward stroke. Screaming as well, Andrea slapped at it with the knife, driving it in with short, quick arcs. Still burning, the pain spiked before the creature finally did let go, shaking its hand in an effort to dislodge the knife.

Teeth gnashing together, it gave one more flick of its

tongue with an angry hiss, then lost interest in Andrea. She took the advantage and climbed in two giant steps against the side of the crevice and into Darren's arms as he caught her. She looked down, far enough away from the edge to avoid any more intimate relations with the skinless monster below and to make certain it wasn't about to follow her. Muscles tight, adrenaline pumping in explosive torrents, she was ready to run.

It had found something else to keep it busy.

Andrea saw its backside, muscles contracting, glistening as it reached for the leg dangling in the doorway. The final piece of flesh snapped like a rubber band as the beast twisted and pulled the leg from the kneecap and jammed it into its mouth, gnawing on it like some starved animal. Andrea turned away, sickened.

Prying herself from Darren's arms, she limped lightly to-ward Earle and looked him in the eyes, noticing the slighter shade of white he had become and the way he ignored the baby pulling at his beard in what had to be painful tugs. Andrea's box of gravestones was still clutched in one hand, and it didn't surprise her that he didn't ask what was inside.

"That was only one of them, and if we don't find the source of the others pretty soon, the entire world could be in some trouble," Andrea said in a monotone. She looked to the thing feeding below her, knowing she didn't need to prove anything. As though it knew it was being watched, the beast disappeared into the hole it had emerged from. A stench was left in its wake, along with a ragged shoe that once belonged to the mother inside the car. Andrea covered the bottom of her nose with the backs of two fingers.

Earle only stared back at her with a blank face. "Could be worse I guess—it could have been having *you* for lunch, instead," he said, trying to smile. The corners of his mouth rose briefly then fell as if exhausted.

Darren took the baby from Earle's large hands.

"What do we do with our new friend?" Darren asked, letting the baby wrap a small fist around his index finger. Andrea saw that the rest of the baby was hidden beneath a blanket sparkling with gathering moisture. So much so that the ducks really did appear to be swimming. They needed to get him someplace warm.

The sirens came to a halt after the final wails from an ambulance and two state trooper vehicles. A helicopter flew low to the ground, possibly searching for a suitable landing pad. The remnants of the fog were whisked away by the speed of the rotors.

"We've got to get out of here without too much questioning, so don't mention the critter we just saw." She knew they would all prefer to forget the thing in the ground as soon as possible. Although, the way the back of her leg was on fire, it wasn't going to be today. "I think I'll give the baby to the paramedics and explain the situation with his parents, maybe even get a bandage for my leg," Andrea said, peeling her pants away from the wound. "Then we need to find a way out of here."

Two paramedics were trying to evaluate the situation before climbing into the crooked smile of a fracture in the ground, clearly something they weren't used to dealing with. They had yet to see the hole beneath the car, and Andrea wasn't about to help them with that particular detail just yet.

She spoke with one of the paramedics briefly, receiving a nod of understanding. Andrea gave the boy a farewell hug and kiss on the forehead before placing him into two rubber-gloved hands. She wiped her eyes, then followed the paramedic back to the rear entrance of the ambulance and received a roll of gauze from an EMT readying the ambulance for some passengers who would probably need only a black, zippered bag.

People started to get out of their cars, able to finally see through the haze and realizing they wouldn't be leaving just yet. State troopers were questioning groups that were huddled together, trying to determine what had just happened, as if they couldn't see the gaping crack in the highway. Reinforcements could be heard in the distance.

Darren and Andrea used this time to make a slow exit, out of view from the authorities, without being too secretive. They'd wait for someone to be through with questioning, so they could hitch another ride.

"Sorry I can't help you any more than I have," Earle said. "I gotta tend to my truck and find a way to give the boss a call and help get my rig back on its wheels. Please tell me you'll find whatever the hell was under there and kill the goddamn thing. You seem to know more about it and I'd rather stay as far away from *that* as I can. Don't plan on staying nearby for any long period of time, if you know what I mean." He was talking fast and curling at a length of beard with a finger, but did produce a very genuine smile.

"Thanks Earle. Thanks for everything, and we'll try," Andrea said.

"Thanks for letting me toot the horn," said Darren, blushing.

"No problem, son, you take care now." He turned and headed toward his truck while removing his John Deere hat, scratching the top of his head as he looked at his truck lying on its side. It looked like a giant beast slain by a mighty sword. They saw Earle's shoulders rise in a tired inhale, then watched as he reached for a cigarette and rubbed at his pockets in search of a lighter.

"Oh shit, my notebooks," Darren said in surprise.

They were near the edge of the crevice. One book was open, its pages turning in the breeze before being weighed down by drops of rain. The other was beneath it, teetering on the edge. He ran to get them.

Andrea sat down heavily onto the embankment on the side of the interstate, leaning against the rough, paper-like surface of a birch tree, which marked the edge of a small forest between the interstate and the outer edges of Durbin. She had one pant leg up, wincing as she wrapped the gauze around the fresh wound in her calf. Darren joined her and together they watched the aftermath of what had placed them here. They listened to the drone of activity, still not believing what they had seen. The rain slowly tapered to a soft drizzle, but a look to the darkened sky hinted at more to come.

Andrea rested her chin on the edge of her box of gravestones. Watching people huddled together, some leading children ahead to prevent losing them, and others keeping their children within the safety of their vehicles, she realized she and Darren were part of something completely different from what the lives of the others contained. They had no idea what was going on, but Andrea suddenly wished she were as ignorant as the rest of them. She was holding a box of gravestones for Christ's sake! And Darren held within his hands a diary written by the dead. What were they doing and what the hell was the world coming to? She had no desire to spoil the tranquility of ignorance the others were swimming in, didn't want to involve anyone else if she didn't need to. God knew Earle would have quite a few sleepless nights ahead of him.

"How far is it to the pit?" she asked.

Darren was picking at the papery sheets of bark from the

tree Andrea was leaning against. One of many that seemed to guard the entrance to these woods. Beyond them, Eastern white pines dominated the forest, darkening an already gloomy interior.

"Couple of miles, I guess. If I remember right, the edge of the cemetery where I first met Albert also borders this same patch of woods. But the trail I had taken then is probably hidden beneath the overgrowth by now," Darren said.

Andrea stood up, favoring one leg, hissing in discomfort as she brushed away loose dirt and pine needles from her butt and legs. The gravestones rattled inside the box.

"Let's go, shouldn't be dark for a while."

Darren grimaced, but followed.

With clouds getting a darker shade of gray and drizzle returning to rain, the forest just beyond the interstate swallowed Darren and Andrea within two steps. They were thankful for the thick ceiling now hovering over them as they created their own path.

They listened to the rain, but felt not a drop.

Chapter 42

Heavy layers of pine needles covered the forest floor, like a protective blanket draped over the vulnerable earth below, and cushioned their footsteps. The rain had silenced any critters lurking about, leaving them feeling alone in another plane of existence, a world dominated by things much bigger than they were. An occasional tree that had finally given in to age was heard with a violent snap every so often and made them jump every time.

They used casual conversation to fill the silence.

"Do you still know how to get there?" Andrea asked while stepping over the gnarled skeleton of a fallen tree. A few dried-up leaves clung on to their mother branch in a desperate attempt at survival. Her leg kicked a branch and one leaf fell to its death. *And then there were three,* she thought as she clutched the trunk of a living tree for balance. She heard branches crunch as her foot came to rest on another tree's weathered remains. It sounded much bigger than it actually was.

"I don't know. It's been a while. Looks like everything's changed," Darren replied. "I used to see stuff people had left behind through the trails. Cigarette butts, wrappers, that kinda stuff. Doesn't look like many people travel through the woods much anymore. I don't even see anything that looks like a trail."

"Too much TV in the world I guess. And computers, of course. No one wants to live with the basics of life anymore. They only seem determined to create some alternate dimension with a blinking cursor as a gateway. Except for term papers, kids don't visit the library or even seem to want to read anymore. They'd rather have someone read it to them and be able to pause the story with a click of a mouse." Andrea was disheartened, remembering the look, smell, and feel of the library. She hoped her assistant was taking good care of the place she termed her second home. Her mood brightened somewhat and her pace increased, as she knew she would walk through those doors very soon. Tomorrow, if she were lucky. Unless . . . She stopped the thought before it could develop. Everything was going to be just fine.

But still, her stomach tied another loose knot.

Another tree took the leap of faith and crossed to the other side in a crash that lingered in their ears. Or was it something else? Andrea thought she heard faint rustling sounds coming after the snap of the tree. Everything was magnified tenfold in the woods. It was probably just animals scurrying from the noise. She imagined a chipmunk running to another and exclaiming, "The sky is falling! The sky is falling!" in rambling chipmunk chatter.

Her fingers came upon something softer than the bark she thought her fingers were touching. She snatched her hand away and looked to where her fingers were moments ago. Now they were sticky. Thick, shiny sap oozed from a misshapen, knotted area of a pine. It looked like some sort of deformed face staring back at her, swollen cheeks hiding the eyes and drool seeping from the lips. The sharp odor of pine made her grimace. She wiped the sticky substance on her pants, but the harder she tried, the more the sap spread, making her other fingers just as sticky. She reached to the ground and found some moist dirt to rub into the substance.

"Hey look at this," she heard Darren say. He was kneeling by a small stream and holding something. He turned a skull over within his hands, peering at the teeth. "Must be a deer, no canines," Darren said. A tooth fell into his hand. "Must have died a long time ago. I guess scavengers took the rest of it away."

Andrea raised an eyebrow, but didn't offer to touch it. She was still occupied with getting the rest of the sap off her fingers. Something bit the back of her neck and she slapped at it without thinking of the sap on her fingers. Now it was also in her hair.

"Damn sticky shit, it won't go away."

"Only lots of hot water and soap will get rid of it." Darren smiled at her antics. "I used to come home covered in the stuff, if I was lucky. I had the habit of finding poison oak or ivy instead."

"Please don't find any today, this is quite enough for me."

Swarms of mosquitoes seemed to rise from the small banks of the stream, apparently realizing they now had visitors.

Darren swatted at a cloud of them hovering in front of him and let the skull fall back into the stream. "Time to go," he said between forced breaths that tried to push the mosquitoes away from his face. No use. They landed on his face and lips, swarmed around his head. Andrea shook her head from side to side, switching the box of gravestones to her sticky hand to prevent making the same mistake twice.

They crossed the stream in a hurry, unmindful of steps that landed in the water. The bugs died down the farther they moved away from the water, but reminders remained in the form of swelling, itchy bites. The thickness of the woods diminished somewhat as they continued up a small incline. Raindrops were now penetrating the thinner ceiling above them. *Can't have the best of both worlds,* Andrea

279

thought. She blinked away a few drops of rain.

The top of the incline was short-lived as they found themselves heading back down into thick woods—woods that appeared to contain a darker shade of black. As they got closer, they felt their feet slowly sink into the ground. Darren almost lost a shoe, but pulled his foot out with a giant sucking noise before the ground took it as ransom.

As if to welcome them in way that asked why they had been gone so long, more swarms of mosquitoes hovered around their heads. The mosquitoes had also apparently sent messengers to pass along the news of visitors to their friends, the black flies.

"This only seems to be getting worse. How much longer do we have to put up with this?" Andrea asked in short gasps, hoping not to swallow any bugs. She swung wildly around her head.

Darren slapped his forehead and looked at the bloody smear that ran across his fingers. "I thought I saw the top of the church steeple from higher up, so we have to be getting pretty close," he said. "If that's true, then the trail I used to take home from school can only be about a mile ahead."

"A mile!" Andrea shouted, smashing something against her forearm. It already began to itch.

"Sorry, I told you it'd be a couple, at least," Darren said.

But nothing could alleviate the madness the bugs brought with them. They came in droves, undaunted by waving arms and the deaths of their friends, relentless. They thrived in the darkness and damp of the woods, hatching by the thousands.

Darren led the way, looking for a way out of the soft ground, knowing they were treading on the edges of a swamp. The number of bugs and smell of standing water proved it. He already had one leg stained black up to his knee from the thick, moist ground and that was plenty. Flies were already landing upon the slick surface of his jeans, somehow attracted to it. He veered left and felt the ground sink, but it held his weight better than the way they were previously headed.

"What's that?" Andrea called from behind.

Darren looked around his immediate area, but couldn't hear what she was referring to.

"Do you hear that?"

Darren tried to hear the source of her concern, but heard only the pleasant gurgle of the stream they had recently crossed. "I don't hear anything." He continued ahead.

"Wait, listen," Andrea said. "There it is again."

"Really, I don't—" he began. Then heard it. Goose bumps riddled his flesh, hiding the bug bites.

Something big cried in pain. The baritone wails were clear now. Long, winded cries of an animal caught in a position it didn't want to be in. He had heard the sounds of animals in the woods quite often when he was younger, but this was a sound that could never be duplicated.

"Sounds like an animal, hurt," Darren said.

"Can we help it?" The cries were increasing in intensity.

"Might be dangerous; we don't even know what it is or what it'll do."

"We have to at least try; maybe it's just caught in some old barbed wire or something."

"All right, but don't get too close once we get there, at least until we see what it is."

Andrea nodded, determined to take the lead toward the painful cries. The louder the cries became, the faster she seemed to go, ignoring the sinking ground and the bugs as she pushed hanging branches out of the way, marching forward. Darren was having a hard time keeping up with her and more than once got smacked in the face by a branch that had been pushed away by Andrea and allowed to snap back into its previous position. He slowed his pace to avoid losing an eye.

The wailing continued. It caused his hair to stand on end as he imagined the misery it must be in. He looked toward the source of the cries, but the thick foliage could hide a person in full hunter-orange gear. Then saw the slightest movement of a bush, followed by the sound of something being dragged. He pictured a deer with a broken leg trying to crawl to safety. Maybe it had fallen, broken its back, leaving only the forelegs able to move. His stomach curdled. They were close enough to feel the vibrations of its mournful cries.

Andrea finally slowed down, stopped. She was taking careful steps with her face thrust forward in an attempt to determine its location.

When her head snapped away from whatever she was looking at and she took some hurried steps backward, he picked up his own pace and ran as fast as the tangled forest floor would allow him. He reached her with heavy breaths, almost falling into a newly formed crack in the surface of the earth, and followed her gaze. He didn't need to ask what she was looking at.

It was starting again.

A wedge of soft earth appeared to have been taken away like a giant piece of pie. Bare roots, ripped and frayed at the breaking points and gleaming white at their centers, stuck out from the sides of the crack with clumps of dirt so moist they actually hung from them.

Measuring about five feet across and six feet deep, it was large enough to allow a moose to be dragged into it. Its black eyes barely expressed the pain as a skinless monster tore at its legs and sunk pointed teeth into its hide. The moose bellowed from deep within its lungs, its forelegs making desperate attempts at clawing the earth and being released from the creature's hold. In between wails of pain, its body convulsed. Waves of dark hair stood on end like that of an alarmed cat. The moose had no doubt been taken by surprise as the ground separated below its feet, only to be greeted by a thing it certainly had never seen.

Darren gawked at the living nightmare as it feasted. Like the previous one they'd seen, half of its body was still hidden beneath the earth. It ripped and tore at the backside of the moose, undeterred by the thick hide and massive size of the animal, seemingly anxious to bite into the fresh meat beneath. The beast's eyes registered their arrival, but it kept on chewing with guttural grunts. It snarled at them, then kept eating.

Without even knowing she had left, Darren felt Andrea slap him on the shoulder upon her return. "Here, you're stronger than I am, kill the damn thing." She held a sizeable branch, broken at its base, sharp teeth of splintered wood at the end. Darren took it, still not believing what he was about to do with it. The look in Andrea's eyes told him to be quick about it as well.

He looked into those lidless eyes and wondered if the thing even knew what was going to happen. It only watched him with mild curiosity, too enthralled by the living meal within its claws, an animal of its own sort. It pulled at the moose, sinking yellowed dagger-like fingers into the hip.

The moose fought hard, but couldn't gain any ground against the force that pulled it, only bellowed in pain and scraped frantically at loose dirt. The black eyes seemed to cloud over, sinking into someplace where it felt no pain.

Soon it ceased any type of resistance and waited for the inevitable, groaning only when it felt itself move another inch.

Darren handed his notebooks to Andrea, took a few furtive steps backward, and pulled his arm back as if he were about to throw a javelin, or a harpoon more likely. He closed his fingers tightly around the branch to get a firm grip. He would only have one chance.

It was all he needed.

Darren thrust his arm forward with the strength of a Hail Mary in the last play of a football game. The branch slid from his hand with an ease that surprised him and glided along a path that amazed him even more so. He viewed the spinning of the branch through the air in slow motion, eager for it to strike the snarling monster below him. The few seconds it traveled through the air crawled through time. Small pieces of bark and drops of water fell away in mid-flight and seemed to float to the ground.

The branch pierced the thing's chest without resistance and embedded itself into the ground behind its victim, spearing it. The skinless beast quivered for a few seconds, eyes unable to get any wider due to the absence of lids. Its scream was similar to that of a dying rabbit—so close to the screaming cries of a baby as to make Andrea cover her ears.

They both watched in surprise as the beast decomposed at an alarming rate, all but melting away from the branch sticking through its chest. Small tendrils of steam were released from exposed muscle and dissipated. They covered their noses.

The moose had since stopped breathing, perhaps willing its heart to stop, choosing to be the master of its own destiny. Black eyes stared beyond the heavens. Andrea reached down and rubbed its large snout, stared down at the shell of a once majestic animal.

They were able to catch one breath, allowed the one chance to calm their nerves and relax. And that was all.

Darren spotted a pair of eyes peeking from behind a tree, then another. Saw a bloody hand—with nails that made him cringe—grasp the trunk of a tree to pull itself out of the ground. He grabbed Andrea by the arm as one revealed the rest of its body. He would ask himself later why he looked below its waist and find no answer. His eyes were drawn there, and he noticed it possessed no genitals distinguishing it as either male or female.

They ran . . . or tried to.

Chapter 43

Extended roots and fallen branches reached for their legs and tried to hold on. They ran, ignoring jabs and scratches of intruding branches and the hot pain of occasional thorns. The rain continued to fall harder, though they couldn't see it. The harsh sounds of thunder shook the ground, but they didn't feel it. Though the sun failed to penetrate the clouds above, shadows grew longer with a life of their own, bringing an early darkness to the forest. It crawled on their skin and they tried to escape it.

Darren had no idea how long they had tromped through these woods, but they were clearly behind a schedule that had been set by someone else. Or *something* else. *If there's more here,* he thought, *how far do these cracks go and where?* He already knew where they originated from, but how could they seal the source? He couldn't help but think of his home sliding into a hole in the ground, his parents clueless as to what was going on around them. He ran faster, images infusing his mind with muscled, glistening beasts climbing out from under his house, his town, invading it.

Sweat burned in his eyes, threatened to close them. He fought to keep them open and wiped at them with the back of his hand. It came away with something other than sweat smeared across his fingers. He felt it ooze back into his eyes.

He fell, looked behind him with a quick glance, and got up before Andrea could fall on top of him. He heard his rasping breaths and felt the burning in his chest, a stitch in his side. The notebooks splayed in front of him as his sweaty palm released them, pages fluttering in the wind. He recovered the fumble and kept running.

Three pairs of eyes chased them, lured by the thrill of the hunt and led by the foreign blood that pumped hard within their veins. They seemed to be connected to a single brain, knowing nothing other than hunt, kill. Take over. Behind each pair of eyes, a small portion of brain that once belonged to them knew of another life, but that thought would never make it to the conscious level. It only hinted at the way things used to be. They were now hunters and gatherers, prepared to claim their piece of a new world and make it their own. They couldn't turn back, knew the result if they did. The freedom they felt as they marched ahead was enough to keep them going.

Andrea imagined the hot breath of one of the beasts behind her neck, sniffing before it decided to take a chunk out of her. As each branch brushed against her, it suddenly became the finger of what had once been wrapped around her ankle.

Like some new, primitive species, they didn't just chase them, but stalked them. On the chance times that she did steal looks over her shoulder, she noticed how they ran: sometimes on all fours, sometimes on two crimson legs. They sniffed at the ground, snarled, ran a short distance before hunkering down behind thick bushes. They moved within the safety of a pack, occasionally fighting among one another for the role of the Alpha. The shining, crimson surface of their bodies stood out against the darkening background. She counted three, but wondered when more would show up, aggravated by the scent of her and Darren. In their favor, the beasts were just as unfamiliar to the terrain, stumbling at times. It allowed the distance between them to increase.

Come on, Darren; get us the hell out of here, she thought, her brain running way ahead of her body. The contents of the box she held tightly rumbled with every step, sounding like she was shaking a box of marbles. She knew it would be much easier to run without them and almost dropped them to the ground. *No, they have a purpose,* she thought again, and reapplied her hold. For what, she hadn't the faintest notion.

She saw Darren fall and went wide before tripping over him. They were going uphill again and she felt the burning in her calves, one more so than the other. It looked like a clearing above—she could see no trees inhabiting the top of the hill. Head down, she concentrated on holding onto whatever her hands found, pulling herself up, sometimes with small trees, sometimes with weeds protruding from the side of the hill, hopefully to safety.

At last, they both stood at the top, feet balancing on small planks of wood in between two railroad tracks. Out of breath, Darren bent over, resting on his knees. "Holy shit . . . how far are they?"

She looked to the edge of the woods below, but couldn't see any movement. "Still inside the trees somewhere," she wheezed. Trying to get rid of the burning feeling in her lungs, she coughed and spit a glob of green mucus to the ground. It landed on one of the tracks with immediate adherence. She could have been that great glob of goo—that's exactly what she felt like inside and out. "Probably not for long though." She cleared her throat again, deciding to swallow the phlegm instead.

"Your head has quite a cut," she said, now able to talk with less effort. She went to touch it, but Darren pulled away from her reach. She dropped her hand.

"It'll be fine. I think it's stopped bleeding," Darren said, scrunching his forehead to get a feel of the gash. He looked to both ends of the railroad track, to the sky, with closed eyes, letting the rain cool his forehead. He scanned the edge of the woods. "I think I know where we are."

That was the best thing Andrea could have heard. Her eyes lit up with sudden sparks of interest. "How much farther?" Andrea asked, not knowing if she wanted to hear the answer. The words seemed to come before she had the chance to retract them.

"Not far," Darren said with an attempt for a tired grin. He unbuttoned his jacket and slid the notebooks inside, placing the edges of them inside the waist of his jeans, away from the rain.

A rusted heap of a bicycle lay on its side nearby, blades of long grass coming through the bent spokes of the wheels. Soon, the bike would disappear completely.

Another section of forest waited for them on the other side of the tracks, but the outlines of buildings rose above the trees—the edge of town. Andrea saw the top of the school and the church steeple Darren had mentioned earlier, almost hidden by the overcast skies. If they didn't have to go by foot, it wouldn't be far at all. Still, it was a welcome sight.

Andrea thought she could make out the vague outline of the library. It made her eyes water. Everything seemed so different traveling on foot. She was completely turned around, had no idea they were this close. Now, if they could only find the warehouse Darren had spoken of, it would almost be over. Maybe.

Sheets of rain at both ends of the railroad tracks decorated the gray sky like taut black veins. The tracks faded into the mist. What was directly above them seemed only a small sign of weather to come. It looked as if, at any moment, the two systems would collide over Durbin, raising the floodwaters of the Androscoggin River.

They waited.

They were learning the tactics of a successful hunt and knew they had to catch their quarry off guard. Motionless, they remained behind the edge of the forest, in order to give their prey a small sense of safety before they pounced. Inside exposed muscle, they seethed. When they saw them gradually vanish from sight behind the other side of the hill, they crept out into the open, sniffing at the air. They separated on instinct, ready to trap them from either side should they veer from a direct path.

The tree line was thinning, allowing Darren and Andrea to walk without constant looks to their feet. Waist-high grass and willow branches brushed against them instead of gnarled branches. A stone wall came into view, the remnants of an entrance. Boulders were stacked neatly together on either side of the six-foot opening. It appeared to be a structure that had once been made with the caring and patient hands of its creator, but had never been completed.

As they went through the entrance on a dirt road hidden beneath the grass, the first headstone appeared. It took Andrea by surprise and she paused in wonder. It was one of the few stones able to stand above the lengthened grass. Its surface was cracked and brittle to the touch. Brown stains oozed down all sides, making it appear as a rusted block of stone. The name on the stone was all but invisible, the etchings erased by time.

The small cemetery looked like so many of the others she

had seen, but she dug deep into her mind, wondering why she had never seen this particular one. Of all the research she had done, all the town and county records she had perused laboriously over, one cemetery had still slipped through. As if it were meant for someone else to find.

She moved clumps of grass with her feet in search of more headstones, but looked behind her every so often. They didn't have time to spend looking for the hidden stones perched along the rippled ground. Not with things hunting them down like they were field mice instead of people. She looked for Darren and her heart lurched. He was just beside her a moment ago. In place, she did a complete circle, holding her breath and not realizing it.

She found him only a few yards away, kneeling beside one stone in particular. His body in the crouched position was all but consumed entirely by long strands of grass in varying shades of yellow and brown. She could barely pick out the blue of his denim jacket.

She traversed the space between them with long strides and a wary eye.

The "A" of the name was the only carved feature of the stone that was legible. Her mind went back to the day she had first read his obituary at the library, many years after his death. She remembered the change in Albert's eyes after Darren had mentioned he had already met the man.

Darren flattened the grass around the stone with his hands, allowing it to have a clear view of the skies above. He used the moisture of the rain to wipe away layers of grime with the sleeve of his jacket. Even after the years that had passed, the memory of his first visit was still clear. What he didn't understand then was a puzzle almost completely solved now. Perhaps some part of Albert still remained within his burial site, but Darren only felt the smallest hint of him. He must have departed the day he had made his first visit.

Others still needed to be remembered within this cemetery. He heard them as he would whispers in his ears, soft voices calling out to him and Andrea. Listening required an effort. He was exhausted physically as well as mentally. All the same, he could hear the whispers getting agitated, like the swarming buzz of bees had he knocked over a hive. But they weren't trying to sting him at all. They were giving him their combined effort and passing a message.

They were warning him!

As he looked to where they had come in, at one time the entrance, he saw the first beast climbing over the wall. It crawled on the stones, slithering, but when it knew it was spotted, decided to stand up straight and walk slowly to where he and Andrea crouched beside the headstone of Albert Fontaine.

Darren stood up.

Three came from the entrance, one over the other wall and one in between the two structures. They seemed confident in their eventual success, prolonging the inevitable with slow, arrogant strides. They had their prey trapped and knew it.

The cemetery was an obstacle course in itself, and Darren knew if they chanced the run for it like their hearts told them to, they would only stumble among the hidden stones and that would be the end. They would be fed upon like the bounty of a pack of wild wolves, only worse. He had the uncanny feeling these creatures would take their time and enjoy their terrified screams as they were pulled apart, piece by tasty piece. He sensed Andrea thinking the same thing as she moved closer to him.

"What are we gonna do now?" Andrea asked, barely above a whisper.

He only mumbled his frustration.

Darren tried to maintain eye contact, as he would an opposing football player, getting the first sign of movement from their eyes. He backed up, but could go no farther as another tombstone nudged his backside. One beast was clearly in the lead, the other two holding back a pace or two, looking more than anxious to have their share. If there were more, they were remaining well hidden, probably surrounding them, somewhere.

Darren focused on the leader, now only feet away, and placed a hand upon the headstone behind him for support. Brittle pieces of stone fell away. He clutched a piece within his shaking hand.

They couldn't run, but had to do *something!*

The creature was close enough to smell—unpleasant at best. Andrea backed up a few paces, unhindered by a headstone. She managed to pull the notebooks out of Darren's other hand, should he need it to fight with.

Darren felt hot burning breaths reaching for him, observed the creature sniff from where there was supposed to be a nose. Rain hitting its exposed muscles evaporated on impact, creating small puffs of steam. He could think of nothing to do but throw the one thing he had in his hand at it, as a distraction at the very least. He didn't know what a two-inch piece of stone would do to such a thing, didn't feel comfortable with it at all, but it was all he had.

Pulling his arm back, Darren fumbled the stone within slick fingers and it fell, along with Darren's stomach, to the beast's feet and landed upon one of them.

Not only did it land on top of the foot, but passed through it completely!

As the stone came in contact with the foot, it shimmered like a small sphere with an electrical charge, turning muscle into the equal of butter under a hot knife. One-half of the foot separated from the beast entirely. Snarling in pain, the beast fell in awkward, flailing movements, caught unsteady without toes to balance upon.

Darren could only stand mesmerized and suddenly knew the value of what Andrea held in her box. He looked at her with the biggest grin he could manage. She must have seen it, too . . .

But he couldn't figure out why she was pointing, mouthing something, eyes glued to the ground below him. Couldn't hear if she was trying to speak.

She pointed to the ground and backed up slowly.

He looked.

The amputated foot began to dance upon the ground, stirring the grass. The creature once on the ground was now starting to get back up. On two good feet!

Darren didn't know which to look at: the dancing foot or the beast with one newly formed. Both were equally amazing in some disgusting, yet fascinating, way. His brain failed at trying to explain to him what was happening.

The other two creatures still stood back a pace, looking just as surprised at what had just happened. Yellow drool dripped down one's chin in a steaming trail.

The severed foot stopped twitching as a small mass began to grow from the stump. Fleshless muscles crackled in extension as the shin of a leg began to appear—then a kneecap.

Darren's mind went back to the spearing of the first one. He had hit it square in the chest, destroying whatever black heart pumped within its body.

The heart.

Next time he wouldn't make the same mistake.

The single foot quickly developed to the point of a lower torso, with muscles and veins stretching along a fully formed leg. The thigh of another leg pushed its way out of the torso from what was to be the waist.

The ground started to rumble.

Pieces of loose shards and dirt bounced on the tops of visible stones. One headstone fell victim to a stress fracture, toppling over and separating into two pieces.

The two systems had finally met above them, causing the wind to howl a woeful tune and droplets of rain to land upon Andrea's face like hundreds of pellets. The sudden gusts were heavy enough to lay down every strand of overgrown grass, revealing the entire population of the cemetery. All headstones were now visible.

Andrea knew the power contained in the small cardboard box she was holding, but her gut told her they would be needed later. This was only a small battle in the war. Best to conserve her resources, as sheepish as it might sound. She kept one hand in front of her eyes to protect against the rain and a tight hold onto her box and Darren's notebooks, not knowing what to expect next.

Especially what actually *did* happen next.

Above the howling wind, above the sound of the stinging rain, she heard every stone that surrounded her falling apart. The tall stone near the entrance wobbled in response to the vibrations of the ground beneath it. It, too, cracked down the middle and split like a tree under a bolt of lightning.

On instinct, Darren jumped back when white, glowing orbs rose from all of the gravestones except Albert's. His stone remained intact. They crackled in the air as though aggravated by the falling rain, sounding like dozens of tiny bug zappers you'd keep on your back porch. They rose from the cracked sections of aged stone like they were coming out of eggshells, and hovered as if waiting for the others to do the same.

Then they attacked.

In one movement, the orbs rose to the center of the cemetery, above all of their heads and staring eyes and a few slack jaws. They combined to create a single giant ball of energy that sizzled in the air and made Andrea and Darren squint their eyes shut. The beasts turned their heads away in pain, unable to protect their eyes from the searing brilliance.

As though breaking from a huddle, the orbs separated into tiny spheres of light and, like swarms of hornets, flew in separate groups to the individual creatures.

They paved smooth paths in and out of each body, riddling them like tiny bullets, harvesting the smell of burning meat, only to come back and do it again. Each beast fought its own war with the swarm of orbs surrounding it. Eerily familiar cries of agony poured from their mouths as they flailed at the balls of light with frenzied arms and kicked at them, only to find the orbs pass through them like sharp needles. The torso of the partially reborn creature was cauterized at chest level, denying its birth.

Seeming to be satisfied they had tormented them enough, each group of orbs joined as another singular mass and drove a burning path through each beast's chest, coming through their muscled backs with steaming trails behind them. Each creature fell in a hideous mass of burning, steaming muscle.

If there were more beasts waiting, they had disappeared.

The dazzling orbs of light separated and combined one

last time before disappearing into the thick sky above. Andrea and Darren watched the ball of light extinguish from their view before looking to the mess at their feet. The remains were decomposing in a steam of silence.

The wind died down, but the rain continued.

Uncontrollable shivers ran through Andrea's body, from fear or hypothermia, she couldn't distinguish. She let Darren place his arm around her as they walked a path he had taken before. She could have sworn she saw a pair of panties hanging from a branch and a scattering of rusted beer cans below them in tribute. Then again, it could have only been her mind trying to make sense of everything.

Chapter 44

They exited the path, maneuvering different routes through rocks and debris that had gathered at the edge of the woods. To their left, a park stood forlorn, awaiting children in the rain. Streams of water fell from the top of an aluminum slide. Two sandboxes were turning into mud, and a set of swings gently swayed in the wind as if invisible children sat upon the hard, plastic seats.

Ahead of them, a paved road led to the beginning of the residential houses and apartments of Durbin. Trees outlined the sides of the road and bent at their tops. The wind pushed the bottoms of the leaves up, giving the trees a silver color as though the sun wasn't hiding behind a thick layer of clouds, but casting bright rays upon their surfaces.

They left the darkness of the woods only to be welcomed by a town they barely recognized as their own. The temperature had dropped—it could have been October. Even as rain continued to plummet from above, there still should have been people going to and from work, or getting groceries, or kids playing in the rain against their parents' wishes.

Instead, a traffic light swung above an intersection and blinked a yellow rhythmic pattern while the drains beneath the curbs of sidewalks gurgled, almost in overflow. A flattened pack of cigarettes, pulled by the small river it floated in, scraped against a curb. Cars could be seen in the distance, parked in front of houses or occupying driveways, but a single vehicle didn't hiss upon wet pavement, even in the distance. The town seemed to sleep, though sundown

was still a few hours away. Only the wind, rain, and their footsteps on the pavement punched holes into the stillness of the air.

"Where is everyone?" Andrea asked, tucking her chin against her chest, letting her chin warm beneath the front of her shirt.

Darren had his hands deep inside his pockets. He turned an ear toward her voice, against the wind. "I don't know, but I'm definitely not getting a good feeling."

"Maybe it's just this section of town. We'll probably see more once we get closer."

"Yeah . . . maybe," Darren said.

"Where's the warehouse?"

"Couple blocks ahead, on the right."

"You ready to do this?"

"I don't even know *what* we're doing, but I'm ready to get these clothes off and jump into a hot shower," Darren said.

"Me too. Soon," Andrea said.

And hoped she was right.

They walked with quick steps down the center of the street, not bothering to look behind them to see if any vehicles were coming. The small river hugging the curb was slowly spreading past the bicycle lane, the white line barely visible beneath the brownish muck of flowing water. The lone pack of cigarettes fell victim to the water's force and disappeared inside the rusted bars of a storm drain.

An apartment building, once white, now a shade of stained brown, stood silently as if in punishment. The rain threatened to peel away more of the paint and soak it with its dismal wrath. With dusk approaching, lights still couldn't be seen in any of the windows, nor could the bluish glow of a television. A wind chime clinked under the roof of a small porch and a screen door slammed with each gust of wind.

They passed a small house with toys strewn about the front lawn. A tricycle and a battery-operated truck a child could sit in were both on their sides. One wheel of the tricycle creaked unevenly about its axle and colored strands of plastic danced from the end of a handlebar. This house was also quiet, with no sign of activity within its brick walls. The daily newspaper stuck out from the mailbox to the right of the door and a closed curtain covered the inside of a picture window.

As they gazed upon it, the picture window shattered, the sound of breaking glass exploding into the silence and lingering until every shard of glass bounced on the front lawn and came to rest within strands of wet grass.

Along with a body.

"Holy shit!" Andrea shouted, jumping at the sudden noise, words caught on her tongue at the sight of the man coming through the window.

A man dressed in only his boxers crashed through the window, back first, and bounced limply among the slivers of glass. His head was the last to stop moving as it pounded into the ground and bounced before remaining still. A green curtain followed in trail and tangled about his feet.

He lay among the glass, unmoving.

With the seal of the house broken, screams came from somewhere deep inside. A woman shrieked and children screamed for their daddy.

Andrea started to run toward the man on the front lawn, but Darren held her back.

"What the hell are you doing? We have to do something!" Andrea shouted, pulling her arm from Darren's grip with a defiant glare in her eyes that demanded he let her go.

Chills pummeled her body at the sound of the children. She could no longer hear the woman.

"Hold on! I don't think he jumped out himself. Look at his throat."

She did and her feet locked themselves to the pavement. Her heart wanted to help, reached out to the children screaming inside the house, but her mind told her to be cautious and her eyes told her to turn and run like hell.

"Oh, my God!" A shaking hand muted her gasp.

The base of the man's chin to his collarbone was torn away, flaps of skin hanging loosely to the ground. Lifeless eyes stared into the clouds above.

"The kids, the kids," Andrea stammered.

Soon, they too were silenced.

A loose piece of glass fell from the picture window with a dull ring. More followed. Bloody hands were placed on the sill of the window and a hideous face looked at them from the darkened interior of the house, seeming to smile and produce hollow grunts of satisfaction. Its teeth chattered.

"Let's finish this FUCKING thing!" Andrea yelled. She turned and started to run, but soon realized she didn't know which way to go. "Hurry up! Get us there, fast!"

Darren assumed the lead without comment.

Their feet slapped against the pavement and their arms threw fists into the air along their sides. Drenched from head to toe, Darren found running with sodden clothes harder than running laps in full football gear. The weight was staggering to begin with, and with the physical exertions they had been thrown into throughout the last few days, he felt as if he were crawling, his knuckles pulling his body forward through quicksand. He felt Andrea pushing at his back, urging him forward, and wondered where she

301

found the strength. He heard the rustle of stones from behind him and almost laughed at the fact that they were going to a battle with only a box of gravestones.

He tried to force his breathing into some type of steady rhythm, but felt the burning in his lungs just the same. Pins and needles scratched at his throat. Puddles erupted into large splashes around his feet as he made his way through standing water and developing streams. He didn't look both ways as he crossed the streets, dared not glance into the windows of any houses they were passing.

Thoughts of his parents teased his mind and he tried to push them back. Were they getting ready for dinner? Had they set a plate out for him? Did they have any uninvited guests attending? He swore at himself for not giving them a call every night, prayed that it wasn't too late to apologize, hoped they would understand if he ever had the chance to tell them the entire story.

He only lived a few blocks from where they were, yet it could have been a hundred miles. If he looked in a certain direction, he would probably see the walkway, the front porch. The picture window decorated with white shutters. He forced his gaze forward.

A few more turns along the way and the hulk of a decrepit warehouse took shape in the mist, growing in mass like some weird disease. The grayness of its peeling surface almost matched the color of the clouds, as if it belonged to the same dreary substance. If the surface appeared this way, he could only imagine what the inside was like or what was living beneath it.

He was about to find out. And refused to imagine what was under there, deciding to let reality present itself at the moment, as odd as it might become. Or horrific. Or both.

He came to an ancient set of railroad tracks that sat

rusting alongside the warehouse and slowed his pace. The town had grown around it, but at one time, the warehouse was a hub for transporting and receiving supplies from around the state, standing alone against the countryside. Now, it sat in sagging heaps along the roof and the darkest of black beneath its wood floors and support beams.

Looking into the darkness below the unleveled structure, Darren was reminded of other times, when to venture underneath this same building was to welcome the joy of an adventure, scouring every inch of the ground in hopes of finding a treasure that hadn't been touched in years.

In contrast, to look into the darkness now was like looking into the mouth of a dragon, about to be swallowed into the depths of its throat and boiled in the fire of its belly. He had received a taste of this beast the last time he had visited with his friends. But then, it had been in broad daylight. Shadows had still enveloped the area, but were always made less threatening by the sunshine of the summer day. And they could always see clearly once their eyes got used to the change in lighting.

The darkness under the warehouse now seemed impenetrable, thick, and heavy. The sun had all but set somewhere behind the clouds, losing the power of its rays as they were collected by the thickened layers of overcast gloom before being able to shine underneath the edges of the warehouse.

They were without flashlights, and the thought of taking that first step into seeming oblivion terrified him. Darren imagined himself in some cheap horror movie, where the hero or heroine knew what was on the other side of the door (something clawing against the wood and ready to go for his or her throat), yet had this immediate need to open the door and experience the terror.

And here he was now—ready to pull the door open.

Andrea had asked him a question, but he only heard the squeal of rusted hinges, saw a shadow leak from between the door and its frame.

The door creaked open another inch and released an invisible cloud of trepidation that found its way into Darren's gut like a breath of fetid mist.

He knew what was on the other side and was going to open it, anyway.

Chapter 45

"We're here?" Andrea asked between heavy breaths.

As small as their town was, she couldn't help marveling at this section of town she had never been to, except in passing. Nor was there any reason to come here. The warehouse and the few buildings next to it were like failed attempts of Durbin trying to expand, an eyesore in need of removing. She pressed a soaked sneaker against one rail of the tracks and watched water seep from the edge of the sole in a foamy-like substance. *Armed with a box of gravestones and a pair of rabid tennis shoes,* she thought, *we are unstoppable.* She suppressed a weary chuckle.

Darren only offered a blank stare. "You with me?" Another question, louder than the first.

"Oh . . . yeah. Just thinking about the door," Darren replied.

"What?"

"Nothing." He shook his head. "It's under there," he said, a shaky finger pointed toward the darkness beneath the towering structure before them. It could have been shaking from cold or fear, but Andrea didn't think it really mattered at this point. Her own body shook with each.

"Lovely. Got a flashlight?" She tried to get a laugh out of him, bring him back from wherever he was, but received only a slow blink of his eyes.

"Flashlight? Hah—good one!" He was back.

"How far in there is this place?"

"Way back there," Darren said.

"Only gets better, huh?"

Darren ducked his head and took the first step under the building. Welcomed by the dank smell of moist earth that hadn't seen direct sunlight in many years, Andrea followed Darren with a small leap, as though if she didn't jump into the darkness right now, she never would. A few yards into the underside of the warehouse, available light seemed to all but extinguish as it was pulled into the darkest of corners.

They paused their advance, letting their eyes adjust as much as possible. Darren seemed to be hunched over, but she had no problem standing almost upright. Only the rough outline of him and the whites of his eyes were visible as he stood only inches away. She reached out and held onto his jacket, needing to know he was there with her, but mostly to prevent him from leaving without her knowing.

If there was an end to the darkness, Andrea couldn't see it. She felt as though they were descending through undiscovered caverns into a subterranean city where light hadn't yet been invented, an unmapped land where certain species of creatures remained to be discovered—along with the way out.

Something scurried away and she was thankful she couldn't see what possibly crawled around her. With some effort, she pushed away visions of giant spiders, bugs, and unidentified concoctions of both. But nothing could compare to the creature that had stared at them from the picture window earlier. And there could only be more . . . somewhere.

Something fell into her hair and she brushed at it with quick strokes. Torn between the crawling feet of some unseen critter and the thick, matted hair her fingers struggled to pull through, she didn't know which to grimace at. Placing heavy strands of hair behind her ear, she strained her eyes and tried to see something, *anything* in the sheet of darkness that now covered them.

Empty spaces gradually became shades of heavy gray and the supporting beams for the floors above stood out in a darker shade of black. Twisted metal remains that littered the area appeared as silhouetted blotches against the gloomy background.

Their vision was as good as it was going to get, leaving all the room for something to sneak up on them.

"I think it's time to open the box," Andrea said. Her voice traveled into the recess ahead of them, but didn't echo. Instead, it fell flat, lingering only an instant before dissolving into the shadows. She lowered her voice to a whisper. "We'll each take a few and keep the rest in the box."

"Let me see your shirt," she said, and the whites of Darren's eyes grew larger. "I need it to put inside the box. The noise these things make under here will sound like we're coming through with a big band in tow, and I don't want them knowing we're here until I'm good and ready."

"Good idea, hold on a minute," Darren said and took off his denim jacket, giving it to Andrea while he pried his wet shirt from his body. He also gave her the notebooks—the cardboard covers were getting flimsy, but still held together.

His skin seemed to glow and he put his jacket back on quickly, buttoning it up to his neck, with the notebooks once again tucked inside the waist of his pants.

Andrea grabbed his hand and placed five small stones inside his palm. He put four inside the pocket of his jacket and kept one in his hand. She did the same and placed his shirt inside the box before closing the lid, to prevent the remaining stones from rattling like Mexican maracas.

She gathered strength from the surface of the stone in her hand, pulled at the power inside. She felt the remnants of memories it still contained. It belonged to an elderly woman who had died of natural causes, leaving no family behind, no family to remember her passing. She had out-lived her entire small family and welcomed death as a form of release from the loneliness. Instead, the woman had found herself being pulled in a different direction, unable to resist for much longer when Andrea had paid her first visit to the cemetery.

She rolled it between her fingers, squeezed it, and en-joyed the feel of the rough edges against the inside of her palm. A few more squeezes and she thought herself as ready as she'd ever be.

Darren took the first step forward. Andrea could see the shape of his body move ahead of her, but held his jacket tightly between two fingers just the same. They proceeded slowly, as the blackness seemed to get thicker with each small, quiet step. Andrea looked behind them and realized the edge of the building they had stepped under was already gone. Heavy rain pounded against the aged wood slats of the building above.

Drips of water fell from the edges of the building and sounded like small waterfalls cascading into gathering pud-dles, but soon diminished into a dull roar as the void in front of them sucked them in. Their footsteps were softened by moist ground, but soon met hard-packed earth, allowing for easier travel, though Andrea didn't feel any more com-fortable than when the muck pulled at her feet.

Darren pulled her into different directions with his jacket. She felt the pull of fabric change as they went around abandoned bicycles, a shopping cart, and oddly enough, the axle of a vehicle. Shapes barely recognizable until they were just about tripping over them.

"Is there a party going on or something? Can't y'all just

leave me alone?" The slurred voice stopped Darren in his tracks and Andrea felt her face bump into wet denim.

"Hello?" Darren called to the voice.

"Y'all best be leaving. Seems to be a popular place the last few hours. Weird things crawling round here," an elderly, crackled voice told them. "Course, could be the wine."

A bout of laughter, the rustle of a paper bag, the small gurgle of liquid being swallowed, and the exaggerated sound of a refreshing sip being taken. The clink of a bottle falling to the ground and muffled thuds of staggering footsteps got their hearts beating, blood pumping. They couldn't tell if he was coming or going.

"Watch your step," the voice warned them, then silence.

"What do you make of that?" Andrea whispered into Darren's ear.

"Don't know. Couldn't see him. Sounds like he was just drunk." Darren did his best to keep his voice calm, but Andrea still detected a small change in pitch.

"What about things crawling around here?"

"Let's hope he was just drunk."

She felt the pull of fabric and followed.

If someone had placed a cloth over the lampshade upon entering, the same person now saw no use for it and pulled the plug, leaving them to utilize all senses but sight. Andrea swallowed hard, her throat producing a rough, croaking noise. A thudding pulse beat within her ears.

She found it difficult to imagine how blind people were able to do it, relying on intuition and sharpened senses of touch, sound, and smell. She took a deep breath through her nose, closed her eyes, and tried to picture what the underside of the warehouse looked like.

A familiar smell tinged her nose.

She took another breath in as deep as it would go and her mind seemed to clear. She could see the supporting beams of the warehouse spaced in even distances apart from one another, the splintered wood above her head, junk left behind by previous visitors, and cobwebs hanging in wispy sheets.

What she thought was a cobweb grazed her cheek and she almost pulled back. Not in disgust, but as an inconvenience—her hair had enough things in it.

Except, cobwebs weren't cold to the touch. And this touch still remained, as if caressing her face.

She opened her eyes.

Faye!

She pulled hard on Darren's jacket. Felt him resist.

"Can you see them?" Andrea asked, barely able to contain her excitement. Around her were more transparent shapes of those she had released. Faye was at the forefront, smiling that beautiful smile again, yet her eyes drooped as if in concern. A child was at her side, crying tears of joy or sorrow, tucking her face into Faye's side. Faye rubbed Sarah's shoulder in comfort, held her close.

Others produced a faint glow as they surrounded Darren and her with clean, welcome light. She recognized faces she hadn't seen in years. Behind a group of three or four, she thought the faces of her parents took shape, but couldn't be certain.

"Darren, can you see them?" she asked again.

"See wha—" The piece of jacket she was holding onto snapped free and Darren fell. Darkness immediately filled in every pore of the glow she had seen, invading it, conquering it. She didn't understand. She followed Darren's voice and stared into the void, frantically searching for the people she had just seen.

They were gone, but a dancing light ahead of them revealed the crack Darren had fallen into and illuminated the area with a fiery radiance. The ground was ripping, the crack in the earth being pulled farther apart.

The ground trembled beneath their feet and the floorboards of the building above began to creak and moan with bitterness.

Something knew they had arrived.

Chapter 46

"Help me up!"

Darren grabbed at her feet, reached for her grip with blind sweeps of his hands. Her mind still raced with the images of people she knew she had seen, some of them still embedded within her vision like the after-effects of a bright flash.

Behind Darren, a supporting beam glistened as crimson drops of moisture fell in sluggish trails. For a fleeting instant she thought water had leaked from the cracked pipes above, let loose by the shaking of the building, but knew in the next instant the only thing occupying any rusted pipes of this warehouse would be dust.

She reached down as movement caused shadows to dance around them in a feverish, almost nauseating kaleidoscope of activity.

"Come on, come on!" she cried.

The first finger appeared from behind the beam.

The yellowed claw attached to it scraped against the surface, peeling away slivers of wood that had dried over time.

More fingers appeared.

A grotesque face slid out from behind the beam—slowly, as if playing a horrific game of hide and seek. Muscled flesh spoke with the moist sound of movement and extension as more of the beast was exposed. Lidless, glaring eyes pointed toward Darren and sharpened their glare with shrinking pupils. It salivated with a quick slither of its tongue along serrated teeth.

"Darren, behind you!"

Darren turned and a yelp caught in his throat. He backed against Andrea's side of the edge, his feet knocking away loose dirt as they tried to propel him to the surface. Like a hamster churning endlessly along the small steel bars of a circular cage, knowing it was going absolutely nowhere, Darren gave up, and prepared for the inevitable.

The creature slid from behind the beam to all four limbs, ready to jump on a morning snack. A deep growl grew from within its chest as it cocked its head to one side and crawled closer to the edge. Its body quivered with tension, muscles twinkling with each contraction as it lurked forward.

Darren pulled an arm back, with a piece of headstone pinched tightly within his grip. Waited as though sure he would hit the mark—the center of its shining chest. If he didn't, Andrea knew there would be two of these things to deal with.

Arm cocked with her own weapon of a distant past clutched within unsteady fingers, she waited, and kept a watchful eye out for more movement within the shadows.

The creature bent on all fours, its muscles going rigid in preparation, then leaped into the air above Darren. It snarled in anticipation of a quick kill, spreading its claws and pointing them downward, ready to tear Darren open upon impact.

He was expecting it, waiting for it.

The chest above him gleamed with muscle and sinew, but left itself exposed. The stone flew a short distance in the air before turning into a bright mass of surging white light as it struck the creature's chest. It burned its way through to the other side and fell at Darren's feet in its original form of brittle stone.

As the creature fell on top of him, one claw tore through

his jacket and ripped at his shoulder.

Darren howled against the spread of fire permeating his shoulder, the tearing of his skin. He pulled at the ghastly arm still connected to his shoulder, felt exposed muscle sticking to his hand. The claw separated from the creature's finger, dangled from his shoulder like a loose tooth clinging to a last piece of shredded gum, then fell to the ground.

With eyes squinted tight against searing pain, Darren saw he held only the arm of the creature. He threw it to the ground in disgust as it began to hiss beneath a growing shroud of steam. The rest of the creature had crumpled around his feet and was disappearing into a pile of steaming, foul air.

The ground rumbled and the crack widened.

He made sure of his grip on Andrea's hand with his good arm and pulled himself out. Then fell to his knees clutching his shoulder, pressing his jacket into the wound in order to stop the blood he felt oozing down his left arm.

Andrea went to his side, placed a soft hand on his back. "We have to get moving, there are others out there," she whispered. He made a cursory glance into the oppressive murk surrounding them, expecting to see the reflection of light upon glistening muscle.

"I'll be all right, just give me a second," he said between clenched teeth.

Movement rustled around them. Shadows flickered within a glow that shimmered along the rotting floor above, like something dancing in front of the flames of a fire.

Darren thought he heard a rush of air expel from a craving mouth, but tried to steal enough time to let the pain subside. His shoulder throbbed, but the pain was becoming bearable. At least it was keeping him alert, responsive.

When he heard Andrea suck in a quick mouthful of air,

he struggled to his feet, legs shaking from exertion but still holding his weight.

The proverbial door stood wide open. It was now time to face whatever came at them from within its darkened chambers.

Chapter 47

The glow surrounding them grew brighter, enough to reveal a multitude of similar crevices spreading from a common center in the short distance ahead. The yellowish radiance pulsed from below this central source, allowing shadows to create deeper shades of black at the edges of the territory.

It seemed as if they were walking among the ruins of a prehistoric time, able to watch first-hand as evolution took place before their eyes. As if a surreal landscape were being born from the pregnant, molten caverns below, pushed out of a fiery womb.

Along with its children.

New life forms pulled themselves from the jagged veins of the earth, bodies glistening with something similar to the mucus surrounding a newborn infant, shining in crimson splendor. Their eyes searched for food, seeking the elusive mother's nipple of human flesh from which to pull the essence of their existence while their jaws clacked together, testing them. Strings of steaming drool stretched between upper and lower jaws as they opened and closed, opened and closed.

Rotten slats of wood, unsettled by the constant rumbling that coursed through the ground, began to shake free of the structure above. Previously undisturbed layers of dust dispersed and permeated the air, sparkling in the subtle light. Wooden beams, once straight, now bent and threatened to snap and topple over, bringing whatever they supported down upon their heads.

The groaning of twisting wood caused Darren's stomach

to twist along with it. A sick sound, as if the wood itself were alive and being tortured, stretched beyond its limits. Slowly. Soon, he knew, they would hear it give way under pressure and begin to splinter.

He looked to all sides and was greeted by fleeting movements from every direction. Some creatures were already standing, testing the strength of new legs. Others still had their lengthened nails carved into the surface, pulling, their hungry eyes becoming visible as they clambered over the edge of a new territory like soldiers dug deep inside a trench.

They were outnumbered and Darren's mind ran with possibilities, not liking the way any of them would turn out. The door was about to be slammed shut behind them, of its own accord, trapping them within the utter blackness where the darkest of nightmares were born. The peeled tomatoes of his dreams were about to make sure they left a lasting impression and a gruesome aftertaste.

He looked at Andrea and saw the same expression he felt dominating his face mirrored in hers: eyes frantically moving within their sockets, tight-lipped, veins at her temples throbbing in fear. She reached for the other stones inside her pocket and placed them into the hand of the arm still clutching the box. She kept a single stone within her free hand and rolled it within her fingers.

Darren wanted to say something, but realized she wasn't even looking at him. Andrea appeared to focus on things beyond the present, perhaps in search of the final outcome, a way for her to face whatever was going to happen. Darren wanted to say that it was going to be all right, had to be—that they were the heroes, out to avenge the evil that had found its way into their world. But his heart ached at what could only be determined a lie. That wasn't the way things *really* happened.

Darren reached for another handful of ammunition, winced at the pain of newly-opened flesh, then used his other hand to pick the stones out of his jacket pocket with fumbling fingertips. He almost dropped them all into a crevice that seemed to be creeping its way toward his feet, patiently waiting to slide underneath him and swallow. He took a few steps away from it and found a position behind Andrea, covering her backside.

They were surrounded.

Skinned, peeled tomatoes sniffed at them, took slow steps forward.

Wood above them continued to stretch, scream in pain, and splinter with crackling bursts similar to knots exploding under the heat of a roaring fire.

The fiery glow became brighter still, its source thundering with activity.

With each change of shape the shadows produced, the creatures appeared to get closer, jumping in frames as though illuminated by a giant strobe light. The large whites of their eyes pierced through the shadows, fixating on an immediate food source.

Darren and Andrea held each other up, backs together, waiting, feeling the shaking tremors of each other's bodies with each passing second.

A putrid smell entered her nostrils and brought Andrea back to the harsh reality that enveloped her with decaying arms. It made her gag, her head reel. Facing the central source of this madness, she knew its spreading had to be stopped. She looked for the glow of familiar faces, but couldn't see them—instead felt them there watching, waiting. She kept thinking of Sarah tucking her head into Faye's side, but wondered why she appeared so sad. And

Faye, smiling yet concerned.

The closest creature to Andrea was almost within range. If her pulse could add another beat to its feverish rhythm, it did. The intense pounding in her ears all but drowned out the unsteady building above her and the explosive cavern ahead. She had to get there, but that meant going through at least three of the creatures, watching her step among the cracks and crevices, and avoiding other monsters hunting her from behind the veil of darkness.

The creature in front of her bulged its eyes even more than she thought possible and opened its mouth. The shadows upon its gleaming body made it look as if it were growing, then shrinking, then growing larger, changing shape. Its eyes locked onto hers, but she didn't look away. Instead, she whispered to it, drew it closer with the hardest stare she was able to produce by shear willpower alone.

"Come on, come on, you *motherfucker!*" she screamed. The profanity made her feel powerful. She said it again, almost relishing the change from her normal behavior, feeding from its vulgarity and letting the anger flood her body. It tilted its head at her as if in misunderstanding, but Andrea thought she saw something familiar trapped within its eyes.

Her hand quivered around the stone, but not from nervousness. Or fear. Her grip increased and drew upon energy from all parts of her body and displayed the pure anger she was feeling in the form of tremors rattling her body, in the stinging cut that opened in her palm as she squeezed on the edges of the stone. In the sharp, pinpointed circles of her pupils. Hatred tightened the muscles of her jaw line and clenched her teeth. She pulled back her arm in a stiff retraction, her muscles too tight to allow a flexible, smooth motion.

She began to see the pulsing veins decorating its muscles, appearing like black webs spreading from the darkened center of its chest. Andrea locked onto this center like the sensors of a guided missile, and threw the stone, forcing all of her contained energy into an explosive release.

The creature took two small steps without realizing it had a shredded hole within its chest, no longer containing a blackened heart. Its flesh melted, oozed into the subterranean earth it had climbed from. Two steaming, dirt-stained cowboy boots were left in its place.

The quick victory gave her the boldness to walk toward the burning center. She felt unstoppable. Her legs knew where to step and her body knew which way to lean as the ground trembled and tried to knock her off balance. She continued on, the glow getting larger upon her cheeks as she moved forward. Though sweat streamed from the pores of her skin and joined together in sweaty puddles that fell along her sides and the center of her back, she didn't feel the increase in heat upon her flesh.

Another creature appeared to her left and she did away with it with another stone, quickly turning her head to greet any others that attempted to cross her path.

Darren felt the pressure lift from his back as Andrea took her first steps away from him. He wanted to look back, but was busy battling his own monsters. He took one down with a single throw, but missed another altogether and required a second attempt to do the job. There were others creeping from the shadows, but he was running out of stones and Andrea had just walked away.

"Andrea!"

No response.

A crimson silhouette sauntered toward him with staggering steps and steam emanating from its body in wispy filaments. But it was far enough away for him to take a single glance to the rear of his position.

It was all he needed to determine that Andrea was well out of his shouting range. The outline of her figure lost its definition, seemed to blend into the ethereal creation surrounding them. To shout to her would be like calling along a vast expanse of barren desert with a throat only moist enough to utter a single scream.

Andrea.

The thought only developed into a whisper. His body tingled at the mention of her name, as if there was something special existing in just the thought of her. They were at a pivotal point in their journey, and he knew they were only two beings in a master plan and could only let the pieces fall where they may. A puzzle fit together by unseen hands, with Darren and Andrea the final two pieces to be inserted, creating the end of one puzzle and the start of another.

Stepping along an edge of crumbling ground, Darren kept an eye on things moving toward him, things that would surely haunt him for years to come. He was able to keep Andrea within sight for a few steps, but the fading edges of her shape were soon completely lost within the shaky mirage of heat rising from below. He jumped over one crack without thinking what would happen if he missed. The depths of each crevice deepened the closer he came to the center. Upon landing, to lose his balance in one direction or the other would mean a fall to whatever existed beneath—something he didn't want to think about.

Darren's heart dropped as he felt the leg of his jeans pull against him, preventing another step forward.

With eyes that only wanted to stare ahead, he looked down.

Expecting a clawed hand ready to rip into his leg, he let his eyes adjust to the shadows at his feet and was relieved to see a rusty nail caught in the fabric of his jeans. The piece of wood attached to it was connected at an inappropriate angle to the floor of the warehouse, having succumbed to the shifting ground. Relief made a swift departure as he looked up and saw other slats hanging from the floor, some swaying as the warehouse refused to settle its slight motion. The creaking of the wood now seemed much louder.

Another slat fell to the ground, then another.

"Andrea!"

He removed his pant leg from the nail as the smell of rotting flesh mugged him with its thickness. Looked quickly to his left and right, but saw nothing. A strong breath of foul air swept across his ear and made the hair at the back of his neck stir. He froze. A moist tongue licked at his ear lobe with the fine ends of its forked tip.

"Andrea," Darren whispered.

He clenched a fist around the remaining stones in his hand. And turned, feeling frenetic energy pummel the palm of his hand with a thousand pinpricks. Light shone through his flesh, awaiting its release, its purpose. Darren refused to look at the creature's face as he pushed his hand through the center of its skinless chest.

The sharp scream was eliminated as quickly as it had begun. Darren's fist found the heart and destroyed it, his hand passing though bone and muscle with an ease that surprised and disgusted him at the same time. He felt the cool of the night air as his fist pushed through the creature's back. Then pulled his arm back through a heated pile of mush dissolving even as his hand was still the inside its body. He looked into the creature's eyes and saw life fading quickly, hostility losing to bewilderment, before they melted and slid down the remains of its face.

He was about to be ambushed. Dozens of eyes stared at him—more soldiers peeking over trenches. The number of stones he held wasn't even close to matching the number of creatures those eyes belonged to.

Darren continued toward the center, almost losing his balance on more than one occasion. Rotten slats continued to fall around him and the entire building shifted its weight with a muted thud.

He reached the source and looked into a hole about ten feet in diameter, the sides near the surface containing large, exposed roots from plants and trees that had not yet made it to the surface. He didn't see the origin of the fiery glow, only an endless chasm of yellows and oranges. He looked up at Andrea staring into the center as well, the glow casting alternating shapes of shadows across her face and a fire within her eyes.

She was on the other side, clearly within hearing distance, but only looked into the world below her, hypnotized, as one would be while looking into the molten top of a volcano as it was about to erupt.

"Andrea!"

She heard her name being called, but could not pull herself from the abysmal depths seeming to beckon her.

She remembered the first day she had met Darren as he looked over the library counter with wide eyes, waiting to be filled with knowledge and take on the world. She had turned around to type up his library card and was instead delivered to this very same cavern of Hell. But in her trance-like state, it was a tunnel she had traveled by foot, with images of Darren appearing at different stages of his life. She remembered seeing him in a sports uniform, which she now placed as a football jersey, and a suit and tie. She hadn't actually seen him in a two- or three-piece suit, but could easily picture him as an executive of a company in the future. Or even a librarian.

She heard her name again, this time a bit louder, and raised her head to Darren. She saw his arm pull back and release a stone at a creature directly in front of him. Saw the thing fall into the depths and Darren quickly focus his attention on more beasts using exposed roots as a ladder and pulling themselves out of the central cavern. They were coming in full force now, going in for the final kill.

Darren's hand previously holding the stones fell to his side, empty. Eyes once squinting in concentration now relaxed and seemed to sag with infinite sadness. It was now up to her.

One stone remained in her hand. She threw it at a silhouette whose features were shadowed by the fires gleaming off its backside, and missed, the ball of white light falling, falling.

Andrea opened the box and discarded the lid, exposing dozens of chipped stones. Once belonging to the dead, they were now the only weapons she had to save their lives, each stone containing the essence of a previous life.

Andrea ridded the earth of two more parasites with precision aim of two brittle stones, their explosive brilliance causing her to turn away as she reached for a third. A snarl came from behind and she turned to face it. Realized with a quick gulp of air that it was not soon enough.

This creature had gained some understanding of the way this game was being played and counteracted with defensive maneuvers. It stayed low to the ground on all fours, claws digging into the ground if it should need to pounce or flee. Moving back and forth, it prevented direct exposure of its chest and snarled in excitement, its forked tongue all but hanging out of its mouth in pleasure, occasionally licking at its teeth. Once close enough, its jagged nails reached for Andrea's legs.

And found purchase.

It grabbed at the backs of her legs and knocked her off-balance before she realized what was happening. Andrea tried to kick its clawed hand away, but only worsened her situation. Too late to come into contact, with its swift movements, her foot struck upon air alone. Panic began to creep its way into her bones. Her arms went out to catch herself and the stones came free of the inside of the box, floating in mid-air as she made a feeble attempt at catching them on their way down.

Teetering on the edge of the central cavern, feeling the heat of it on the back of her neck, Andrea had no choice but to take one step backward to regain her footing on the edge.

Almost all of the stones fell back into the box, but a few tumbled into the abyss. In the fury of activity, Andrea thought she heard the distant thuds of small explosions.

Her foot landed on the crumbling edge of ground inches before she would have fallen into the fathomless depths. A deep breath of hot air burned her lungs but still provided some relief as her senses told her she was okay.

Until a clawed hand swiped one leg from the edge of the cavern. Her eyes bulged in surprise as she hopped backward on the leg she still had under control.

Her foot searched for the ground.

And continued to search as her toes pushed on the inside of her shoe to find the feel of solid ground.

And searched as she fell, the stones following her and illuminating before her eyes, glowing with the explosive energy of the memories contained within each shard.

The cavern grew on all sides, rising.

In that instant, she knew her destiny, saw the meaning of her existence and the purpose in each of the stones that fell with her.

Familiar faces were smiling at her, waving her forward.

Andrea reached for their hands.

Chapter 48

Taking nimble steps in Andrea's direction and fighting a dizzying spell of queasiness, Darren watched, horrified, as she battled against the thing at her feet and tumbled backward into the waiting depths he had first stumbled upon with his friends, years ago. He saw the stones rise from the inside of the box and slowly rotate as they followed Andrea out of sight, then saw each of them begin to ignite and fall like distant stars.

Nausea turned into a heavy bag of rocks inside his stomach and told him he was too far away to make any attempt at catching her, but he fell to his knees just the same and thrust an outstretched arm over the edge. And watched her fall.

His life fell with her.

A life that, up until now, held the most meaning he had ever experienced in his eighteen years. A purpose he had searched for and found, through Andrea, was now gone.

More newborn creatures, still bathed in the unearthly fluids they had spawned from, crawled out of the central cavern and the crevices that spread from it like giant tentacles.

As Andrea disappeared within the dancing shades of yellows and oranges, so did Darren's hope of getting out of this alive. Without any type of ammunition, there was no way to wage any sort of battle against the things that hunted him. His mouth contained a sudden dryness and his stomach plunged even further. He refused to look at any of the skinless beasts lurking in his peripheral vision, deciding only to stare at the space of air Andrea had so recently occupied. It was the only thing that mattered.

It was time to face the unfortunate truth that he had been defeated. The fairy tale was over. The creatures living behind the door of his nightmares were about to drag him deep into the basement. If he chose not to struggle, the pain might not be so bad.

Darren closed his eyes, waiting for his flesh to tear open and be ripped from his body with violent shakes of pointed teeth. He almost willed it to just be over, the weight of this journey lifted from his shoulders. His pulse weakened, and his breathing got slower.

Then a slow rumbling injected his nerves with anxious energy.

As if all subterranean creatures living in the soils of the earth were migrating upward, those on the surface waited in eager anticipation of their arrival. A gentle tingling entered Darren's toes as the rumbling continued. He tensed, allowing only his eyes to move.

Drooling beasts around him also paused in reaction, not knowing what to do next or which way to go. Chattering jaws ceased their tumult. Heaving chests held onto a final gulp of air.

As the frequency of vibrations increased, Darren's muscles instinctively readied themselves for his command and quivered from their tautness. To his right, two creatures hunched on bent legs, slowing their chatter with infrequent clicks of their teeth, confused.

An explosion from deep within the central cavern lit up the underside of the warehouse. Darren pulled his head into his shoulders, expecting to be bombarded with fragments of wood, earth, and stone. When nothing of the sort happened, he pried open his eyes.

The sound of the explosion faded, but a milky radiance still remained, infusing the air beneath the warehouse with a thick cloud of sparkling fog. The creatures around Darren shrieked in disgust and pain, wiped at their arms and legs as though they were trying to rid themselves of a dousing of biological chemicals.

Shapes began to appear, then dissipate, and appear again as the fog condensed into a more solid definition. People started to form within the glow: arms, legs. Faces.

As a familiar face made Darren's heart leap from his chest, he was thrown to the ground. A violent succession of explosions sent shock waves through earth and granite, rocking the surface. His head slammed into moist ground that seemed to be flowing with surging waves, momentum almost pushing him into the ragged grin of a crevice.

Through clumps of soil covering his eyes, Darren turned to see the air shatter with rays of dazzling white light. He covered his head for protection, used his feet and legs to claw away from the edge.

Darren heard the world crumble around him.

The warehouse had taken all the beating it was able to. Creaking groans of stretched wood turned into a deafening, raucous shriek as the wood splintered, shattered. Exploded. The entire building seemed to be crushed beneath the foot of a giant as it caved in.

Shards of wood fell upon Darren's back and legs, one missing his head but sticking into the ground a breath away from his ear. One of the supporting beams finally collapsed to the ground with a jarring crash.

Silence stilled the air, but was soon replaced by the sound of the ground moving, adjusting.

Heaps of wood, steel, and pipes surrounded him. At first

thinking he was slowly being pushed into the ravenous cavern, he felt his body move upon the ground and immediately tried to fight against it. A squeal attempted to crawl from his throat as the cavern came closer, but he swallowed hard, kept it suppressed, when he realized the opening was also getting smaller.

The ground was closing!

As a seamstress would sew a tear in a child's grass-stained corduroys, the ground was mending itself, pushing all openings together again.

Darren looked for the creatures behind him, to the sides of him, in front of him.

Nothing.

He looked into the central cavern, now only a hairline fracture in the crust of the surface, but saw no peering eyes or clawed hands pulling at the edge. Small mounds of earth traveled the length of the ground where the crevices had so recently gaped.

Darren climbed from the debris and got to his feet, still feeling the ground move, but not enough to be dangerous. Taking large, unsettling steps over rusted pipes and something that resembled an old office chair, he went to the seam that had been the central cavern. He kneeled and touched the mound of dirt as if to prove to himself he wasn't imagining what he was seeing. He scooped up some of the dirt and let it sift through his fingers. The dirt fell freely, but a yellowed, cracked nail remained. He toyed at the edges of it with his fingers, squeezed it before placing it into his pocket as an unsettling reminder—as proof.

The ground at last ceased to move beneath his feet, as though it had received its fill for the day and was taking an afternoon nap.

Silence, save for a single piece of glass falling from a

warped window frame somewhere inside the rubble, and the rain.

His emotions balled up inside his stomach and rose to his chest, until they were finally transformed into painful sobs and hot tears. Darren let them out, needing the release, until his eyes wouldn't allow the salty substance to gather and fall down his cheeks anymore.

Darren rose to his feet, wiped his eyes.

Stared into the apparition of Andrea.

A lone figure amidst the rubble of the warehouse, she smiled.

Placing a hand upon his cheek, she said his name, which came as a pleasant whisper to his ears.

And handed him two notebooks he had dropped during his struggles.

Chapter 49

Legs quivering and sluggish, forcing them to move ahead, Darren kicked away chunks of wood and steel, returning the way he had arrived. Without the warehouse as cover, the rain fell upon his body in a comforting shower. He raised his face and let it cleanse him. The gray light produced from a setting sun veiled by clouds eliminated most of the shadows, lifted the weight of the oppressive darkness that had previously saturated him, and made his sodden clothes seem lighter as he walked.

His feet slapping against the pavement was a welcome, familiar sound. But it wasn't enough to rid his mind of the heavy thoughts of a woman he had begun to love.

Sirens wailed in the distance. People were coming out of their houses, inspecting the damage, as if a major storm had recently passed through and cleanup would commence.

Darren heard the murmurings from small groups of people; some mentioned an earthquake, while others didn't know how to describe horrible creatures they knew they had not imagined. Those who hadn't seen them nodded with small grins perched upon their lips, being polite. Conversations for the years ahead were created.

He maintained a slow pace to avoid drawing attention, his mind trying to piece together the bizarre events of the last few days. He went unnoticed.

When he turned the corner and the front porch of his house appeared, Darren's heart beat hard and he picked up his pace. The small walkway to the front steps seemed to be miles long, stretching with each jittery step he took. In a way, he wished the path would get longer, further out of reach, enough to delay the discovery of what might be lurking inside his house. Cracks riddled the concrete foundation, and the house it supported seemed to lean to one side. The screen door swayed in the breeze.

The front porch beckoned yet pushed him away, appeared as a holy shrine and the gates of Hell in the same shimmering image he viewed through exhausted eyes.

He imagined and hoped his parents were still waiting for him—his mother at the kitchen table with a box of Kleenex, his father pacing back and forth, peeking through the curtains to see if he was coming down the sidewalk. The front door still locked against gruesome things that had scratched against it . . .

The screen door slammed behind him. It swayed back open when the skewed frame of the porch couldn't hold it in place. He noticed the windows were boarded up, nailed with haste. Broken glass crunched beneath his feet.

He tried the doorknob to the front door. A sheet of plywood covered the space reserved for the window.

Locked.

Backing up, ready to slam his shoulder into the door, it opened.

Two silhouettes appeared behind a gold chain that prevented the door from opening beyond its length. His mother was hugged tightly into the back of his father, looking over his shoulder, eyes glossy from fresh tears.

The door closed momentarily, before it was flung wide open.

"It's over," Darren said, and rushed into his mother's arms. His father hesitated before joining in the embrace.

When a large hand lay upon the back of his head, Darren was again able to deliver warm tears.

Tears of relief.

Between hitching sobs that left his throat too tight to utter anything coherent, he thought of what he wanted to say, amazed at how much there was to tell. But the two most important words did fall from his lips—words that had waited too long to be delivered.

"I'm sorry."

Afterword

Wearing a suit and tie he thought he'd wear to a first job interview, Darren let his hand rest upon the mahogany casket and looked longingly into Andrea's eyes. She stared back from a picture resting atop the closed section of casket where her head would have been if she were lying inside.

In silent conversation, he told her he would continue the journey and spread the word about those that were, and will be, forgotten. Darren knew she heard him, knew she was there, felt her presence beside him, probably chewing on her lower lip, heavy in thought.

Very few of the local residents appeared at the funeral, aside from her assistant and a small number of teenagers who frequented the library. Probably just the way Andrea would have liked it: a small, quaint ceremony with those that were close to her.

Darren's parents sat on the church pew behind him, hands clasped together, letting him have his peace with Andrea's memory. He was surprised to learn they believed his every word, only gazed at him with eyes that had seen more than they had ever wanted, nodding in agreement at the mention of the creatures—unlike the local authorities.

Brought in for questioning, Darren had held nothing back, and told all. When they thought his story a bit over the edge, the state police were brought in and he reiterated the same tale, giving them no proof or reason to hold him in custody. Even showed them his two notebooks filled with entries from beyond the grave. Darren brought them to the site of the central cavern, but the rubble from the warehouse covered all evidence of his story.

He chose not to show them the jagged nail he had kept.

His story could have been supported by sightings of the same creatures by other residents of the community, but were quickly dismissed into the realm of local folklore, possibly for sanity's sake.

For the man that had his throat ripped out before being thrown out of his window, the authorities blamed a rabid dog that had been on the loose. Remains of the man's family were not found. Nor was the rabid dog.

Once able to rest, enjoying a cool night beneath sheets he had craved for some time, Darren immediately began writing about the journey he and Andrea had started and transcribed all the entries of his notebooks into a well-woven tale for others to read. To support his documentation, he had called what family members he was able to contact, connecting them to those in his notebooks. The facts were identical to what each had remembered or heard about their deceased relatives.

He hoped to find a publisher for this strange story, wanting to bring awareness to the world, and deserved attention to the deceased. Something, he knew, that had to be done.

To remember the dead.

Most of Andrea's belongings were sold at auction, but a will had been found in the rear of her refrigerator freezer, leaving a substantial amount of money to Darren, along with the house, and a car still sitting in the parking lot of a Super 8 in Bangor. Andrea had also requested to have Darren take her place as town librarian, if he so desired. He agreed without hesitation, shocked by the fact that the will had been written a few years ago, shocked more by the way fate had provided him with a future he was in search of not so long ago.

Rain continued for days afterward.

As Darren watched the rain continue its cleansing from behind a library window, he thought about the days ahead and where they would take him.

He studied a moth dancing around the beacon of a streetlight in early dusk; saw its wings become drenched with rain and the moth fall in a downward spiral to the pavement, twitching once before becoming eternally still.

It was the end of a life and the start of a new beginning.

Continuing to watch the sky replenish the earth with its nectar, allowing others to be born, die, and be remembered, Darren heard the library door open with a small squeal—a last patron for the day, in search of information.

A hot flash soaked his body as he met the eyes of a young girl.

Though her steps were hesitant, her demeanor nervous and timid, her cheeks soon blossomed into a scarlet flush and eyes sparkled with the well-kept secret of hidden knowledge.

Darren turned to greet her with the casual grip of his trembling hand.

About the Author

Originally from Auburn, Maine, T. G. Arsenault is currently in his seventeenth year of service with the U.S. Air Force and hopes to retire deep inside the Maine woods to write full-time in the near future. He currently resides in California with his wife, Diana, and son, Christopher. His short fiction has appeared in two anthologies: *R.A.W.— Random Acts of Weirdness* and *Octoberland*. His short story, "The Eighth Day," received an honorable mention in the *Year's Best Fantasy and Horror, Sixteenth Annual Collection*. Visit T. G. Arsenault online at www.tg-arsenault.com for contact information, news, and fiction.